D0871728

A Complete State of Death

JOHN GARDNER

A Complete State
of Death

The one certainty in Life is Death;
And Death is the most complete state.

Words attributed to Brother Frances
of Shrivingfold (1424–1501)

New York   The Viking Press

Published in 1969 by The Viking Press, Inc.
625 Madison Avenue, New York, N. Y. 10022

Library of Congress catalog card number: 76-83228

Printed in U.S.A.

ACKNOWLEDGMENTS
The author and publishers gratefully acknowledge permission to
quote from the following songs:
"Last Night When We Were Young" by Harold Arlen and
E.Y. Harburg, © Copyright 1935 Bourne Co., New York,
N. Y., Copyright renewed, used by permission of the Copyright
Owner. "These Foolish Things Remind Me of You" by Strachey,
Marvell, and Link, © Copyright 1935 by Boosey & Co., Ltd., all
rights for the U.S.A. assigned to Bourne Co., 136 West 52nd
St., New York, N. Y., Copyright renewed. "April in Paris"
(Vernon Duke–E.Y. Harburg) © 1932 by Harms, Inc., used by per-
mission of Warner Bros.–Seven Arts Music, all rights reserved.
"Button Up Your Overcoat" by De Sylva, Brown, and Hender-
son, © Copyright 1938 by De Sylva, Brown, and Henderson,
Copyright renewed, reprinted by permission of Chappell & Co.,
Inc. "When the World Was Young" by Philippe-Gerard Vanier,
English words by Johnny Mercer, © 1950-51 by Enoch & Cie.,
words reprinted by permission of Criterion Music Corporation,
rights controlled in U.S.A. and Canada by Criterion Music
Corporation.

To E.H. with thanks

I ... being appointed a Police Constable of the Police Force of the Metropolitan Police District, do solemnly, sincerely and truly declare and affirm that I will well and truly serve our Sovereign Lady Queen Elizabeth in the office of a constable for preserving the peace, and prevent robberies and other felonies and all offences against the peace, and in all respects to the best of my skill and knowledge discharge the duties of the said office faithfully according to the law.

Oath taken by Police Constables on being accepted
into the Metropolitan Police Force

I will never act officiously or permit personal feelings, prejudices, animosities or friendships to influence my decisions. With no compromise for crime and with relentless prosecution of criminals, I will enforce the law courteously and appropriately without fear or favour, malice or ill will, never employing unnecessary force and never accepting gratuities.

United States Law Enforcement Code of Ethics

A Complete State of Death

1

A BLACK HUMBER saloon took them to the waiting VC10
Armitage was in the back, pale, between Torry and a uniformed
inspector. He gave the impression of being a man near to death.
A man uncertain of his whereabouts. Blown out of his mind.
The skin of his face taut and translucent, like dried and aged
parchment. His hands were never still, the fingers scratching and
pulling at his clothes, as an old man, left with the one sense of
touch, will pluck and scrabble at his bed sheet in a vain attempt
to avert the inevitable.

As the car drew up below the steps leading to the economy and
tourist class cabins, Torry, leather-skinned with restless eyes,
leaned forward to Armitage.

'Let's have your hands then, "Shoelace".' He sounded weary.
Diffident. 'If I've got to deliver you in one piece we might as well
stick to the rules.'

Armitage nodded vaguely, as though hearing Torry from a
great distance. He held out his hands in subdued co-operation.

Torry snapped the handcuffs over the man's bony wrists.

'No Press, thank God,' observed the uniformed man.

'The Press wouldn't be interested in this bit of refuse.' Torry
looked at Armitage as though he was a typhoid carrier. 'Ten
years ago, Shoelace Armitage. Ten years ago and we'd have had
the Press here. You'd have drawn crowds like Sammy Davis, eh?'

Armitage did not reply. His total attention seemed to be centred on a point some five inches from his eyes.

'Come on then.' Torry dug his elbow into the man's ribs. 'Let's get you aboard the giant bird and slide you home. My God, the things one does for money.'

'I'd give a couple of months' pay for the trip,' said the uniformed inspector.

'Done,' said Torry. 'New York's like anywhere else. When you dig under the surface the people are all the same. Like H-bombs. When you've seen one you've seen them all. Anyway, I'll only have time for a couple of hamburgers.'

'Have one for me.'

'With mustard?' Torry raised an eyebrow.

'With mustard and pickles.'

Torry shook his head. 'You couldn't afford it, not on your salary.'

'I've got savings.'

Torry shrugged and led Armitage to the steps. At the foot he turned back to the uniformed man.

'You want me to bring back a Tony Rome official detective badge for you?'

'Make it Dick Tracy. I'm old-fashioned.'

Detective Inspector John Derek Torry mounted the steps with his charge. During the transatlantic flight he would be forced to make some conversation with the paltry piece of human flotsam that he was returning to its country of origin. It was a chore to which Torry did not happily turn.

Yet, high above the ocean, it was Armitage who talked while Torry listened with a mounting interest.

2

'NEW YORK'S the only city in the world where a guy can be arrested on the sidewalk for impersonating a human being. And I'll tell you something: in this city always expect the worst.'

The cab driver was jostling for a position on one of the television late-night shows. Torry twisted his lips. Consciously it was meant to be what they call a wry smile.

Outside, the Great White Way was at its garish worst. In New York they did it with more panache, the sets bigger and the lighting extravagant. A lot of people thought it exciting, only you could find the same things around Shaftesbury Avenue or in Soho. You just had to look harder. New York did not have the monopoly on vice, pornography, sudden death, obscenity, theft, or shops where you could buy plastic vomit with plastic flies. It was just that the city's pulse tripped with a greater urgency, and violence was more apparent. It was there in one out of every ten faces if you looked for it and knew what to look for. Torry knew.

In Times Square, George M. Cohan, stony on a plinth and dappled with pigeon droppings, was giving his regards to Broadway. So was Derek Torry, tastelessly from the back of a Yellow Cab. The driver continued his monologue.

'Take this big Chrysler. Well, it stops quick at a red light and,

13

okay, I guess maybe I'm a little close to him. Anyhow, I hit his fender. Just sort of gentle like. No real damage. But I'm worried because, like I said, in New York City, always expect the worst. So the feller has a big car and naturally he gets out and I think he's goin' to make with the pencil and paper to take my number. So, he comes over, leans in the window, then whispers kind of soft—and this'll kill you—"Christ, buddy," he says, "if you're goin' to hit me, make it hard—it's better for the insurance." '

They stopped at an intersection, steam rising from the gratings like marsh gas. A prowl car jumped the lights, its siren giving one quick wail. A couple of cars with right of way braked horrifically. 'Tired of waitin', so he presses the button on us. Cops,' spat the driver. Torry did not say it was more likely the prowl car had to answer a ten-thirteen, and that could lead to anything.

The driver shifted, turning right round in his seat to face Torry. 'Say, what's a nice guy like you doin' ridin' down to the Fourth Precinct House? You're not a cop.' It was not quite a question. The lights changed.

'You want to put money on it?' It had been a long time. Fifteen, sixteen years? That long since he and Joey Donalta had answered a ten-thirteen only a few blocks away. He really should call old Mrs Donalta. Maybe down at the Precinct House; there would be little time later at Kennedy.

'Not like any cop I ever knew.' The cab driver still probed.

'I'm English; it makes a difference.' Torry had lost interest. He should not have taken Armitage seriously. After all this time. It was asking for trouble, like taking a knife to an old operation scar.

The cab driver had slowed in the traffic. He wanted to talk. 'Say, I figured you weren't from New York, but I couldn't get the accent. You don't sound like English.'

'It gets a bit muzzy.'

14

'An English cop, huh? I got a real live Sherlock in the cab.'

'Let's cool it, eh?' Torry did not mean to sound unpleasant.

'Okay, okay, just trying to be friendly.'

'That's all right. Bit edgy, that's all. I used to work here and it's been a long time.' Torry bit his tongue, knowing he should not have said that to a complete stranger, to a cab driver of all people. The flight and time change had got him off balance.

The driver nodded. 'Sure. Old home week. Me it doesn't affect any more.'

The Precinct House had the same smell and the décor did not seem to have changed much: a mixture of polish and work and sweat and close contact with corrupted humanity. The smell that rubs off and, for Torry, now chopped away the years. He could not put a name to the desk sergeant, but he knew the face and saw the man's brow crinkle in response. The sergeant was trying to place him, probably going through the mug shots in his mind. You get like that after a time; see a face and go straight to the criminal file locked in your brain. You never start by assuming it could be the face of a colleague.

'Don't I know you?' The sergeant had good strong grey eyes which held like an arm lock.

'Could be. Captain Lorenz around?' Torry felt the quiver in his voice. The anticipation of seeing the past.

'Who wants him?' The sergeant was not letting go until his curiosity was appeased.

Then, the half-forgotten voice. 'Torrini. Derek Torrini. What the hell are you doing ... Well I'll be ... ' And Guy Lorenz was standing in the doorway where it was marked CAPT. LORENZ in gold lettering fading against the wooden plaque, those big hairy hands clutching the jamb. When they were training down at the Police Academy they used to call him King Kong because of those hands. Maybe it was not original, but in those days the jokes did not have to be sophisticated.

'Guido.' Torry started towards the door, he wanted to hug the big captain, pound his shoulders with his fists and go through all the ritual emotional equivalents of the kissing, embracing and tears of reunited females.

'Course I know you.' The sergeant relaxed and grinned. 'Torrini. I was a second-grade patrolman when you came down here. How've you been?'

'Fine.' Torry still could not remember his name. In any case he had little time to bother about anyone else but Lorenz, who was now motioning him towards the office.

'Coffee, Dutch. Get us some coffee,' Lorenz called to the sergeant. The name came back to Torry, 'Dutch' Schaefer. Lorenz had his arm round Torry's back, one big paw resting on his shoulder. 'Look, I got some British C.I.D. man dropping by any minute, but he can wait. You're like Ma's apple pie, baby. Where've you been all my life?'

It was as though he had never been away. The office had a feeling of constancy, unchanged through the years. Same desk, chairs and pictures on the walls. A forgotten police captain. The Precinct Team that had won the Pistol Trophy in nineteen hundred and thirty-something. But now the captain was an old classmate.

The first time Torry entered this office it had been with a mixture of trepidation and the inexperienced enthusiasm of youth (*I will constantly strive to achieve these objectives and ideals, dedicating myself before God to my chosen profession … law enforcement*). The captain then had been a little runt of a man with the Hollywood dream-cop name of O'Brien. His greeting to new patrolmen also came straight from the scriptwriter's notebook. 'This is a tough precinct. But never forget you're dealing with human beings out there. Even the most hardened criminal still has some human dignity left in him ... ' A good Irish cop, just like the movies.

Torry closed the door behind him. The desk was neater than he remembered it, but then Guido always had a neat mind. Brains, perception, experience, tact. He had them. The prerogatives of a police officer. Easy words with no hint of the blood, grind, exhaustion, boredom, frustration and the million temptations. But they were also just words. Words, thoughts even, could not come near the reality. They were as far removed as the pictures which only mirrored the truth of violence, pain, deprivation and grief, never coming close to the jumble of mental misery and warped actions which spreads, like a thick mucus, round the core of crime. Words, thoughts or pictures cannot capture that revolting stench that is the afterbirth of criminal action.

'Good to see you, Torrini. This make you homesick?' Now alone, the two men faced one another, embarrassed and conscious of the abyss time had created between them.

'I was thinking about Captain O'Brien.'

'Oh yea, you worked under him. Long gone, Dereko, long gone.'

'Dead?'

'Made his pension, then got himself killed in an auto wreck about a year later.'

Torry mentally crossed himself. *Eternal rest give unto him, O Lord, and let perpetual light shine upon him.*

'Stupid accident as well. Made it worse.'

'They all are,' Torry mumbled.

'What?'

'Stupid. All accidents are stupid.'

Lorenz nodded and motioned towards a chair. 'I still can't believe it. Say, how long's it been?'

'Around sixteen years.'

'It can't be.'

'Then you work it out.'

'Fifteen years.' Lorenz placed his hand on the latest copy of *Spring 3100* which lay open on the desk. 'Fifteen years it takes you to come back and see your old friends. No letters, not a word, except Torrini's resigned and gone back to England. His old man is dying. What gives, Dereko?'

'You've got some English cop coming in?'

'He'll keep.'

'Unimportant?'

'You in trouble?'

'What's his name, Guido, the British copper?'

'Torry.' Lorenz glanced at the memo pad on his desk. 'But ... look, what is this, pal? You got ... ?'

Torry leaned forward, warrant card cupped in his outstretched palm.

'John Derek Torry,' read Lorenz. 'Detective Inspector? Am I nuts?'

'You knew I'd gone back to England.'

'Sure, but the crazy name. Torry? You've got a good Italian name, boy. Torrini. What's the matter with Torrini? You ashamed or something?'

'You sound like my mother and my brother and my brother's wife. No, I'm not ashamed. But you try saying Detective Inspector Torrini, C.I.D., Scotland Yard. It doesn't have a good ring to it. The nice people look down their noses and the clients immediately think if you're a wop you'll be a pushover for dropsy.'

'Dropsy?'

'Payola. Anyway, I anglicized the name. Deed poll. Easier.'

'So you couldn't keep away from it.' Lorenz's voice took on a goading tone. 'Once a cop.'

'I tried.'

'After you went back to London? After Joey?'

Torry nodded. 'After Joey. My father died the following week. I took up British nationality again. Went into the Army for a spell.' He rubbed his chin with the right-hand knuckles. 'As you say, once a cop. I had to learn again, right from the beginning.'

'And now you're a real live detective. An inspector. Big deal, I'm happy for you. You marry?'

Torry shook his head. Negative.

'Still chasing ideals?'

'Come off it, Guido. I just want to be good at the job.'

'At it or because of it? Derek baby, I haven't seen you in years and I can still read you blind. Torrini the white knight, galloping through the bad giant's territory, righting wrong and saving the young maidens. You make one mistake so you've got to atone for it. Life sentence. No remission and solitary on each anniversary of the crime, like the judge gave to that guy down in Illinois. Milani his name was. Killed a girl, so the judge gives him life with the proviso, on each anniversary he sits it out in solitary.'*

People do not change. They could be back at the Police Academy arguing through the night. How many times in those days had Lorenz called him a white knight? Lorenz the professional. Torrini the professional idealist.

Torry shrugged. 'Maybe you're right. It's how I'm made.'

'Me,' Lorenz sighed, 'I'm a good husband, a good father, I go to Mass, make my confession, try to do a job, and that's as far as it goes. You still think a cop should be like a priest? Celibate?'

* Joseph Harry Milani: shot and severely wounded John Bryant Jr and kidnapped his fiancée, Mary Lilly Ellen Roberts, at Crab Orchard Lake, Illinois. Later murdered Roberts. Sentenced to life imprisonment. The sentence contained the proviso that he spent each August 25th (anniversary of Roberts's murder) in solitary confinement.

'I think, for me marriage might get in the way. But look, Guido, at one o'clock I have to catch a plane back to London. I got in at five. I'm tired, jumpy. All right, coming back, driving through Manhattan, it's stirred up all the old things. But I'm not going to start a discussion on the ethics of law enforcement because I just haven't got the time.'

The sergeant came in with the coffee in paper cups brought up from the canteen.

'You know,' said Torry, 'I laugh when I watch the shows on television. People ask, is it really like that in the States? I laugh and say, what do you think? Then I come back and it *is* like that. It always has been.'

'They're in here all the time making movies.' Lorenz chuckled. 'Shoot, then, what's the problem?'

'I knew you were here. You're the only contact with rank I've got on this side. You have any *in* with the Feds?'

'Oh sure, J. Edgar flies in from Washington twice a week and we do the town. Latin Quarter, Rainbow Room. You name it.'

'Seriously.'

'I know a couple of people.'

'I've just brought an old friend back for them. We picked him up in London a couple of weeks ago. Forged visa, false name in his passport. Someone in Customs and Immigration's going to be chopped. He'd only been in the country a week. In his hotel room there was enough Dextromoramide to make him a millionaire. He also had a neat little arsenal: two automatic pistols, one revolver and a throwing knife.'

'A one-man revolution. Who is this nut?'

'Shoelace Armitage.'

'Shoelace? I thought he was dead years ago. Big time. Never mixed with narcotics when we knew him. He must be past it by now.'

'The man's a wreck, Guy. Not a junkie. Alcohol mostly, with a little tertiary syphilis thrown in. They found him drunk on the Embankment. Coincidence, I happened to have a feeling about his face.'

'You always did. Shoelace Armitage,' mused Lorenz. 'Once he was poison. Finger man, button man, trigger man, whatever. You know how he got the name "Shoelace"?'

'Tied up a couple of patrolmen with their shoelaces, in Denver, after they'd arrested him. He's still wanted on suspicion of murder in three states. Two are Federal jobs.'

'You got trouble with the Syndicate over there?'

'We've got trouble with everyone, but the Syndicate wouldn't use a clapped-out drunk like Shoelace. Their boys wear clean collars and carry slim brief-cases. Shoelace isn't their style. I've just spent seven hours with him on a plane.'

'And what's worrying you?'

'He's been giving the impression he's tied in with something big. I don't know. It could be delusions. But he seemed frightened stiff. Said he needed special protection.'

'And the boys from Washington weren't interested?'

'Messenger men. Western Union. Thank you, Inspector Torry. Sign here please. Thank you for doing us the favour, hope we can help you some time. You know how it is.'

Lorenz nodded. 'But you're still worried?'

'He said he had information for me if I helped him.'

'We've all heard that.'

'I suppose you're right. It didn't amount to much.'

'How much?'

Torry flipped open his notebook. 'In the next ten days he reckons there's going to be a happening at the Scrubs—that's Wormwood Scrubs, one of our ... '

'One of your principal London prisons. We get the British programmes. A break?'

'I don't think so. He said that after it's happened we should go for a man named Wexton.'

'Wexton? Ring any chimes?'

'Not a tinkle.'

'Sounds imaginative to me, baby, but I'll speak around, find out who the interrogating officer is and put him wise. We can do a run on the name Wexton as well. Anything comes up I'll send it direct to you, huh?'

'Thanks, Guido.'

'And you?'

'I'll report it.' Torry paused before adding, 'I think.'

Torry waited while Lorenz made his calls and changed into civilian clothes. They drove back to Times Square and ate at the Howard Johnson. Steak and a salad, strong coffee going down as they picked away at the past. At eleven, Lorenz called the precinct and they sent a car for Torry. He checked in at Kennedy with plenty of time to spare.

Around midnight, the B.O.A.C. Departure Lounge at Kennedy International Airport has a tired, unloved look. Expressionless, waiting passengers sip coffee or calm themselves with the endless Martini belt. A brace of bored waitresses thread their way through the tables taking orders with the enthusiasm of lethargic robots. One or two dubious travellers sit on the red-leather bar stools. The only ones who look comfortable are the ground stewardesses who move with cool haughtiness, firm buttocks and living breasts.

Torry sat alone with a cup of black coffee, pondering on the untouchable image of the stewardesses, until five minutes before his flight was due to be called.

'This seat taken?' He was a man in his mid-thirties, a bland grey face matching the uncrushable suit.

Torry indicated, without speaking, that he was alone. He had decided that the hygienically self-sufficient sensuality of the stewardesses held out more temptations than the blatant displaying of a human body. He would have to talk to Father Conrad about it when next he saw him. The grey-suited man sat down, placing a copy of the *Daily News* on the table, and ordered a Martini from the passing dead-eyed girl. Torry, as his job required, instinctively wondered why the grey man had chosen his table when the room was only half full. Then the flight was called. Torry pushed back his chair. The stranger leaned forward. 'Don't go for a moment, Inspector. A friend has his eye on you. He also has a small automatic pistol.' The voice was flat. Torry looked hard at the face, noting each feature for later. 'I am leaving. I'm also leaving the newspaper.'

Torry's ears strained to catch any intonation which might place the man on a map. Nothing. Flat, without distinctive accent. The grey man continued.

'There's something of interest to you on page one. It's marked, but don't pick it up until I've gone.'

He rose, turned and walked casually towards the exit escalator. Passengers were moving quickly through the departure doors. Torry could not afford to take chances. Slowly he got up and took the newspaper. Underneath lay an oblong white envelope. His name typed, neatly centred. Torry slipped the envelope into his pocket and joined the procession heading down the cold white corridor, the floors decorated with empty cigarette cartons and jettisoned tabloids. Through the tall observation windows one could see the winking lights, blues, reds and greens, and far off, the roar of engines sifted through the night. The taste of long hours of travelling hit the back of Torry's throat in a wave of bile.

It was not until he was aboard the aircraft, with seatbelts fastened and jets grumbling, that Torry ripped open the envelope.

There must have been the best part of three hundred pounds, in ten-pound notes, together with a slip of white cardboard. The message was typed. 'This is a suggestion for you to remain silent about the late Mr Armitage. See page one of the Daily News.'

Torry knew what would be there. Only the details needed filling in. William 'Shoelace' Armitage and the two Federal men had died in an inexplicable accident on the Pennsylvania Turnpike that evening. The picture, twisted steel and wood, bore no relation to the facts. All accidents, thought Torry as they took off, are stupid. In London it would now be six in the morning. When he arrived there would be an awful lot of writing and talking to be done.

3

THE house was as uninspiring as its surroundings; and Willesden, London NW 10, is not noted for poetic revelations. From the window, overlaid with smoke grime, on the top floor, the boy looked out across Willesden Junction: greasy jagged gables of carriage and engine sheds, the puzzling network of railway lines. On a clear day you could literally see for ever — right into the borders of the Roman Catholic Cemetery and of famous Kensal Green, last resting place of Thackeray, Wilkie Collins and Trollope; only the boy did not know that. To the right, farther on, obscured now, lay the 'Scrubs'.

The boy was about nineteen, tight jeans, black turtleneck and long blond hair thick with cream. Cheap hair cream, a comb heavy with the silt of scurf and a plastic bottle of after-shave decorated the dressing-table, its edge marked with black burns where cigarettes had been left to brand the wood.

He could smell the bacon cooking downstairs and wondered what time they got them up in the 'Scrubs'. Gus was in the 'Scrubs', and tonight he would be ... who knows? It could wait. Best not to think.

'Alf, ain't you bleedin' ready yit?' Robey's voice from the stairs. An old voice, as though the throat was lined with wet cement.

'I'm coming.' Bloody old fool, he knew I was up. Alf bent to look in the mirror. 'Bloody old fool,' he repeated aloud. Robey had told him Zam-buk was good for spots. What a dump; dirty, miserable, stinkin' dump. If it weren't for the money he'd have been off. Tonight anyway he'd be off. The Smoke's all right, but when it comes to birds and gettin' it regular, Birmingham and Coventry every time. Bloody dump. Warped door with a panel cracked. Worn patch of lino on the stairs, all the fibres showing through; and the walls hadn't seen fresh paint since the bloody Boer War.

'Y'breakfast'll be cold.' Robey was already halfway through his, mopping up the slimy uncooked egg white with a bit of bread.

Alf slashed across the yolk with the tip of his knife. Wonder if that's how the blood comes out when you really do someone? What they call oozing. 'Jumper gone then?' he asked, dipping the bacon into the egg's yellow blood. Sacrificial rites. One piece of the victim's body, virgin of course, crunched between his teeth.

'Went before you was even awake.' Robey looked dirty, unshaven, tiny half-moons of grit under cracked fingernails, dried globs of fat staining the filthy pullover.

'Garage open?' Alf swilled the slice of virgin down with tea the colour of liquid sackcloth.

'Course the garage is open. Wotcher think they pays me for?' A tiny rivulet of yolk was starting to congeal among the stubble on the right of Robey's mouth.

'They pay you to use your loaf, old man.' Alf wiped his lips with the back of his hand. 'Use your loaf, cook decent food, not this filthy muck, then keep your horrible mouth shut.'

'I don't know nothin',' grumbled Robey. 'Nothin'. They tell me nothin' so I can't talk about nothin'.'

'I should bloody well think so and all.'

Jumper was older than Alf. Two, three years older. Slim body, quick eyes, slow confident walk. 'Another good day's work done. Breakfast, Robey.' He stood, smiling sarcastically, in the kitchen doorway, rubbing his hands.

'Christ, you came in quiet.' Alf did not look up, still intent on the remaining fragments of bacon and egg.

'Best way, Alfie boy. Quieter the better. Robey, I said breakfast.'

Robey shuffled past the newcomer, into the kitchen, grumbling to himself.

Alf pulled his eyes away from the plate. 'What d'ya get?'

Jumper slid into Robey's chair, pushing the plate to one side. Minimum effort as he moved. 'Nice black Austin Cambridge. Tank's full. Changed the plates. Can't be more'n seven or eight months old.'

'You earn your money easy.'

'And you, mate, get twice as much as I do. Mister anonymous Smith arrived?'

'Plenty of time. Only hope that bloody replacement's all right.'

'You must've said that two hundred times since yesterday. All bloomin' day you were on about him. Even in the pictures.'

'Yeah, well you wouldn't be too keen either, would you? After what's gone before. Armitage.'

'I wouldn't bloody do it at all, mate. Knock off a car, change the plates, pick up me money and scarper: that's me. Right out of the way I'll be.' Jumper let his eyes rove around the room. Squalor. You'd think they'd have taught Robey to keep clean. He'd done enough bird. Why did Smith use him? Perhaps he's done Wexton a favour. Christ, don't even think the name. Bad luck. Even the television came out of the ark. Good that, all those elephants and lions sittin' down watching telly on the ark. Zoo time. Bet it was nicked though. Alf had cleaned off the screen when they arrived yesterday. All that muck on the duster. Gawd, and the carpet. Stand up by itself if you took it outside.

Hate to look in the cupboards, and what the hell were those pictures meant to be? 'The Childhood of Sir Francis Drake', or whoever it was, and 'When Did You Last See Your Father?' When the copper dragged him off screaming he never done it, mate, and Ma shouting every swear word you ever heard.

'Smith's here with the cruel one.' Alf was by the window, admiring a maroon Rover 2000 outside. 'He's a big boy, too.'

'Then you'll be all right, won't you.' Jumper did not move— then Ma breaking down and having hysterics. The ride on the train to his auntie's house. The boys at school. 'They hung your old man this morning, Jumper. Bet he jumped, Jumper.' Black and red. Red. Black. Willie Jarvis, that was the boy's name, funny how it comes back. Bastards. No. Bastard father. Hope they stretched him proper, silly git, getting topped for some poxy barmaid or whatever she was. Auntie. Up her and all. There were enough uncles to play off the World Cup.

'Morning, Jumper. Alfred.' And Smith was in the room. Jumper stood up. Smith could have been a copper. One of those who do the firm father bit. Pipe, raincoat, plain red tie. Chosen carefully.

'Morning, Mr Smith.' Alf always felt he ought to stand to attention when Smith spoke. He looked past Smith, at the replacement. Jesus, but he was a big one.

'Everything all right, Jumper?'

'Austin Cambridge, Mr Smith. Full tank. Changed the plates.' Jumper's litany.

'You packed?'

'All ready.'

'And the original plates?'

'Top of me case.'

Smith nodded. 'All right, lad. Single ticket to Reading and your money. Get rid of the plates. Really get rid of them. Understand?'

Jumper took the ticket and envelope. 'Don't worry, Mr Smith.

Nobody's going to find those plates.' He began to tear open the envelope.

'Not here, lad. Or don't you trust Mr Wexton's generosity?'

'No, I mean yes. Sorry, Mr Smith.' Jumper stuffed the envelope into his pocket.

Robey was shuffling back into the room. 'Mornin', Mr Smith, want some breakfast?'

'We've had breakfast. Haven't you got anything else to say, Jumper?'

Jumper's eyes flitting round like glow-worms. 'Goodbye, like. And, well, see you.'

'Nothing for me to tell Mr Wexton?'

'Oh, yeah. Thank you. Tell him thank you very much.'

'Watch it, Jumper. We'll be in touch.'

'Don't he want his breakfast then?' Robey looking as though someone would drop a tip on the outstretched plate.

'He'll get breakfast on the train, Robey.'

Alf could see that Smith even put Jumper off. You could tell, the way he sort of sidled out. Like some geezer in one of the old movies, what'd they call them? Period, where the men were all dressed up like in Robey's picture over there, in the long knickers and that. Jumper left, going backwards as though Smith was some kind of a poncey king. Alf turned his attention to the big lad with Smith.

'You'll want to meet your partner then, Alfred.' Smith smiling. Christ, honour your partners.

'Yeah. Yeah, Mr Smith.'

'Graham, meet Alfred.'

'All right then?' Strewth, he's got a grip like an octopus. Tight and clammy.

'All right.' Geordy accent.

'Graham was in Aden with the Army. Had plenty of experience and finds life rather dull now.'

'I'll bet he does. That's good, the experience.' What else can you say? 'He knows it all then? Got the whole thing taped.'

'I hardly do anything, do I? It's you that has to do the hard work, gettin' us in and out.' He pronounced 'work' like 'walk'. 'As long as we gets out, that's all I'm worried about.'

'We'll get out all right.' Alf was always a positive thinker.

Big Graham turned to Smith. 'It's a Sterling, you said?'

'Yes, they're quite easy to come by nowadays. Alfred's had charge of it. A Sterling.'

'Best have a look. Make sure it's in good nick.'

'It's in perfect condition, Graham, brand new. But, if you want to. Alfred, get Graham his gun, will you.'

Torry lay panting on the lip of his nightmare. Hospital ward? No. But it was night, and the long aisle seemed dotted by green glowing lights. People sleeping and the hum of engines. He was sweating in spite of the cold. Sense returned and the dim outlines of the aircraft's cabin took shape. He reached for his blanket and lifted his left arm to the light. Eight o'clock. Eight o'clock in England. A stewardess passed between the huddled rows of restless passengers like a nurse in a children's ward. Torry saw that she knew he was awake, but purposely ignored him as she went by, avoiding any awkward duty.

Torry, always a light sleeper, never travelled well. Now, after six months, the nightmare had returned. He had almost taken it as a premonition of death, the first time.

'Do you ever consciously feel any deep sense of guilt about anything?' Father Conrad asked him when he recounted the dream. 'Our guilt, you know, as much as our hopes and fears, comes to the surface during sleep. Psychiatrists say that boils and rashes are outward signs of inner worries, neuroses. One might say the same of nightmares.'

High over the Atlantic, Torry had a vivid picture of the presbytery; Father Conrad's study, battered roll-topped desk, the prie-dieu under a simple crucifix and the books, millions of words, years of time, eternal ideas bound in leather, calf, cloth and stiff paper. Did that study really exist? One's detachment, when far away, in flight, was incredible. The nightmare existed, still clinging round him, a wet shroud. This made three times in all. Always the same, and always remembered with intense clarity.

He was at a reunion of his class at Hendon Police College. Everybody happy. Then he upset a glass of beer and looked up into the eyes of Harcourt. Only Harcourt was never in his class at Hendon. Harcourt died long before in the sweaty shade of the Malayan jungle.

Awake, Torry could never be described as a neurotic, yet, in the nightmare, panic caught him by the throat, tearing him from the dream prison. He fought to get out, away from Harcourt.

Then the horrible moment, the realization that this was not just a reunion of his Hendon classmates, but a lifetime's reunion. As he pushed his way through the crowd, faces, long-forgotten, appeared, mingling with old friends.

Torry wiped his brow. The aircraft gave a slight lurch. Hitting the jet stream? One face was always missing. Now he could bring it to mind like snapping his fingers, but Joey Donalta never appeared in the nightmare. What was it Lorenz had said? 'You make one mistake so you've got to atone for it. Life sentence.' Could be. Often he had spoken to Father Conrad about Joey. The priest's reply was the same as all the others. 'You can't go through life reproaching yourself for something that might have happened anyway.' Torry knew it need not have happened on that night.

To begin with he was tired when he went on duty. You tire easily during the summer in New York, and on the previous evening his behaviour had not helped. He could even remember the girl's name. Evelyn Haynes. Blonde, hard as a diamond and, to a young fourth-grade patrolman, just as expensive. It was that night with Evelyn Haynes which disgusted Torry almost as much as the following events.

They were there within four minutes, out of the car almost before Torry had secured the handbrake. The patrolman was a young, red-faced New Yorker. A large, spotty sort of mole on his cheek. The cornered youth did not seem frightened — thin, arrogant in a stained pinstripe nearing the end of a chequered career.

'His partner's in the store. If you guys can watch this one I'll get him out.' The patrolman gave them no chance to argue. The grey wall. The thin youth, leaning and watching Torry with rodent eyes. The feel of the Police Positive in his hand. Joey's voice. 'Watch him. I'll call in.' Then, the distraction. The patrolman shouting from round the corner. His eyes moving away from the boy. Flash. An explosion close. Joey gasping. The thin youth whirling towards him and firing a second time. Glass crunching and a tug at his sleeve where the bullet ripped the cloth, then the Positive jerking and the young killer screaming.

The rest was a twisted blur, as though Torry's mind had tried to scramble the memories. Joey's shirt being torn away to reveal the ugly wound pumping blood. Joey's breathing. Blood smearing the sidewalk. People. A babble. Joey's breathing changing to the laboured wheeze, then nothing.

Torry came out of the daydream, back to the aircraft cabin with its dimmed lights and spectral stewardesses. The day after Joey had died beside the police car in downtown Manhattan, the cable arrived. Torry's father was dying, in bed in the Earl's Court Road, above his delicatessen.

Derek Torry lit a cigarette, hand trembling while his mind recited the prayer, automatically, like a magic incantation:

Incline Thine ear, O Lord, to our prayers, in which we humbly entreat Thy mercy bring to the country of peace and light the souls of Thy servants Michael Torrini and Joseph Edward Donalta, which Thou hast summoned to go forth from this world and bid them be numbered with Thy Saints. Through Our Lord Jesus Christ ... Torry paused and added another name, for the thin youth had died also.

The table was cleared of breakfast debris. Instead of cups and plates there were pieces of metal. Graham mumbled phrases like 'breech block assembly' and 'return spring cap' as he put the pieces of metal together, working smoothly, happily, pleased with himself. A final click as the triangular metal skeleton butt snapped into place.

'There you are.' The corporal he had always wanted to be. 'The L2A3 nine-millimetre submachine gun, commonly called the Sterling.'

'Very clever, Graham. Very clever with guns Graham is, isn't he, Alfred?' Smith spoke quietly. 'Gives you confidence, Alfred, doesn't he? Now all you have to do is wait.'

Alf looked at the weapon which Graham handled with firm tenderness. It could have been a living being. Graham's baby. At a distance you might have mistaken it for a greyish bit of stick. Hard to believe that a simple-looking metal pipe could spew death—would spew death. Gawd, the things you did for money.

Jumper came jauntily on to Number One Platform at Paddington Station. The big clock showed two minutes past eight. Just missed the eight o'clock. Never mind. Another one at quarter past. Time to get a paper and a couple of magazines. Just over ten minutes and he'd be out of it. *Mirror*, *Mayfair*, haven't seen this month's *Mayfair*, and one of those women's magazines, *Nova* or something like that. Funny how he got excited over women's magazines. Always felt a bit guilty about it. Kinky? Suppose so. 'These please. I've only got a quid note.' Must ask someone about women's magazines. Bring it up in conversation. Casually. Don't really go for the glossy monthlies for men with the coloured pictures of birds showin' their tits. 'Thank you.' Put *Nova* on the inside. No, with the women's magazines you know you're lookin' at pictures and adverts and readin' stuff that isn't being ogled by a load of yobs. Which platform? Oh, bloody hell.

'Mornin', Jumper. Early for you to be out.'

It was that tall red-haired copper who'd nicked him last August.

'Hallo then. They got you down this way now?'

'I'm not walking round the station for fun, Jumper. And I don't collect engine numbers. You haven't met my mate?'

The other copper was a big bloke and all. 'How do.' Smile and look relaxed, Jumper, you've done nothin' wrong.

'Police Constable Philips, this is Lionel Jumper, known in the trade as The Jumper, 'cause he has a nice habit of jumping into people's cars and driving away.'

'Useful bloke to know.'

Jumper did not like the look of P.C. Philips. Bit too keen. 'Well, I got a train to catch, so ... nice seeing you.'

The red-haired policeman stood his ground. 'Oh yes, and what train might that be?'

'Reading train. Eight-fifteen. Look, I'm goin' to miss it.'

'You've got a minute. What's up, Jumper? You're usually a co-operative gentleman. Been on a caper, have you?'

'Have I hell.'

'What're you going to Reading for then?'

'Me auntie. Going to see me auntie.'

'Jumper.' Admonishing. 'Your auntie's in Liverpool.'

Christ, you got to be quick with them. 'Moved. Me auntie moved to Reading.'

'When?'

'Last week.'

'What's her address then?'

'What's in the suitcase, Jumper?' Police Constable bloody Philips.

'Me gear. What do you think I got in here? A bloody bent drag?'

'I'll give him that.' The one with the red hair, only you couldn't see it because of that bloody great helmet covering his bonce. 'Jumper's strictly a drag man.'

Lord bless you, constable. 'Look, I told you. I got a train to catch, so piss off and … '

'Using offensive language, Jumper? Perhaps we'd better have a look at the case after all. You being a convicted felon.'

'Come on, Jumper. Open up.'

Bloody hell, what can you do? Convicted flipping felon. Run? Yea, here we go, Jumper lad.

He got about five yards. It was Philips who tackled him, and Philips was a rugger man. Jumper went down hard. He thought he would never breathe again it was so hard, with the suitcase scraping along the platform and the magazines flying. *Nova*. They'll think I've turned poufy reading *Nova*. It was like an echo of Ma, 'What'll the neighbours think?' and his old man up for doin' a bit of skirt to death.

When they opened the suitcase, the number plates were on top.

'Funny gear you've taken to wearing, Jumper,' said Philips. 'Tin shirts with numbers and letters on them. Very *avant garde*.'

'I only stopped him to be sociable to an ex-con,' said the redheaded constable later.

Torry's aircraft got in just before noon. He checked through customs and put in a call to Ticker. Practically out on his feet, Torry had a nasty feeling that Ticker was going to insist on his going straight into the office. The money would have to be handed over. There would be a full report to make.

But Detective Superintendent Tickerman was in a helpful mood.

'Go home and get some kip, Derek. Come in before five though, would you? I'll pass the facts on to the gaffer in case anything comes up. Can't say I've had any association with a Wexton, though.'

'Thanks, Tick, I'm bushed, but I'll be in around four, four thirty.' The telephone booth was getting hot, his eyes red and watering from lack of sleep and the drifting smoke from his cigarette. A blue-and-white notice had been stuck to the inside of the booth. PLEASE DO NOT SMOKE IN THIS TELEPHONE BOX, it said. On the coin box somebody had scratched *Donald Duck The Con Man*.

'Okay, Derek, but for Christ's sake be careful with that money.'

'I haven't reported it just to slope off on a bender.'

Ticker chuckled. Outside, Torry looked for an airport bus that would take him to the B.E.A. Terminal in Cromwell Road, only two hundred and twenty regulation paces, at two and a half miles per hour, from his door.

The flat was as he had left it. You are supposed to be able to read a man's personality from the décor of his home or the books he collects. The furnishings in Torry's flat gave the impression of an uncluttered life, the actual furniture sparse, chosen with care and an eye to economy. A large circular glass table, a pair of deep leather chairs, a sideboard and bookcase, both picked up from a second-hand dealer near the delicatessen, were the major articles in the living-room. Bed, side- and dressing-tables, upright chair in the bedroom. Above the bed hung a large brass crucifix; its twin (he had picked them up as a unique pair in the Portobello Road) caught the eye instantly on entering the living-room, gold against the olive wallpaper to the right of a long oblong window.

Torry looked at the crucifix, his head moving in an automatically reverential bow. Then his gaze switched lovingly to the fireplace and his one self-indulgence: a large, fine reproduction of 'The Haywain', Hieronymus Bosch's masterly bizarre triptych, in which that prolific old Dutchman sets out the Fall of the Angels, the Creation, the Fall of Man and Mankind's avid determination to progress towards Hell. The afternoon sunlight fell across the centre panel, slashing brightly on the bulging haywain of life being plundered, surrounded by the deadly sins and used as a couch for voluptuous lust.

Torry had paid twenty guineas for the painting. The complexity and emotion of the thing remained a continual source of amazement to him. In it he found, again and again, faces and incidents familiar in his daily work. It seemed incredible that man's inhumanity could have changed so little since the end of the Middle Ages.

Out of habit he checked the small kitchen and the bedroom before running a bath. Twenty minutes later, clean, shaved and naked, Torry asked G.P.O. Telephone Information for a call at three thirty, and slipped into bed. The telephone would ring before his requested alarm call, anyway.

Gus tried to control his breathing. Running had winded him and he felt the clawing stitch in his side. But it looked as though it was going to pay off. They had told him the screws would never think of lightning striking in the same place twice. Walk now, don't run any more. The same way as Blake, they'd said. Force the window on the second floor of D Wing. Eighteen foot drop. Thought he'd done for himself then. Foot still hurt. Sort of tingled. The rope over the wall. Right on time, these boys were really organized. Two thirty. Straight down the road. Over the second wall and on to the railway lines. He was in overalls, the cloth cap and plumber's tool bag were there, just where they said. Straight up and left into Primula Street. Nice name. Nice timing. The car would be there at two forty. It would wait until the quarter, no longer.

Kids were playing in front. Pushing, falling, charging all over the road. Plastic machine-guns and pistols.

'Hey, Charlie. Bang-bang. You're dead.' Dirty little face and filthy T-shirt.

'I'm not dead. I gotcher first.' Snot running from a small red nose.

'You're bleedin' dead, I tell yer.'

Come on, Gus. Now, into Primula Street. As he turned the corner all the bells of hell seemed to start ringing.

Alf, behind the wheel of the Austin Cambridge, heard the prison alarm bells. 'Christ, that's it, Graham. We'll have to get out.'

'No, man, he's here. He's coming.' Graham from the back of the car.

Alf glanced over his shoulder. Gus walking towards them. The window coming down. Into gear. Two bloody women at the end of the street. They'd never have a go anyway. 'For Christ's sake, Graham.'

'He's not near enough.' Graham leaning out of the window, shouting. 'Gus. Run, Gus. Run.'

Gus dropped the tool bag. The bells. Run. They were calling from the car. He could still hear those kids in the street behind him.

'Bang-bang-bang.'

38

The Sterling came up to Graham's shoulder. Alf heard the chatter. Doesn't make as much noise as you'd expect.

He couldn't run. Why couldn't he run? Oh Gawd, the pain in me chest. Jesus, Joseph and Mary. Backwards. I'm bein' knocked over. Christ. Blood. What ... why? No ... no ... no ... no ...

'You're bleedin' dead, I tell yer.'

'All right, Alf. Go now. For Christ's sake, get us out. Go fast.'

Alf had not watched Gus being cut down. He only had to do the driving and try not to think about Gus lying there in Primula Street. He thought of his breakfast egg yolk. Straight up into Westway. Let Graham out, then on as far as the White City and leave the car. Just walk away. Buy a packet of fags and then walk away.

At three fifteen Detective Inspector John Derek Torry's private telephone rang, and an ambulance waited to remove the shredded body of Gustave Lipperman from the roadway in Primula Street where, together with several police vehicles, it was obstructing traffic.

4

THE appointment was for five thirty. The lean-faced, grey man, suit crumpled from a long day spent sitting cramped at a desk, waited patiently. At five thirty-two the trim civilian secretary came out. She had good legs and a breastline that would have shaken the Venus de Milo.

'He'll see you now,' she said.

The room did not have the same character as the office back in the old building, but already its occupant was placing the stamp of his particular style on the place.

'Thank you for bringing it down yourself.' The man who filled one of the warmest chairs in London smiled as he looked up. The weary executive smile.

'There it is then, sir.' His visitor held out the red file with a distinctive yellow disc in the top right-hand corner. 'I'm afraid you'll have to sign for it, even if it is your property.'

'How's the wife?' asked his superior, poising pen over form. He made it sound unlike a standard senior-officer question.

'Fine, sir, thank you.'

'There you are then. All signed for.'

'Good. Hope it's what you wanted.'

'If it's not, you'll hear about it.'

The file was dropped into a slim brown Samsonite brief-case which lay open on the desk.

At nine o'clock that evening, after he had dined, the Commissioner of Metropolitan Police went to his study, settled into a favourite chair, thought twice about lighting his pipe, and opened the red file.

CONFIDENTIAL

TO: COMMISSIONER METROPOLITAN POLICE
FROM: METROPOLITAN POLICE RECORDS
REF: BM/1/ JDT

For the Commissioner's Eyes Only

NEW SCOTLAND YARD

TO: COMMISSIONER METROPOLITAN POLICE
FROM: METROPOLITAN POLICE RECORDS
DATE: APRIL 15TH, 1969
REF: BM/COM/1
SUBJECT: DETECTIVE INSPECTOR JOHN DEREK TORRY

SIR,

REGARDING YOUR INSTRUCTIONS, FOLLOWING THE INQUIRY INTO THE INCIDENT CONCERNING DETECTIVE INSPECTOR JOHN DEREK TORRY, I HAVE NOW COMPLETED THIS FILE PERSONALLY.

CHIEF SUPERINTENDENT
METROPOLITAN POLICE RECORDS

SECTION ONE

NEW SCOTLAND YARD

MEMO: 429/1
TO: COMMISSIONER METROPOLITAN POLICE
FROM: ASSISTANT COMMISSIONER, C

41

DATE: JUNE 17TH, 1968
SUBJECT: DISCIPLINARY ACTION AGAINST DET. INS. JOHN DEREK
                TORRY, C.I.D., C ONE
ENCLOSURE: PERMISSION FOR DISCIPLINARY HEARING WITH REGARD
                TO INCIDENT AT FULHAM POLICE STATION, S.W.6,
                F DIVISION, ON NIGHT OF JUNE 13TH, 1968.

                                        NEW SCOTLAND YARD

MEMO: 429/2
FROM: COMMISSIONER METROPOLITAN POLICE
TO: ASSISTANT COMMISSIONER, C
DATE: JUNE 17TH, 1968
SUBJECT: DISCIPLINARY ACTION REFERENCE DET. INS. JOHN
                DEREK TORRY, C ONE. THIS OFFICER SUSPENDED FROM
                DUTY UNTIL HEARING AND INQUIRY. ACTION IM-
                MEDIATE.

                                        NEW SCOTLAND YARD

MEMO: 429/3
TO: COMMISSIONER METROPOLITAN POLICE
FROM: ASSISTANT COMMISSIONER, C
DATE: JUNE 18TH, 1968
SUBJECT: DET. INS. JOHN DEREK TORRY. THANK YOU FOR
                RULING. NECESSARY TO PASS TO YOU IN VIEW OF
                TWO EARLIER COMPLAINTS OF A SIMILAR NATURE.
                BOTH INCIDENTS REPORTED BY THIS OFFICER'S CHIEF
                SUPERINTENDENT. BOTH INCIDENTS PROVED TO BE
                UNFOUNDED. HOWEVER, I STRONGLY FEEL THAT FACTS
                SURROUNDING THE PRESENT INCIDENT SHOULD BE
                INVESTIGATED WITHOUT DELAY, PARTICULARLY AS
                ACCUSED SUSPECT, WILLIAM EDWARD WARD, HAS
                MADE AN OFFICIAL COMPLAINT AGAINST DETECTIVE
                INSPECTOR TORRY.

42

PRECIS OF INCIDENT INVOLVING DETECTIVE INSPECTOR JOHN DEREK
TORRY AND FINDINGS OF BOARD OF INQUIRY

At 21.00 hours on Thursday, June 13th, 1968, Fulham Police
Station received a 999 call from 'The Pilgrimage' public
house, Queen's Road, Fulham, reporting a serious disturbance on the premises in which one man had died of knife
wounds.

Inspector Torry was leaving the station following investigations in Case No. 6853 (see Closed Case File 1009/56/M).
Inspector Torry agreed to visit the scene of the disturbance
with Police Constables Dawlish and Crispin. On arrival they
found that two beat constables had taken charge, preventing
anybody from leaving the premises. The weapon was
found lying beside the body. (See Exhibit C in Regina *v.*
William Edward Ward. *One ex-United States Army fighting
knife.*)

Victim recognized by Detective Inspector Torry as Ralph
Ernest Chisholm, a known ponce.

All five officers interviewed persons on premises and
Inspector Torry picked out Alfred Charles Wilson and
William Edward Ward, both known to be associated with
Chisholm. Wilson and Ward were asked to return to the
station for further questioning. Both men resisted at first but
finally accompanied officers.

On arrival at Fulham Police Station the suspects were
separated and placed in No. 1 and No. 2 Interview Rooms.
Each was accompanied by a police constable.

Police Constable 832 Barraclough was with Ward when
Inspector Torry began his investigation. After approxi-
mately fifteen minutes Detective Inspector Torry asked
P.C. Barraclough to get tea for the suspect.

P.C. Barraclough went to the canteen, returning with the tea approximately ten minutes later. As he approached No. 1 Interview Room, Inspector Torry came out and said, 'He had a go at me. You'd better get a doctor. Anyway, he'll talk now.'

P.C. Barraclough went into the Interview Room and found Ward unconscious on the floor.

Dr Edward Furnace examined Ward twenty minutes later and diagnosed slight shock. Ward had a badly bruised face and marks of heavy bruising on the right shoulder and upper arm, all consistent with blows from a fist. He also examined Inspector Torry and pointed out grazing and a red puffiness on the chopping edge of the right hand.

Inspector Torry commented, 'The man's a maniac. I had to defend myself.'

Ward later made a statement admitting to the murder of Ralph Ernest Chisholm following a quarrel over money. He was then charged. At the same time Ward made an official accusation against Inspector Torry, accusing him of unprovoked assault.

Complete report already in your possession with details of Board of Inquiry held on July 10th, 1968.

Evidence given by Dr Edward Furnace; Mr William Madox, Consultant Psychiatrist; Detective Inspector John Derek Torry; William Edward Ward; Detective Sergeant Adam Parker, F Division; Sergeant Edward Gordon, F Division; Police Constables 749 Reading; 928 Paton; 209 Dawlish; 837 Crispin and 832 Barraclough, all of F Division (see File EN/MP/262).

Detective Inspector Torry completely exonerated on account of both lack of evidence and the psychiatrist's report on Ward's unstable, violent nature, congenital untruthfulness and confession to the murder of Ralph Ernest Chisholm.

Detective Inspector Torry returned to full duties with C One on July 11th, 1968.

SECTION THREE

DETAILED PERSONAL BACKGROUND OF JOHN DEREK TORRY, DETECTIVE INSPECTOR, C.I.D., C ONE, NEW SCOTLAND YARD, AS CALLED FOR BY THE COMMISSIONER METROPOLITAN POLICE

NAME: Torry. (Family name Torrini. Change of name by Deed Poll to Torry, August 22nd, 1956. See below.)
CHRISTIAN NAMES: John Derek
RELIGION: Roman Catholic
DATE OF BIRTH: May 20th, 1929
HEIGHT: 6' 1"
COMPLEXION: Dark
HAIR: Black
EYES: Dark brown
WEIGHT: 13 stone (182 lbs)
DISTINGUISHING MARKS: Scar on left shoulder running down chest and ending above left nipple
FATHER: Michael Torrini (deceased October 3rd, 1952)
MOTHER: Maiden name, Florence Angelica Tibbits

Parental Background

Michael Torrini immigrated to England from Riccione, Italy, in the autumn of 1923.

Worked for his uncle, Luca Torrini (deceased). After eighteen months borrowed money from uncle and opened delicatessen in Earl's Court Road.

May 14th, 1926, married Florence Angelica Tibbits.

Three sons:

ROBERTO: Born March 12th, 1927. Now runs Torrini's delicatessen, Earl's Court Road. Lives on premises.

JOHN DEREK: Born May 20th, 1929. Present address: Flat four, 286a Cromwell Road, sw5.

PAUL JAMES: Born December 3rd, 1930. Commercial artist employed by Cortatex. Address: Somerset Mansions, Flat 38, w1.

John Derek Torrini educated at private school, St Peter's, Newbury Villas, w8. School has ceased to exist.

On outbreak of World War II, St Peter's School negotiated evacuation scheme with Hartford, Connecticut, U.S.A.

John Derek Torrini billeted with Donalta family (Italian-American, Roman Catholics) in Hartford. Donalta boy, Joseph (Joey), six months Torrini's senior. Torrini and Donalta inseparable. At age of sixteen Torrini persuaded father to allow him to stay in U.S.A. in order to study for a pre-law degree.

1947, Torrini entered Albany University. In spite of excellent results only remained there for a little over two years.

January 9th, 1950, became American citizen (see file M/28749278/LN, New York City Department of Justice, Office of Immigration) and was accepted for training with New York City Police Department (see Section Four). Joseph Donalta had already entered Department.

April 11th, 1950, Torrini posted to Fourth Precinct where Joseph Donalta was already serving.

September 30th, 1952, Donalta and Torrini were teamed for night duty in a prowl car. During an incident that night Donalta was killed (see sections four and seven).

On the following day Torrini informed his father was dying. Immediately applied for compassionate release, returned to England two days later and in the following year renounced American Nationality (see Home Office file HM/243/505) and applied for a three years' tour of duty with the Special Air Service Regiment (see section five).

Torrini left the Service in 1956 and on August 20th changed name by Deed Poll to Torry.

August 25th, 1956, made application to join Metropolitan Police. (For Metropolitan Police record see Section Six.)

SECTION FOUR

SELECTED DATA ON DETECTIVE INSPECTOR JOHN DEREK TORRY'S SERVICE WITH THE NEW YORK CITY POLICE DEPARTMENT

(I) EXTRACTS FROM FINAL APPLICATION AND SELECTION BOARD NEW YORK POLICE DEPARTMENT
(*Note:* Basic information listed in Section Three has been omitted.)

New York City Police Department,
Headquarters,
240 Centre Street,
NEW YORK CITY,
New York.

FINAL APPLICATION BOARD IN SESSION, ROOM 221, AT 10.00 HRS JANUARY 15TH, 1950.

NAME OF APPLICANT: John Derek Torrini
NATIONALITY: United States citizen (papers taken out 1/9/50. Office of Immigration file M/28749278/LN)
PHYSICAL: AI
APTITUDE: AI
CREDIT RATING: B3
PSYCHIATRIC: Clear
LANGUAGES: Italian. French
SOCIAL SECURITY NUMBER: 295-36-5470
FBI, ALL POLICE AGENCIES: Nil
COUNTRY OF ORIGIN FORCES: Nil

47

BOARD CONDUCTING FINAL APPLICATION INTERVIEWS:
  CHAIRMAN: Chief Inspector George K. Wellman
  OTHER MEMBERS: Lieutenant Peter Sobesto
                 (Director Legal Bureau)
                 Captain Joseph J. Younger
                 Sergeant Paul Barefoot (Special Assignment)

CHAIRMAN'S REPORT:

The candidate is of well above average intelligence and has specialized knowledge which could make him a particularly fine asset to the Department. Some of the Board felt that, with his special qualifications, it would be better for Torrini to return to Albany and finish his pre-law studies—in which he is advanced. But upon examination the candidate was adamant that he should try to make a career in law enforcement. Our final recommendation, therefore, was that John Derek Torrini should be accepted for recruit training at the New York Police Academy as soon as possible.

LENGTH OF INTERVIEW: One hour.

(2) FINAL REPORT ON JOHN DEREK TORRINI BY THE COMMANDING OFFICER NEW YORK POLICE ACADEMY ON GRADUATION

NEW YORK POLICE EXAMINATION RESULTS
John Derek Torrini

PENAL LAW	
CODE OF CRIMINAL PROCEDURE	
ADMINISTRATIVE CODE	82%
CRIMINAL LAW	
STATE LAW	
INITIATIVE:	84%
GENERAL INVESTIGATION:	80%

48

SCENE OF CRIME INVESTIGATION:	83%
SOCIOLOGY:	90%
ABILITY AND CONFIDENCE ABOVE AVERAGE.	
COMBAT TRAINING	
BOXING: DRIVING: UNARMED COMBAT:	
JUDO:	84%
RIOT CONTROL:	80%
PHYSICAL TRAINING:	83%
FIREARMS:	
PHASE ONE:	36 (Possible 40)
PHASE TWO:	300 (Possible 600)
PHASE THREE:	360 (Possible 600)
PHASE FOUR:	230 (Possible 300)

Probationary Patrolman Torrini has attained the highest grades in academic, physical and firearms training of his class. On two occasions he has shown great personal coolness and courage, as follows:

On the night of February 4th, 1950, while unarmed and in civilian clothes he was passing a small food store on 29th Street. Glancing in, he saw the owner looking frightened and the one customer standing in a menacing attitude. Without thought for his personal safety, Torrini entered the store. The customer turned out to be carrying a revolver and was in the process of a hold-up.

Torrini, taking him by surprise, disarmed the man, who was arrested and is now serving a sentence of five years.

On the second occasion Torrini was returning to the Academy at 22.00 hrs on March 15th, 1950, when he heard shouts from an alleyway located off 42nd Street. He immediately went to the assistance of a sixteen-year-old girl who was being assaulted, overpowering the assailant and probably saving the girl's life.

49

For these actions Torrini has been awarded the Mayor's Trophy. He also received the Academy Award of a police revolver. In my opinion Torrini is a born and dedicated police officer who should go far in the Department and is certainly to be watched for accelerated promotion.

COPIES TO: District Attorney, New York City. Chief of Police, New York City. New York Police Department Records. Captain O'Brien, Fourth Precinct.

(3) April 9th, 1950   New York Police Academy
POSTING
Probationary Patrolman John Derek Torrini will report for duty at the Fourth Precinct House as from 09.00 hrs, April 11th, 1950.

(4)   New York Police Department
DATE: April 11th, 1951.
FROM: James O'Brien, Capt. Fourth Precinct.
SUBJECT: Probationary Patrolman John Derek Torrini.

ANNUAL REPORT

Torrini is one of the most able patrolmen in my Precinct, showing more tact, discretion, intelligence, and initiative than many of my senior officers. Strongly advise his normal promotion to Patrolman (4th grade) which is now due. Also recommend promotion be accelerated within next six months, preferably to course at Detectives' School. As from this date am placing Torrini with other officers on car detail.

ENC: Copies of Torrini's crime prevention and detection and arrest reports.

(5)   Fourth Precinct,
                                 New York City Police Department
DATE: October 1st, 1952.
OFFICER: J. D. Torrini. Patrolman (4th grade).

On the night of September 30th, 1952, Patrolman (3rd grade) Joseph Donalta and myself were on car detail, 23.00 hrs to 8.00 hrs.

At 01.28 we received a ten-thirteen to proceed to Pekov's Liquor Store off East 13th Street to assist patrolman dealing with illegal entry.

On arrival we found Patrolman (1st grade) Hawkes had one youth (later identified as Rodney Charles Fenham) under control outside the store. Fenham had his back to the wall and Patrolman Hawkes was standing over him, gun unholstered.

Both Donalta and myself left the car with guns unholstered. Patrolman Hawkes said, 'His partner's in the store. You guys watch this one and I'll get him out.'

I stayed with Fenham while Patrolman Hawkes moved round the corner of the building.

Patrolman Donalta said, 'Stay with him and I'll call in.' He then went back to the car.

As Patrolman Donalta was leaning inside the car to make radio contact Patrolman Hawkes shouted from the corner of the building, to my left. I was momentarily distracted. In that time Fenham pulled a gun (now identified as a 357 Magnum Smith & Wesson, No. 3867) and fired one shot at Patrolman Donalta. I automatically fired at Fenham, hitting him in the chest.

On going to Patrolman Donalta's aid I found him in a critical condition, the bullet having entered the left side of his back with bad exit wound in lower part of chest.

I immediately called for assistance and ambulance, but Patrolman Donalta died within a few minutes. Fenham died in ambulance on way to hospital. See Patrolman Hawkes's report for details of other arrest.

(6) CABLE TO PATROLMAN J. D. TORRINI
PLACE OF ORIGIN: LONDON, ENGLAND
DATE: OCTOBER 2ND, 1952
    PAPA SERIOUSLY ILL REGRET LITTLE HOPE
    STOP ASKING FOR YOU STOP ROBERTO.

(7) Details of John Derek Torrini's application for compassionate leave and discharge, also complete exoneration from blame regarding death of Patrolman Donalta, can be obtained on request.

(8) For details of John Derek Torrini's renunciation of American citizenship, see Section Three.

SECTION FIVE

SUMMARY OF JOHN DEREK TORRINI'S SERVICE WITH 22ND SPECIAL AIR SERVICE REGIMENT

> Commanding Officer,
> Special Air Service Selection Centre,
> Deering Lines,
> Brecon,
> S. Wales

March 7th, 1953

RECOMMENDATION
                    Private 287386 TORRINI, John Derek

Private Torrini has now completed his three weeks' selection training. Reports from my disciplinary officers, the Adjutant, Tactical Training Officer, his Company Commander and Small Arms Instructors show that this man is well above average. On the Cwmgwydi Range he has qualified as a first-class shot in all small arms, while his general level of field craft and initiative is high.

I therefore recommend that Private Torrini is suitable for posting for basic training with 22nd Special Air Service Regiment and should be watched for potential N.C.O. promotion.

(Signed) R. J. Banks
COLONEL
O/C S.A.S. Selection Centre

Officer Commanding,
Basic Training School,
22 Special Air Service Regiment,
Kuala Lumpur,
Malaya

July 2nd, 1953

Private 287386 TORRINI, John Derek

Private Torrini has completed his basic jungle training with this unit obtaining average pass marks. He shows qualities of leadership which should be fostered, and I therefore recommend that he be made up to Temporary Corporal before starting his next stage of training.

(Signed) John Gould
COLONEL
O/C Basic Training

Commanding Officer,
No 1 Parachute Training School,
Changi,
Singapore Island,
Malaya

September 24th, 1953

Corporal 287386 TORRINI, John Derek

Corporal Torrini has successfully completed his parachute training, carrying out the specified nine jumps, including two at night, one into water and two 'tree jumps' into our thick jungle D.Z.

53

October 1st, 1953
POSTING:
Corporal 287386 TORRINI, John Derek, to 'B' Squadron, 22 Special Air Service Regiment, Kuala Lumpur.

May 8th, 1954
PROMOTIONS:
Corporal 287386 TORRINI, John Derek, to Sergeant, 'B' Squadron 22 S.A.S.

February 20th, 1955

'B' Squadron,
22 S.A.S.,
Kuala Lumpur,
Malaya

FROM: Capt. Mellesh
TO: Officer in Command, 'B' Squadron
SUBJECT: Operation Oust

On February 10th, 1955, following information, I was briefed to lead a sortie into deep jungle (Map 4. Ref: B9/6/4). Our information was that a small detachment of M.R.L.A.* were grouping in an area roughly half a mile south of the D.Z. Drop to take place at 03.00 hrs, February 11th, 1955.

The patrol consisted of myself, Lieutenant Kerns, Sgt Torrini, Cpls Wiltshire, Freeman and Powell with twenty other ranks. The drop was accomplished with success, on target, and with only one casualty, Cpl Powell breaking his leg in falling from a tree.

We regrouped, and, at dawn, started to make our way through difficult and thick jungle. At 09.00 hrs one of my two forward scouts reported back that we were approaching what seemed to be a deserted encampment. This proved to be a clearing roughly

* M.R.L.A.: Malayan Races Liberation Army.

100 yards in diameter. There was no sign of life and after watching for one hour Lieutenant Kerns, Corporal Wiltshire and six men entered the area with extreme caution. They reported that the encampment was deserted and I decided to investigate in order to determine the direction in which the terrorists had moved.

We were just breaking cover to join Lieutenant Kerns and his party, who were well spread out in defensive positions, when we came under heavy cross-fire from right and left. I immediately ordered a return to cover. In the ensuing engagement, which lasted until 15.00 hrs, twenty-two terrorists of the M.R.L.A. were killed. Our casualties (see Casualty Report) amounted to seven dead and five wounded.

I would like to make special mention of the action by Sergeant Torrini who, with complete disregard for his own life, attempted to drag Lieutenant Kerns, who was mortally wounded, to cover. In doing so, Sergeant Torrini received serious wounds on the left side of the chest and shoulder.

We met with no other terrorist action on the way back, arriving at Base Fort Three on February 17th.

CITATION: *Mentioned in Dispatches*: 287386 TORRINI, John Derek, Sergeant, 'B' Squadron, 22 Special Air Service Regiment. During action against the Malayan Races Liberation Army on February 11th, 1955, Sgt Torrini endangered his own life in attempting to save an officer of his unit.

DISCHARGE: Sergeant 287386 TORRINI, John Derek, 22 Special Air Service Regiment, having fulfilled his terms of service is honourably discharged this second day of February Nineteen Hundred and Fifty-Six.

For details of John Derek Torrini's change of name by deed poll, see Section Three.

BRIEF RÉSUMÉ OF DETECTIVE INSPECTOR JOHN DEREK TORRY'S
SERVICE WITH THE METROPOLITAN POLICE

(1) John Derek Torry made application to join the Metropolitan Police Force on May 1st, 1956. He was accepted and
began training with course No. 467 at Hendon Police
College. The O/C Hendon Police College notes in his
final report that Torry is an ideal candidate for promotion,
though relies a little too much on the knowledge and
experience he acquired with the New York Police Department whose methods and procedure differ, in specific
circumstances, to our own.

Torry was first posted to Hammersmith, B (now F)
Division. His annual reports are obtainable from records.

(2) EXTRACTS FROM DIVISIONAL SUPERINTENDENT'S (B
DIVISION) FINAL REPORT ON POLICE CONSTABLE JOHN DEREK
TORRY

DATED: August 1st, 1958.

Police Constable Torry has spent his first two years with
this division and proved himself to be a highly capable
officer, both on the beat and, during a six months' period,
assisting the Station Sergeant at Hammersmith.

There are moments when he is pushed too far and on these
occasions there is a tendency to use his initiative rather
recklessly.

Torry now expresses a desire to transfer to C.I.D. With his
previous experience, both police, law and with the Special
Air Service, I can highly recommend this constable's transfer
to C.I.D.

(3) On August 14th, 1958, Torry was posted to C Division
at West End Central as a Detective Constable. His records
here show the same pattern of good behaviour and

dedication. In July 1960 he took his Sergeant's Examination, obtaining a high pass mark. He continued at West End Central where he got the reputation for being a 'hard man'. His Detective Superintendent's report in May 1962 contains the following comment: 'While Detective Sergeant Torry is undoubtedly an officer of unusual dedication, some of his colleagues find him difficult to work with. This may well be due to his particular flair for C.I.D. work coupled with a manner which can, at times, be brusque ... '

(4) In 1965 (June) after a great deal of experience on all types of C.I.D. cases, Torry sat his Inspector's Examination, again obtaining the high average pass mark.

On July 28th, 1966, he was transferred to C One, New Scotland Yard, where he has remained.

(5) CONDUCT AND PROGRESS REPORTS ON DETECTIVE INSPECTOR JOHN DEREK TORRY MADE AT THE REQUEST OF THE COMMISSIONER OF METROPOLITAN POLICE

FROM: Assistant Commissioner, C Dept., New Scotland Yard

DATE: June 21st, 1968

Detective Inspector Torry has, in the two years he has been with C One, established a unique reputation. As you well know, his advice has often been invaluable in a number of major cases. Though not always the easiest man to work with I have heard of no serious breach of discipline until those mentioned in my earlier reports to you on June 17th and 18th, 1968.

In summing up my feelings about Torry I would say that he is a man who knows his own weaknesses and becomes infuriated by them. He is a completely dedicated officer, but with a rather frighteningly deep hatred of crime in all its aspects.

FROM: Detective Chief Superintendent, Crime One
DATE: June 21st, 1968

Detective Inspector Torry is a hard-working and resourceful police officer who, in spite of his invaluable past experience in different fields, tends to use his initiative beyond the bounds of normal police procedure. Suspects and members of the criminal classes regard him, rightly, as a 'hard man', while, with his colleagues, he can be short-tempered, dogmatic and overbearing when roused. This, however, does not alter the facts, which speak for themselves—that he is a good policeman and a good detective.

FROM: Detective Superintendent Tickerman, Crime One
DATE: June 21st, 1968

I have worked with Detective Inspector Torry for nearly four years, both at West End Central and New Scotland Yard. Though I am his immediate senior officer I have nothing but respect for him. Nor have I anything to report that is to his detriment, except perhaps that he pushes himself too hard and expects others to keep up with him. Also, there are occasions when he allows his own hatred of crime to draw him into self-involvement.

SECTION SEVEN

MEDICAL AND PSYCHIATRIC REPORTS ON DETECTIVE INSPECTOR JOHN DEREK TORRY CALLED FOR BY THE COMMISSIONER OF METROPOLITAN POLICE FOLLOWING THE INCIDENT AND COMPLAINT ON THURSDAY, JUNE 13TH, 1968

FROM: J. R. Davis, M.D., F.R.C.S. Consultant, D Dept, New Scotland Yard
DATE: June 23rd, 1968

There have been no physical changes since the patient was last examined by me. He seems in perfectly normal condition, though still refuses to discuss the bad scar running down left shoulder and chest. Relevant information as follows:

HEIGHT: 6′ 1″
WEIGHT: 13 stone
CHEST X-RAY: Normal
HEART: Normal
ENT: Normal
REFLEXES: Normal
VISUAL ACUITY: L.6/6   R.6/6
COLOUR VISION: (Stilling Test) Normal
BLOOD PRESSURE: 110/71

FROM: A. J. Hughes, Consultant Psychiatrist, D Dept, New Scotland Yard
DATE: June 23rd, 1968

I can find no definite evidence of psychological disturbance, nor any latent neurosis in this patient.

His I.Q. is between 153 and 155 and he seems to have a high pressure and tension threshold. His deep-seated hatred of crime and criminals seems to stem from an incident which occurred while serving with the New York City Police Department: his best friend was killed and Detective Inspector Torry probably, subconsciously, blames himself for the death.

The only other decisive comment concerns the tensions of his private life. Detective Inspector Torry was brought up as a Roman Catholic. In moments of stress, guilt or tension, he tends to behave strictly within the dogmas and liturgy of the Church.

Yet here we have a complexity. Torry admits to being a non-believer, openly calling himself an agnostic. Yet he also

59

admits to the fact that the Church often claims his mind and body against his better judgment and will.

This is especially noticeable in his private emotional life. At present he is deeply attached to a young woman who is a militant atheist. They have both agreed to marriage, but, probably because of the girl's views, Torry tends to behave towards her as a totally committed Catholic. He is adamant that they should marry only with the rites and liturgy of the Church of Rome. She refuses, to the extent that their whole relationship now seems to revolve around this one bone of contention.

Torry is a healthy, normal and vigorous heterosexual. Because of the religious situation, Torry has refused to have sexual relations with the girl concerned, though, when the strain is great, he is not averse to using an available professional woman, or even resorting to masturbation.

In either case, he is subject to severe attacks of guilt, the origins of which can be found in his strong Catholic upbringing. This guilt, together with the religious pressures of the past, could well be the cause of his occasional outbursts of ill temper.

5

TORRY could not tell whether he was awake or asleep. Fatigue plays strange tricks, making the brain over-active, holding back the comfort of sleep, or putting one into the twilight world of half-consciousness where past and present merge, memories collide and the mind races across the desert of years, the whole overlaid with only a light cushion of unknowing.

The smell of the shop, the delicatessen. The noise of the bell as he plodded in, heavy with satchel and the everlasting homework. Bill and Rosalie smiling, Rosalie in the cash desk. His father looking up from serving a customer. 'Now 'ere we 'ave the brains of the family. Hey, Derek, what they teach you today, huh? You bin good boy in that smart school?'

And the smell – sausage, cheese, mortadella, prosciutto – the smell, indescribable now, but mixed with wet gaberdine raincoat and the feel of damp grey cloth. His cap. School cap. Red shield with its four segments. Rain gusty in the Earl's Court Road. The trudge daily through Kensington. Christmas, altar boy at the midnight mass. Father Joseph. 'I always think of today being my day, boys – me bearin' the name of the Holy Saviour's foster Pa. 'Tis a wonderful time for children, Christmas.'

Christmas in Hartford, Connecticut, with Mr and Mrs Donalta and Joey. The big living-room with the tree. Snow; warm inside with the phonograph and the presents and tears alone in the white bedroom he shared with Joey. Tears because Mama and Papa and the delicatessen in Earl's Court Road seemed so far away and they were being bombed.

'Doc' Wildy behind the drugstore counter. 'What's it today, boys? You bin to church today? Good, good boys. Chocolate malted, eh?' Who came in with the news? That tall thin fellow, used to work down at Dooley's Garage? Was it him or Dover? Dover, good-looking Dover. After Dover had gone away they said he was the father of Mary Williams's baby, but nobody knew for sure (except Mary Williams and she wasn't certain) 'cause Dover never came back, only the once, all slick in his uniform with the silver wings, when, they said, he had Mary Williams (with her permission. Later everyone had Mary Williams and confessed it regularly) while her Ma and Pa were at the movies. Right there in her front parlour with the dog scratching at the door. It must have been Dover, white-faced. ' "Doc", y'not heard? Switch the radio on. The Japs. They bombed Pearl Harbor.'

War Bonds. Buy War Bonds. Buy Mary Williams. 'C'mon, Derek. I'll help you. Look.' She seemed so much older than him. The deft, scented, soft hand quick with his buttons and it was all over before he even ... 'Bless me Father for I have sinned ... I have used bad language ... omitted to say my prayers, in the morning, twice ... been untruthful ... allowed my thoughts to wander during Mass ... been lustful ... '

'What exactly do you mean by lustful?'

Caught. God, would he really burn in hell? Smells. The delicatessen. Snow. Snow has a smell to the memory, clean and fresh. Main Street on a cold Sunday morning. Then the bell was ringing. The bedside telephone. Ticker on the line. Calm urgency.

*

Torry's taxi took him through Petty France and into Broadway, past Craddock and Slaters where the men in straw boaters were efficiently slicing off the chops for tonight's supper, up to the Broadway entrance of New Scotland Yard. The name had seemed an anomaly to Torry when the Commissioner's Office was in the old Embankment Building so well known to the world's movie-going public. No British cops and robbers film was complete without the camera moving in on that brick archway or one of the telltale turrets. The old boys moaned the passing of the Embankment Building and complained of a loss of character, but Scotland Yard was now really New for the first time since 1890. New and utilitarian. Three ugly great piles of reinforced concrete and grey granite flags, with sealed anodized aluminium window frames. A human ants' nest rising twenty stories above the triangle of Victoria and Dacre Streets and Broadway.

Torry went in through the Broadway entrance, past the marble plinth with the eternal flame burning inside its glass box in memory of the members of the Metropolitan Police Force who died during the two world wars to end all world wars.

Both the constable on duty and the civilian receptionist pretended to recognize him as he flashed his warrant card and headed towards the nearest lift. The Briefing Room was on the fifth floor opposite the big glass trophy cabinet. Grey seats rose tiered against polished wood. A private cinema. The Detective Chief Superintendent of Crime One leaned over the rostrum desk, like a walrus in a striped shirt. In the front seats a huddle of detectives. Ticker was there with Snaith and Broadbent. Broadbent sucking an unlit pipe. He constantly complained about the cost of tobacco. Torry recognized one of the senior men from C Three, the Fingerprint Department. There were one or two he had seen around but did not know.

'Ah, so Mr Torry has decided to join us.' The old man acid.

63

Torry bristled. 'I'm sorry, sir, I've been up all night. Mr Tickerman called me from … '

'All right, Derek, we all know you're a man of experience and you must have a very good reason for taking so long to get here.'

'I came as quickly as I could, sir. I've crossed the Atlantic twice in the last thirty-six hours … '

'So I believe, Mr Torry, and we'll all listen to your exploits at the appropriate moment. That's if you're not too tired.'

Ticker signalled with his eyes, and Torry, seething with anger, crossed the floor to take his seat.

'Careful, Derek.' Ticker spoke without moving his lips, the habitual offender's method of communication. 'The old man's got a big one on his plate. Touchy, and he's gunning for you.'

'So am I bloody touchy. Bonnie and Clyde touchy. If he doesn't get off my back I'll screw him off.'

'Watch it, lad.'

'All right.' Surly. Then, under his breath. 'Chief Super. He couldn't even recognize a duff eleven-shilling note.'

The Chief Superintendent was away. 'Subject: Gustave Lipperman. Anyone have any knowledge, apart from Sergeant Hart and what you've read in the papers or *The Gazette*?'

No one answered. Behind the old man a photograph had been projected on the long screen. Male, indeterminate age, between forty and fifty, hair receding badly as though eaten away by insects. A shabby face. The Chief was talking again.

'On the fourth of April this year, Gustave Lipperman, aged forty-eight, was taken, together with Wilfred Adam Grosvenor and Florence Annie Cust, to West End Central. After questioning they were all three charged with obtaining money with menaces, causing grievous bodily harm and keeping two houses for the purpose of unlawful sexual intercourse with girls between the ages of thirteen and sixteen. Sergeant Hart, carry on, would you?' His eyes lifted to a cherub-faced young man sitting at the end of the row. Hart ambled up to the rostrum full of that irritating self-confidence often the hall-mark of junior police officers. He spoke as though giving evidence in court, textbook style.

'Eric Hart, Detective Sergeant, C Division. Over the past nine months I have been assisting Detective Superintendent Morse, C Division, in inquiring into allegations of assault, demands for money with menaces ... '

It was warm in the Briefing Room. Hart droned on while part of Torry's mind neatly assimilated the important pieces of information and the other part tried to sum up the young detective. The arrest of Lipperman, Grosvenor and Cust had not been timely. They were only fringe benefits. A central, highly sophisticated, criminal organization had been systematically working in well-defined areas. Not one of the known London gangs, nor the Mafia. Information showed that their activities ranged from protection and prostitution to major robbery.

Hart wore a grey single-breasted suit. Unmarried. Hitched he could not afford gear like that, and the shirt, pink and expensive. Unmarried; bent, or with a private income. The information fell from his sarcastic lips as pat as though he was reading it from the telephone directory. He was good and knew it. Dangerous. Unmarried, dedicated. Like you, Torry. Why hate him? Not hate, that's too strong. Dislike. You both probably have the same qualities. The voice began to infuriate him now. Good London, overlaid with a certain amount of precision. In time, if he didn't watch it, the voice might take on that semi-refined tone of outer suburbia. What are you talking about, you wop? Your own voice isn't so hot.

Superintendent Morse had decided they must turn the arrest to their advantage. Both Grosvenor and Cust had previous convictions, Lipperman had none. It soon became apparent that Lipperman would eventually break. The trial was scheduled at the Bailey in ten days' time. By the end of the previous week

Lipperman had almost decided to turn Queen's evidence and name names. Then, over the week-end, he had cooled. The last time Hart had seen him was during a session of questioning that morning. He had been completely uncooperative.

The sergeant had a habit of running his fingers through his hair and then glancing at the fingertips. Worried? Not with beautiful blond hair like that. There was another possibility. Hart could be a palone. Fanny Hart. No. What's the matter with you, Torry? You don't even know him. An exercise in character observation. Eric Hart. Detective Sergeant, Metropolitan Police, C Division. Twenty-six, twenty-seven years old. Height, around six feet. Complexion, light. Hair, light. Eyes, can't see, bluish. Smartly dressed smarty. What was the trouble? This one wasn't just another civil servant with a bit of know-how. This one was a threat. Another John Derek Torry. Was that it? You recognize yourself here, eh Dereko? Fifteen years ago you wouldn't have been thinking like this. Why? Do you despise people you have to work with? Do they despise you? Don't forget you're one of them even though you're half Italian in the blood and spent three years with New York City Police Department. You can't live off that for the rest of your life. You're one of them. A little civil servant with a spot of power, a certain amount of crude experience and some technical knowledge. Fifteen years ago you wouldn't have allowed your concentration to wander and play dumb tricks.

' ... This morning Lipperman seemed anxious. We couldn't get anything from him.' Hart consulted his notebook. 'On several occasions he said, "Give me a day or two. I've got to make up my mind." That's about all I can give you now, sir.' He spoke the last sentence looking straight at the Chief Superintendent.

'Thank you, Hart.'

What had they got? Lipperman was small fry in a seamy

operation. Locked and bolted in the 'Scrubs', changeable about turning Queen's evidence. Not surprising. So?

'What's it all about?' Torry muttered.

'Lipperman murdered.' Ticker mouthed back.

'In custody?' Almost aloud. Ticker motioned quietly with his hand. The old man was at it again. 'Now to the facts ... '

The real meat? Lord, how the gaffer rambled. The facts, true, but not naked, clothed in layer upon layer of asides, confused terminology, and the growth of words which had become part of the Chief Superintendent's habitual character. The result? Total unreality. They were dealing with a dream, not the hard gritty grainy force of life and death. Good was good. Evil, evil. But they never overlapped, met, swamped each other. Lipperman's break from the Scrubs. Primula Street. The car. Austin Cambridge, licence number BAB462D. Children playing. Two women gossiping. (' ... stopped for a chat at the far end of the street. Here,' said the old man stabbing at the diagram, sinister in black and white, projected on the screen).

' ... Lipperman took six bullets in the chest. By the time the women reached him he was ... ha ... er ... in ... as Mr Torry would say, a complete state of death ... ha.'

Chuckles. Why the hell couldn't he leave it alone? Smile, Torry. Pretend you're amused. It had become a running gag. A complete state of death. Just because he'd used the phrase once in a report. The old man had commented, in front of several people, on 'our budding literary talent'. That was about his level. 'Heard the old man's latest?'

Vehicle recovered: abandoned at White City. Sterling submachine gun in the back. What was it? No passion? Or was he, Torry, supercilious and hypercritical of the authority vested in his superiors? It was no new sensation. It gnawed and worried him, even to the extent of discussing it with Father Conrad.

'That's a sin as old as time, Derek.' The gaunt wise old priest, smelling of incense and candlewax, the scent of holiness. 'It's partly pride. One of the besetting sins of priests.'

'Priests?'

'Oh, Derek, come on now, you're a man of the world. We haven't brainwashed you, have we? Priests, monks, nuns. I knew a child once who refused to believe monks and nuns ever went to the lavatory. Do you think zealous young priests don't raise their eyebrows at one another when they hear their bishop pontificating about this dogma or that heresy?'

Torry had smiled. He was always dropping into the trap of thinking of priests and religious as people so apart that they were far out from all things worldly, tucked away among the beauties of carved polished wood, marble and the tinted light streaming from stained glass.

'If we are zealous, if we are professional,' the priest had said, 'we naturally become critical, particularly of the work of those below and above us. The answer is difficult. It's hard to harness the critical faculty, but one must do it, in a way in which we teach those who serve below us, and learn from those above, even from their mistakes and bad habits.'

Habits. Habits. The old gag about the monk saying, 'I must kick this dirty habit.'

The grey seats of the Briefing Room. Oh God, no, he'd missed something. The Austin Cambridge. Reported stolen from outside owner's house in Godolphin Road, Shepherd's Bush, at eight thirty that morning. At nine o'clock Lionel Henry Jumper taken into custody at Paddington. In possession of the car's original licence plates, number DAA465D. The Chief Superintendent was calling on Superintendent Marlow of Crime Three.

Marlow, that was his name, the man he'd noticed when he came in. Fingerprint man. Worked with him last year. A professional. You didn't have to despise him. Succinct. Knew what he was talking about. Iron-grey hair, northern accent, nothing fancy. Determined tread as he walked to the rostrum. Straight into action.

'As the Chief Superintendent's told you, we're making a thorough examination of the car. I've come over here with two sets of fingerprints taken from the false licence plates BAB462D. On the first analysis these prints seem to be identifiable with those of Lionel Henry Jumper whose fingerprints we have on file.' He looked up curtly at the Chief Superintendent. 'I'd like to be getting back ... '

A nod. This is how it should be done. Quick, no messing with pep talks and bilge. The Chief Superintendent was speaking again. His name. Torry's name.

'As it seems to have direct reference to the case perhaps Mr Torry would tell us what happened to him in North America.'

Don't waste time. Give it to them clean. Hart was smirking. Ticker looking interested. Torry went through the whole thing. 'Shoelace' and his fears. The meeting at the airport. Three hundred pounds. The end of 'Shoelace'. Stress the name Wexton. Back to your seat.

The old man began his summing up. They were all relieved of any outstanding cases. This was priority and the Chief Superintendent was handling it himself with Snaith and Broadbent to assist. Ticker was to back up Superintendent Morse. Good luck, he'd have Hart to contend with. And Torry? Blast him, the leg-work. Personal check on all Wextons in C.R.O. files. Interview Jumper now at Paddington. Full written report of American business and interrogation of Jumper by the morning when C.R.O. would have all the Wextons waiting for him in their neat little files.

It was raining. Chaos on the roads, London bunged full of excess traffic, pedestrians caught napping, scattered in doorways or slopping towards subway stations. Underground stations. Torry had never got out of the American manner of calling it the subway. Ticker had to go across to West End Central and Torry hitched a ride on to Paddington. They sat in the back of the big police Humber eyeing the damp parade.

'You never get passionate about it, do you?'

Ticker was taken by surprise. Basically he knew what it was all about. A nice man, broad shoulders, thinning hair, the trick of being avuncular with junior colleagues as well as clients. He took a drag at his cigarette and gave a thin smile.

'With the women you mean, Derek?'

'You know what I mean.'

'Yes. You mean I never get involved. It's the first rule. lad.'

'To hell with the rules. You people go at it like some great game.'

'And occasionally you have to pick a *Chance* card which gives you a routine job. Miss three turns and have a look at all the Wextons in the book instead of chasing villains across rooftops. Derek, grow up.'

'The hell with routine, that's part of it. I don't mind sifting. But you've got to have hate, Ticker.'

'Hate, lad? What is there to hate?'

'A man leans out of a car and cuts down another man with a gun, in daylight, with kids playing just up the street, and you can't find anything to hate?'

'Don't hate 'em, Derek. Pity 'em. Catch 'em. But don't hate 'em.'

'If I don't hate them, I can't catch them.'

They had slowed down in the traffic. A group of giggling girls huddled together in the doorway of a camera shop, thin bars of rain imprisoning them. In the shop window a large photograph in unreal Technicolor, mocking the rain, displaying a gay sexless couple romping on sunny sands with chubby children and a beach ball. Was that the dream of those giggling girls? A man, orange blossom, thrilling sexless sex once a week, bonny, bouncing, painless babies, a nice little house and annual visits to the sea. Safety. Peace. Sun and no smells. Well, it was their right, if that was what they wanted. The disillusionment would come soon enough. It was what Ticker wanted. That's why most coppers simply talk of their work as 'the job'. Emotion didn't enter into it. But, with Torry, it had to. Christ with his scourge of small cords in the Temple, lashing at the crooked money-changers. It was a sin to hate, yet a virtue to hate evil. To hell with them. The criminal had to be hated as one hates cancer.

'Watch it, Derek. No games with Jumper. The old man'll have you quick as look at you.'

There was something about Ticker's voice which made Torry slide the mildly supercilious smile from his lips. He looked straight at the Detective Superintendent and didn't like what he saw in the man's face.

'I'm among friends?' Torry lifted one eyebrow in question.

'That's why I'm saying it.' Tickerman remained his avuncular self.

'Is there more? More I should know?'

Tickerman looked thoughtful, then glanced towards the driver and back again to Torry. 'Step this way. Driver, wait for Mr Torry, will you?' They had stopped in front of West End Central. Torry followed Tickerman out into the rain and up the steps. Together, they sheltered under the short concrete awning. A uniformed young constable, going on duty, eyed them and asked, 'You any business here?'

'Tell him,' said Tickerman.

Torry showed his warrant card and nodded towards Tickerman. 'He's my Superintendent. Mr Tickerman, if you want to check.' The constable departed, flustered. 'You're the senior officer. You should've done it.' Torry was straight-faced.

'It would've meant unbuttoning my overcoat,' replied Ticker equally poker. 'You remember the song? "Button up your overcoat, when the wind is free. Take good care of yourself, you belong to me." You want to take very good care of me, Derek. I could be the only friend you have.'

'So there's something I should know?'

'There's something *I* think you should know. The old man's gunning for you.'

'That's yesterday's weather forecast. He's been digging in the spurs ever since the Fulham farce.'

'Wait, lad. It's not just that. The Chief Super's not the only one. Half the boys in Crime One've got it in for you.'

Torry's eyes narrowed. He felt traces of sweat on his palms. None of this was really new. Like the next man, Torry could sense the feeling of being disliked. Though nobody had nailed him for the Fulham complaint it had become increasingly obvious that a lot of people had changed their position. Men who had simply got on with him before now showed open mistrust.

'So the Chief Super and his goblins want to crucify me.' He tried to make light of it.

'Don't laugh, Derek. You could really find yourself in trouble.'

'God in heaven, Tick, why? Why me? All right, I've played against the book sometimes, but I've always been conscientious. Everything a good policeman should be.' He adopted a mock sonorous tone. 'Friend in an emergency. Friend to the helpless. Friend to youth. Friend to the innocent. Foe to the lawless. Foe to disorder. Foe to pain and misery. Foe to discrimination. 'Strewth, Tick, I've been a policeman nearly all my adult life. Even in the Army, that was like being a copper. I'm a professional. I can't cope with the old-woman routine.'

'That could be the trouble. You've got a difficult reputation. Gimmicky, that's what the old man called you today.'

'He's talked to you?'

'When I went in with your Wexton story. After you phoned in.' Tickerman went on to describe the interview. How the Chief Superintendent sat quietly smirking, jacketless, the striped shirt sleeves pulled high, held above the elbows with shining spring arm-bands. When Tickerman finished, the old man looked up. As though for the first time, Tickerman noticed how ugly his moustache looked, stained and heavy with nicotine.

'And why couldn't Inspector Torry come and tell me all this himself?'

'I told him to go home and get some sleep.'

'Wish to God we could find some way of telling him to go home for good.'

'Sir?' Ticker did not have to feign surprise. He knew how the Chief Superintendent felt, but this was an open showing of hands.

'He'll have to go. Tickerman. Have to go.'

'I'm sorry, sir, I'm not with you.'

'He who is not with me is against me.' He sounded like an impoverished Billy Graham.

'I mean I don't understand you, sir.'

'Don't you, Mr Tickerman?' He tapped his nose. 'No, course you don't. Torry's one of your boys, isn't he?'

'He's on my team.'

'And what's his game now? All this bribery thing. Dramatics at Kennedy Airport. Amateur dramatics. Trying to be a hero, is he?'

'I don't think it's a game, sir. Torry doesn't play games with criminals.'

'No? You know what they call him? Tricky Torry. And Tricky Torry'll have to be eased out, Mr Tickerman, because neither I myself nor the best part of my staff have any time for him.'

'With respect, sir, Torry's one of the best officers we've got in Crime One. You've only got to look at his record.'

'What you mean is that he gets results at the cost of discipline.'

'No, sir. He gets results, that's all.'

'And complaints.'

'There's only been one that I've heard of.'

'And a hundred minor ones that I've heard of in this very office.'

'Then they'd better be passed on to the Commander, hadn't they, sir?' Tickerman cold as a deep freeze.

The Chief Superintendent let out a spitting noise. 'Torry's gimmicky, Tickerman. Gimmicky, a corner-cutter. A detective sergeant reports him for carrying an unlawful weapon while on a case; a detective constable says he deliberately ignored a radio message in order to proceed with his own line of inquiry. A ... '

'Every good officer has a bunch of men who try to jump on him, sir. I'll bet Torry'd chewed up most of the ones who complained to you.' Tickerman laughed, not with, but at his superior. 'Such stuff as dreams are made of.'

The Chief Superintendent eyed him shrewdly. '*On*, Superintendent Tickerman, such stuff as dreams are made *on*. Not *of*.' "We are such stuff as dreams are made on, and our little life is rounded with a sleep." I know what you mean though. Torry can pull all the standard procedure stuff he wants. You can warn him if you like. I'm not going to tolerate him for much longer.'

'Sir.'

'No, Tick, you listen to me. All right, I'm biased. I don't like the man, but I'm not a fool. Torry's a good policeman, that nobody's going to deny. You can't deny the other thing either. Torry's a professional climber and it's landing me with a department split in half. You and your team get on with him, but there are a lot of men who do not. And they're unhappy men, dis-contented men. If I can fault Torry I'm going to have him out of here quicker than a poxed-up solicitor's clerk from a whore-house, and it'll be for the good of Crime One, not just because I find him bloody smart.'

Torry listened to Tickerman in silence. Then, 'Would it be for the good of Crime One?'

'If you got the bum's rush? No, I don't think so, but then I'm not living in the old man's mind. What I can tell you, Derek, is that they're going to ride you hard. Why d'you think you're doing a sergeant's leg-work on this one? The Chief Super thinks there's nothing to it and you'll end up looking an idiot.'

'That's not hard.'

'Under these circumstances you can say that again. Watch it, Derek. For Christ's sake, watch it.'

They both walked down to the car. Inside, Torry churned with anger. 'I'd like to go and stuff my warrant card down his boozy throat.'

'You take it easy.' Tickerman touched his arm. 'And no games, right?'

Torry nodded. No games? We'll see. He'd read Jumper's C.R.O. file before leaving the Yard. We'll see about Jumper. Through the window his eye caught a newspaper poster, sodden, ink running, wording ambiguous: ESCAPING PRISONER SHOT DEAD.

Jumper inhaled and the glowing butt of his cigarette moved towards him, almost touching his lips. He dropped the end and ground it into the stone with his heel, a movement of destruction. The cell did not impress him. Seen better, he thought, arrogance often being the outward sign of fear. At the worst they could only get him for receiving. With a good lawyer he might even ... Footsteps. Snigger. That old movie on the telly the other night where the fella said, 'Hush, I hear footprints.' Key in the lock.

'Come on then, Jumper. Upstairs.' Bugger, thought it was tea or something. He's only a young copper. Young constable. You could take him easy. Mentally and physically you could take him. No, passive co-operation, like those wartime spy movies where they only gave their name, rank and number. Co-operative. Ask him one question.

'What for?'

'You'll see.'

Chatty. Follow the nice gentleman. Christ no, he'll follow you. Perhaps Smith's already heard and got on to Wexton and they've sent a lawyer. No, Wexton wouldn't work like that. Surely he knows I wouldn't ... not like Gus.

'See what? Come on, give us a hint.'

'Someone from the Yard wants to talk to you, Jumper. How about that? You made it this time.'

The Yard? Jesus, they couldn't. Of course they could. They're bound to think he nicked the car. But proving it was different.

'What the hell's the Yard want with me? Who is it anyway?' Not so fast, Jumper, your heart's going. Hear it?

'You'll see.'

Don't press it. Probably only a sergeant. Time to get worried if it's a Chief Inspector or a Super. Bloody lepers they are. Up the steps. Slow down.

'When're you goin' to get carpets in this place then? Stone plays hell with my feet.'

'Comedian. You're all comedians. Ought to be on the telly, Jumper.'

'That's what my mates say.' Corridor. We're here. Interview room. Usual. Stone walls and glossy paint. Table. Three chairs.

'Sit down then. You've been through this before.'

Bloody coppers. Only a kid, standing there with his back to the door. Damn great clodhopping boots. Might've been a copper myself if it hadn't been for the gear. Dead horrible, those boots. Hallo, here we go.

'Lionel Henry Jumper, sir.'

What's he got to look at then? Smoothie, this fella. Bit of a dresser, with the cuffs on his sleeves and that. And the pink shirt. Big bastard though. Bet he does all right with protection from the toms. Been bashed up in his time. Not nice, not nice at all. Christ, stop looking at me like that. No, don't speak, Jumper. Let him do the talking. Name, rank and serial number. Play at bein' a British flier up in front of the bloody Gestapo.

'Okay constable, I'll call you when I need you.'

Christ, what's he doin'? That's not usual. The quiet chat-up, eh? Sounds a bit Yankee in his voice. What you breathin' so fast for, Jumper? Steady. Name, rank and serial number. Dark hair, dark eyes he's got.

'You sure, sir?'

'I'll call you.'

Dark eyes. Like a bleedin' cat. Never takes them off of you. What's up? I got two heads or somethink?

'Detective Inspector Torry, C.I.D., New Scotland Yard. You are Lionel Henry Jumper?'

'Well I'm not Yogi Bear.' Inspector? They can't be all that bothered about me then. Only an inspector. Why doesn't he sit down? Leaning against the table like that. Leaning on his hands, fingers spread wide. Clean hands. Very clean.

'I'm asking the questions. You are Lionel Henry Jumper?'

'Yeah.' Don't get shirty then. You can't prove I done nothin'.

'Lionel Jumper. You're following in your father's footsteps then, are you?'

'You what?' Nasty bastard, startin' right in with me old man. None of them ever done that before.

'You heard, you bloody little pipsqueak murderer.'

'What you talking about? You can't talk to me like that.'

'Why not?'

Jesus,this was a cold one. 'Well, it's intimidatin' me.'

'Who's intimidating you, Jumper? Do you know what intimidating means? I'm just telling you what I think of you. You're a rotten little half-baked layabout who's going to get done for murder and put away for life. They charged you yet?'

'No, and I want my lawyer.' For God's sake, I want somebody. Quick, I want somebody.

'Your lawyer? And who would that be? You've been reading cheap books, boy. You don't even know the difference between a lawyer and a solicitor, do you?'

'I know you can't keep me here much longer without charging me.'

'You're going to be charged all right.'

He's got an edge on him. Chip on his shoulder. What was he on about?

'They'd better get on with it then.'

'Murder.'

Laugh, Jumper, laugh in his face. That's the best way to treat them.

'I don't find it particularly funny. It's what they usually charge murderers with, isn't it? It's what they charged your father with. He was a murderer too, wasn't he?'

'My old man ... '

'The only difference now is the law's changed, so we can't top you. But, by God, Jumper, they'll give you a bad time.'

Tremblin'. You're bloody tremblin'. Rage, that's what it is. Steady now. Answer him.

'Look, Mr ... er ... '

'Torry. T-O-R-R-Y. *Mr* Torry, and don't forget it.'

'Yeah. *Mr* Torry, I wouldn't do anything like that.'

'Like what?'

78

'Like what you said. Murder.' Careful, Jumper, he's tryin' to get you all tied up.

'You wouldn't? Well, why are you being charged with it?'

Thank God, he's sat down at last. 'No, and you bloody know I haven't done no murder.'

'I know nothing of the kind. I know the exact opposite. I know that you are concerned with a murder and that you can be charged with it. You want to talk?'

'There's nothing to talk about. They pulled me in here this mornin' 'cos I bought a set of licence plates off a bloke.'

'You bought a set of licence plates. Well, you tell me about that, Jumper. Who did you buy the licence plates from?'

'I told you. A bloke.' Christ, now he'll ask me what bloke.

'What bloke?'

'Just a bloke.' Christ, it's getting bloody cold in here.

'His name, Jumper.'

'How should I know? Didn't ask his name.'

'Silly thing to do, boy. Very silly. You bought the licence plates of a car that was used to kill a man. You sure you don't know his name?'

'I don't know his name I tell you.' He wasn't goin' to give up. The way he sat in that chair you could tell. Torry. I'll remember all right.

'His name wouldn't be Wexton by any chance?'

Screamin' Jesus. Wexton. What do they know about Wexton? Answer him. Say somethin'. It won't come out ... throat ... Christ ...

'Who?' Doesn't sound like your own voice. Throat's so bloody dry.

'Why are you so frightened of the name Wexton?'

'I'm not frightened.' Stop shakin'. Fingernails. Just like back at school. Get your hand away from your mouth.

'Jumper, you're going to be charged with murder, whatever,

so you might as well tell me all about it. We know quite a lot already. You didn't buy any licence plates ... '

'Don't know what you're talking about.' That's it, the old name, rank and serial number. Nearly had you goin' for a minute.

'That's a pity. They'll charge you and there'll be a magistrate's hearing in the morning.'

He means it. He bloody means it. Or does he? No, it's the old game. He'll leave you alone to sweat it out. They can't charge you with that.

'You can't charge me with no murder. I was here when ... '

Jesus God.

'When?'

'You can't do that ... ' Aaah. Me breath. Christ, that hurt. Swallow. Didn't even see his arm come up. Backhander across the cheek. He's taken half me face away. 'You can't do that. You can't bloody hit me. You can't hit me, Torry ... '

'*Mr* Torry. And who hit you?'

'You did. You hit me, and you can't hit me. It's not allowed.'

'Of course it isn't. I wouldn't hit you, Jumper. It's more than my career's worth to hit a man like you. They'd chuck me out if I did anything like ... THAT.'

Aaah. Bastard. Again. Tears. Shaking. Madman. A mad copper. Locked in here with a mad copper.

'Now, you're going to sit here and tell me all about it, Jumper. You just said you were here when ... when what, Jumper?'

'I never said that. I'm goin' to report you. You hit me.'

'Don't be a fool. Hit you? Where am I supposed to have hit you?'

'You bastard. Across my face. I must be marked. Bruised.'

Christ, what was he at now. The door.

'Constable.'

The young copper again. Never trust bleedin' coppers.

'Constable. Jumper wants to make a complaint against me. He says I hit him on the face ... '

'Twice he hit me.'

' ... twice. You were outside. Did you hear anything?'

'No sir.'

Real surprise. He never heard nothin'.

'Does his face look marked?'

'Not to me, sir.'

'Have a good look.'

'Looks all right to me, sir.'

He's got bad breath, that young copper. Ought to take some-think for it.

'You'd better take him up and charge him. Then, if he wants, he can make out his complaint and statement. He'd better see a doctor. I want him to see a doctor.'

'Right, sir. Come on, Jumper.'

'Constable, have you seen the charge?'

'Yes, sir.'

'What is it?'

Christ, now the copper's lookin' at you funny as well.

'In that ... '

'Not the whole rigmarole. Just the charge.'

'Accessory to the murder of Gustave Lipperman, sir.'

Jesus, he *does* mean it. Wait now, Jumper. Not even for Wexton.

'Mr Torry. Can I have a word with you in private first?'

Why take so long? Can't he make up his mind? Doesn't need any thought.

'Okay, sit down.'

Wait for the constable to go. He's nodding to him. Now, careful.

'Look, Mr Torry, if I happened to make a statement about the car ... '

'Go on.' .

'Like, and dropped the complaint against you ... '

'I didn't touch you, lad. You can do what you like with the complaint.'

'Well, it would save time and trouble all round, wouldn't it? I mean if I did that ... ?' He's givin' you a queer sort of look. 'If I did ... do you think they'd ... well ... would they drop this murder thing?' He's shaking his bloody head. Must be joking. They can't.

'No deals, Jumper. You ought to know that. You're implicated in a very nasty business. But if you want to tell me about the car, things might be easier.'

'All right, so I pinched the car. They said it was for a heist. I didn't know about any murder. What happened, they knock off a watchman or something?'

'You tell me, Jumper.'

'Honest, I don't know nothin' about it. They said it was for a heist.'

'Where did you nick the car?'

Truth, Jumper. This one's got to be the truth. 'Godolphin Road. You know, out in the Bush.'

'That's better. You're telling the truth for a change. Now, why did you nick the car?'

'Bloke asked me to.'

'Bloke called Wexton?'

'I told you I don't know no Wexton.' Hold it. Play the bastard. Not too much of the truth. Just enough. Think for a name ... name ... name ... 'This was a fella called Jones ... '

'Welsh? Jones the Death?'

'I don't think Jones is his real name. They just call him Jones. Jonesy.' Sounded good. Fast thinking. Stop trembling and you'll be all right.

'Sure it wasn't Wexton?'

'Christ, I've told you ... ' What was he doing? Going to bleedin' pieces. Shattered and smashed. It's not you, Jumper.

Put the clock back and let's do it all again. Make it cool, frozen, like usually. And Torry, the bastard, keeps comin' at you. What did Jones look like? Where'd you first meet him? Did he talk about anyone else? Where did you have to take the car? Who was there? What did they look like? What was actually said? Where did you change the plates? What about Wexton? ... Wexton? ... Wexton.

Wexton tipped the papers on end, shuffled them straight and placed them, with fussy precision, on the desk. Strong hands he's got, thought Smith. Strong hands and a worried look. Don't like to see Wexton worried.

'You needn't bother yourself about Jumper, Mr Wexton. Really you needn't.' The soft voice. There were times when Smith felt Wexton needed a nurse. A male nurse maybe. It was something in the man's manner at times of crisis. Anyone who plans and thinks as big as this man had to be a little mad.

'It's not good, Smith. Not good.' Spoken like a professional. Doctor? Broker? Banker? You would never know which. 'We pay for the best and the best never get caught. There's been too much of it lately.' Then, as if to reassure himself, 'You're certain about Jumper?'

'As certain as one can be. Anyway, he's never met you.'

'That's not the point. He *has* met you, knows you, and the other two.'

'You can forget about it. He knows me, that's why you can forget about it. There's one thing though, sir, he doesn't know about the Birthday Party.'

It was electric. Wexton froze, a hand reaching for the leather cigarette box. Outside, a dog barked in the darkness far away, then a light gust of wind blew a splatter of rain against the windows. After that, nothing. A silence which dominated the comfortable room for a good thirty seconds. Thirty seconds in which Wexton relived the telephone call. When was it? Two weeks ago? Or three? He had been sitting at this desk. The operator said, 'A call from New York. Just one moment,' and he felt the cold hand down in his stomach. The voice at the other end did not matter. Whatever the voice, it was always The Man talking.

'Hi. It's Ed. How've you bin?'

'Okay,' said Wexton, sounding cool enough.

'We were wondering 'cos we hadn't heard anything from you for some time. We were wondering about the investments. Mainly the big one.'

'I told you last time I was over that we can't possibly do anything about that until the end of the year. It needs a lot of work.'

'So how's the work going?'

'Fine. Just fine.' In the pause now, the Birthday Party had been born. 'In fact we're planning to make a public announcement this April to show just how well we stand.'

'Ah. That's what we like to hear. You'll let us see details before publication, of course.'

'Naturally.' It had been a mad idea. A mad, spectacular idea, but just the kind of thing those hard gentlemen in New York would like. They were impressed by skilful planning and a dangerous few minutes being navigated accurately. The Birthday Party was a perfect shop window for his wares.

Wexton's hand relaxed with a slight tremor, a smile slowly changing the position of his mouth. 'Yes.' The slim white tube lifted to lips, flick of the lighter and the cloud of smoke exhaled. The house seemed normal again. 'Yes, I wanted to talk about the Birthday Party.' Wexton raised his eyes and smiled at Smith.

'You've got the figures?' Smith's mind full of £ signs.

Wexton nodded. The gleeful nod of a child on Christmas

morning. 'At least a quarter of a million. Between the four of them, of course. Maybe more.'

'They won't get away with that much. Not in the time. Four minutes isn't long.'

'We're not worried about profits. Don't forget that, Smith. This is a training operation under fire. Profits don't count. You done anything else?'

This was more like it. 'I've got the film, but it needs supplementing. Raymond and Archer'll be going down this weekend. I've told them to get shots of the bad corners on both routes out, and a lot of stuff around the actual area.'

'It won't attract attention?'

'In that place? People with cameras are a penny a hundred, you should know that.'

'I suppose so. The cars?'

'We know which ones and where they'll be, and there are duplicates in case someone changes his normal routine. The Humber's over at my place, going up to Birmingham on Friday to be doctored.' Old Wexton certainly gets worked up when one of his jaunts starts to take off. Look at those eyes. Hungry, like a famine relief poster.

'The briefing?'

'Just as arranged. Heads of teams and the drivers.' Smith settled back comfortably. This was a large one. Large and spectacular. That's what made working for Wexton worth while, you never stood still. Now he was doodling.

'I still think we've got too many men on the ground. Twenty-six is an awful lot.'

Keep smiling, Smithy, you've got lots of aces up your sleeve. 'You can cut it down to twenty-two if you make it four sets of three instead of four of four.'

'It's the only place we can cut. Think about it for me, would you.'

'It's the seventeenth already, Mr Wexton. If you're going to lay men off they aren't going to like it. Not at the last minute.'

'Well that's up to me, isn't it? Think about it.'

'All right.' Yes, Mr Wexton. All right, Mr Wexton. Three bags full. It's going to be a right chuckle.

It took just over three hours. Getting Jumper's statement. Telephoning Ticker. Getting back to the Yard. Typing the two reports. Ticker, you could almost see the satisfied smile, said he would get Morse and Hart to go to the address in Willesden. They would find nothing there, but maybe the fingerprint boys could turn up something more concrete than the vague descriptions provided by Jumper: Jones and two nameless men that the whining little car thief had never seen before. Both were short, one rather stout, the other with a scar across the bridge of his nose. Jones, according to Jumper, was tall, thin, used three different pubs in Willesden and sometimes wore glasses. Jumper's description would have changed again by tomorrow.

Torry worried about the whole deal as the taxi grumbled through the late night traffic towards the Cromwell Road. Why worry? Tomorrow is another ... all the clichés. Wexton. Jumper's face, white as a shroud at the name Wexton. It seemed to have a quality of evil about it. There must be hundreds of people called Wexton, but in this context ... the whine in Jumper's voice and the pleading expression. Shouldn't have hit him, though. You psychopathic or something, Torry? After Ticker's warning. You've had enough experience. The old man *would* have you this time—if he found out. Stupid, idiotic, cretinous thing to do. Temper, power. Is that what it's all about? Disgust in his guts, at himself. The big strong cop beating up the snivelling little crook. It's not like that ...

There was a light on in the flat. It spilled out into the passage in a thin line under the door. Torry quietly inserted the key, holding it with his right hand, the arm spread across the door and his back to the wall. A quick twist and a hard kick with the right foot. The door crashed open, then silence. Torry sprang into the doorway.

'So I tossed in a grenade, then let 'em have it with my super silver-gilt Police Positive Special forty-five thirty-eight. Hallo, darling.' Susan sat, in one of the armchairs. Lounged more than sat. Black mini-skirt and white sweater, yards of leg and her hair short, untidy. On the floor a pile of exercise books.

'Dear God, what are you doing here?'

'I've got a key. Remember? I don't use it often, but as we had a date at eight thirty ... '

'Sue, I'm sorry.' You live for the moment, Torry, don't grovel. 'Work.'

'This?' She was on her feet, indicating the *Standard*. Late Final. Diagrams. Photographs. Morse and some uniformed men in Primula Street. Great black headlines, like something from a montage sequence in an old movie. ESCAPING PRISONER SHOT IN STREET. They had given it the whole front page and more. Torry nodded and tossed the paper on to a chair.

'Tell you what.'

'Coffee,' she stated as though resigned. 'Your phone's been going mad so I answered it. Mr Tickerman wants you to call him at home. Sounded no end pleased when I said I was here on my own. Don't think he believed me really.'

'Sue?' A note of reproach. 'What did you say to him?'

'I did a lot of the heavy breathing and said you weren't available. Then he told me who he was and I showed great respect.'

'When was this?'

'Ten minutes ago. Better ring him, darling, he'll think we've finished by now.'

'Coffee.' Torry reached gracelessly for the telephone.

'I'll go and listen in on the bedroom extension.' Susan grinned wickedly, her hair looked tangled and messy, and, for a second, Torry's mind slipped into sentiment, seeing her against downland, a clump of trees, sun and ripening corn. Corn. 'Hear what I said?' The lush tiny dream disappeared. 'I'll go into your bedroom. Bedroom. Where you sleep, Tiger. You know … '

'Coffee.' No smile. Serious to the last syllable. He dialled Ticker's number.

'What's this then, the ever faithful, ever pure Derek Torry with girls in his flat at this time of night?' Ticker sounded comfortable.

'*A* girl.' Torry, irritated, stressing the indefinite article. 'I had a date that slipped a bit because of Jumper. Sue came in to make the coffee.'

'Got a key, has she?'

'Agile mind, sir. Ought to be a detective.'

'All right, Derek.' Torry knew he had gone too far. 'All right. I just wanted you to know Jumper's done the dirty. There's no such address in Willesden.'

'I checked the map.'

'The street's okay, but the numbers end at ninety-four.'

'It was a hundred and two Jumper said?'

'One-zero-two.' Torry heard the fatigue in his own voice. 'I'm not surprised. I shouldn't think there are two short villains and a man called Jones either.'

'Sounds like something out of a motel register, doesn't he? Morse's none too happy.'

'Well he'd better let his boy detective have a go with Jumper, hadn't he?'

'He's doing just that. First thing in the morning.'

'Then God help Jumper.' And me, Torry cursed quietly to himself.

*

In New York it was six o'clock, a traffic-packed evening with the lights just coming on. The bars were full of the commuter trade summoning the courage to take to the suburbs and the waiting wife and kids. The great city brushed off the grime of the day and began to map out its evening. The planners and the nice folk worked out which programme and what channel for TV viewing, or which movie, show, restaurant, night club.

While the nice folk planned or fixed a simple evening meal the plotters carefully began to draw up their order of battle. Decisions were finally made: which maidenhead would be smashed and where. The bad boys already knew which store, bank, dwelling-house would be hit. The night owls bathed, shaved and preened themselves while their young women, fresh from the shower, chose their underwear with care, because they knew, better than those who plotted, what would happen that night.

Reputations stood on the brink, and in a pleasant apartment off Madison in the high East Forties, five men met to the accompaniment of Peter Nero in stereo and the comforting clink of ice in their bourbon.

The Police Department would have been interested to know that these five citizens were keeping company. For that matter there were several Police Departments throughout the United States, not to mention the F.B.I., who would have quietly flipped had someone dangled the information in their direction.

The host, owner of the apartment and chairman of the meeting, was a New Yorker born and bred, though the breeding was a trifle slap-happy. Albert Vescari had come into the world forty-nine years before, via Carlo and Maria (particularly Maria) Vescari, in a four-roomed tenement apartment six aching walk-up flights above a bookshop on Mulberry Street. Vescari's youth had been spent in and around that tenement; then, at sixteen, he escaped from the neighbourhood, like many before him, by way of reform school. Those two years, laid on him at the Juvenile Court, were the only tangible assets on his record. Since that time, Vescari had never been arrested, let alone convicted. Yet many people in law enforcement would have liked to nail him. The Syndicate had almost certainly used him for a long time, but as the years went by nobody could be quite sure if Al Vescari was on his own or part of some larger mob. Outwardly, he was the Italian kid who had made it in spite of a shaky start. Real estate was his business, and he had grown prosperous, with an apartment in New York and a summer villa on the west coast in swank La Jolla. At the age of forty-nine Vescari looked like any other wealthy real-estate man who cared for himself. Short but hard, without any excess fat, he had the air of one who issues the orders.

The four men with him were of the same mould. There was Eddie Kostar who hailed from Tulsa and looked as though he should have been born way back so that he could have ridden shotgun for Wells Fargo. Joe Bertel, the eldest, pushing the late fifties, with a store of memories that reached back into days which most men in his native Chicago would prefer to forget. Little Mike Seymour, a sometime jockey who had got suddenly lucky, and rich, around 1947. The fourth was tall, lean Tony Champion, whose record was worth looking at because it was even cleaner than Vescari's. Champion's origins were in the Bronx. His old man had died there last fall, so Tony had heard in his twenty-roomed mansion outside the City of the Angels. He was also in real estate and his property included two prince-sized clubs bang on the strip at Vegas.

Vescari played with the ice in his glass while his four guests read in silence, each bent over identical eight-page quarto typescripts. Champion was first to finish. He nodded at Vescari and passed over the stapled sheets of paper.

'You like it, Tony?' grinned Vescari.

Tony was not a man for talking. 'Great. If he can pull

that, there shouldn't be any bother with the real big one.'

Little Mike Seymour chuckled as he stopped reading. 'Al, this guy really takes it. Might even make the trip over to see for myself.'

'That might just be an un-American activity, Mike,' growled Kostar. 'What with the President tellin' us how we oughta cut back on tourism.'

'Hell, that wouldn't be tourism. It's business.'

They all laughed. Vescari had collected the papers by this time and was glancing round the ring of smiling faces. All smiling but Joe Bertel.

'What's eating you, Joe? You look as happy as a good piece of tail with a faggot.'

'You're sure of Wexton?' Bertel looked sadly up at Vescari.

'Sure I'm sure. We all know him, don't we?' There was a murmur of assent.

'We all know him, Al.' Bertel flicked a gold lighter and kindled his cigarette, still squinting up at Vescari. 'We all know him but I don't trust him.'

'You okayed him. Like we all did. We've had results.' Vescari's charm had disappeared.

'We've had results but what's he trying to prove with this production number?' Bertel waved a hand towards the sheaf of papers.

'Come on, Joe.' Kostar joined in from behind his glass. 'He spells it out. This caper's a non-profit advertising campaign to test the training of his top students. You know what the British are like for proving themselves.'

'It's a crazy thing, Joe, but it's a gass.' From Little Mike.

Bertel's face remained impassive. 'It's crazy, but it's a waste of manpower, time and energy. Sure we've been getting regular returns from Wexton's end but I'd like to make two points.'

'You're lucky to be able to make one at your age, Joe.' Nobody thought Kostar's comment funny.

'Go ahead, Joe. You got the right like any of us.' Vescari's face belied the statement.

'First, Wexton seems to me to have been giving us the run-around on this big one. I don't deny it's big. Scary big. But if you'll remember he originally planned it for the spring. Now he says it can't be done until the end of the year. We're looking for a higher profit before then. What if this sideshow – what's he call it? The Birthday Party? – what if it comes unstuck and his boys get picked up? He'll take another year to set the big one.'

'And the second point?' Vescari sounded as though he could dispose of Bertel's uncertainty with ease.

'Now that's more tenuous.' Joe Bertel turned towards Tony Champion. 'Tony, tell everybody what you told me coming in from the airport.'

'That's a load of crap, Joe. Just cheap talk I heard.'

'Tell it just the same.'

Champion stretched out his long legs. 'Well, it's nothing. Just, when I was in London last month I had me a night in one of Wexton's cat-houses. There was this little broad, see ... ' As he talked, first Vescari, then the others, began to look unhappy. When Champion finished Vescari sucked his teeth.

'As you say, Tony, it could be nothing ... '

'Could be,' chipped in Bertel. 'But do you want a nut handling the British end? Do any of us?'

Nobody answered. Peter Nero, incarcerated in micro-grooves, played on.

'I'll encourage him on this Birthday Party thing and start asking around.'

'Maybe one of us *should* go over.' Little Mike on the edge of his chair.

'Yes,' said Vescari, balling his right fist and thumping it into his left palm. 'Yes, maybe someone should go over.'

6

TORRY gently replaced the telephone. So Jumper had lied. So? Not the most startling news of the day. He leaned back in the chair, vaguely aware of kitchen noises, and looked up at the Bosch 'Haywain'. Some of his more intelligent clients would probably call it square, living as they did among the synthetic pop-culture Union Jacks and sprawled-paint garishness which seemed to decorate London. But in this one painting, old Hieronymus Bosch seemed to have captured all that was ugly and evil and vicious in the human condition. The tortured faces stared back at him. *De Profundis. Out of the depths I have cried unto Thee, O Lord; Lord, hear my voice.* Wexton was in there somewhere, not crying out of the depths, but in them just the same. Where? The centre panel, among the grotesques gathered around that rich, straining wagonload of hay. He was there all right, sprawled across a dying man, in the act of slitting his victim's throat, a bright yellow hat hiding the unknown face.

The knife had already penetrated the spread-eagled man's windpipe, blood was beginning to spurt. The face behind that bright yellow hat? Did Jumper know the face? Jones? Did anyone? You'd have thought the master-mind would've gone out with Fu Manchu or Sexton Blake, but you only had to look at the way the big syndicates operated, or the carefully planned jobs, the really profitable knock-offs, like the Train Robbery. Masterminds were still well in.

The kitchen noises were louder, joined now by Sue's voice singing 'September Song'. She was hardly Bassey but it was not unpleasant. Torry's smile switched on, then off, almost with a viciousness that he found hard to understand. Susan Crompton. That was another worry he could do without. The ache in his loins, unsatisfied, yet so easily bathed and soothed in her. Simple, until one remembered the mental and spiritual havoc which would be the aftermath.

They had met, almost predictably, just under a year ago in a store: she, knocking over a pile of books; he, hurtling like a paper knight to pick them up. She, thinking he was one of the assistants. He, pointing out that he could not really be confused with all those dim, leggy foreign ladies wearing plastic badges and knowing nothing about the wares they were supposed to sell. She, laughing. He, feeling the sudden swift upsetting loop in his stomach. And the consequence was that they went off for coffee at the Golden Egg or the Burned Sausage – one of those mass-production places anyway, where the décor looked like a National Theatre set. For a month it had been a roller coaster. Sue was on holiday. ('Teaching has its compensations, the leave's good.') Torry was busy, but the hours were regular. So, for a month it had been Susan against a background of London, theatres, cinemas, places they had both always meant to see but never seemed to get around to until now. Neon lights, crowds, buskers, occasional sordid moments, the villains and yobos in dark doorways. He kept off the subject of work and listened to her talk about teaching at North End Primary School, Finchley. Torry did not mean to push religion. Even in the past, when he fully believed the whole Catholic thing, he had never felt the need to be an apostle. He had never felt it his duty to go out and drag converts into the Church's net. Yet, when faced by the

94

moment of decision, he had inexplicably been drawn back to the old feelings, the acts of superstition, the rituals to ward off sin and bring his soul to light everlasting.

It had happened in the very chair in which he now sat. Sue on his lap and the gap between the permissible and the sin of fornication growing smaller every minute. He went hot, now, at the thought. Sue's body pressing closer, the control of two adults swiftly breaking away. Then her hand touching him hard (Mary Williams again whispering 'I'll help you'). Susan's voice. 'Darling, for God's sake take me. Now. Now.'

His head turning away and his voice unfamiliar and throaty. 'Sue, I love you. Marry me.' Words from some cheap romantic novel.

Susan had said, 'Yes. Oh please, yes.'

'When?' Lord, he felt embarrassed now, remembering his maladroitness.

'Yesterday.' Sue all shining eyes like they tell you in the women's magazines.

'I'll go and see the priest tomorrow.'

That was the trigger. No priest. No church. No religious ceremony. He had cursed and gone into deep black depressions many times since then. If only he had probed deeper before asking. But would it be different? It was pig-headed, stupid, foolish of him, yet, with this girl, he felt marriage could only be sealed in one way, the way of his father and mother, his brothers, his family: through the rites and ceremonies of the Church.

'Is it really that bad?' Susan stood by the chair, a cup steaming in each hand.

'What?'

'Whatever you're thinking about. The case?'

Torry paused. 'No, I wasn't thinking about the case, love.'

She handed him a cup and slid down to sit at his feet, the black mini-skirt lifting and showing a long dune of thigh.

Torry nodded towards her legs. 'One of our people says we should ban mini-skirts. Cause too many road accidents.'

She laughed, head back and teeth flashing like in the commercials. 'Miss Rawthorne put me down today for wearing one to school. "Not quite the right influence for the children, Miss Crompton",' Sue imitated. Miss Rawthorne was to her what Torry's Chief Superintendent was to him.

The laugh faded from her face. A sudden symptom which Torry recognized at once, the sparkle dying in her eyes.

'Was it us?' she asked. 'Were you thinking about us?' Fear in her voice.

'Could be.' As he said it, Torry realized his personal pomposity.

'I'm sorry, I didn't mean to goad you.' Prim. The words could turn sour any minute.

'Goad me?' He half laughed. A nervous habit when trouble threatened. 'How'd you goad me?'

'The bit about Ticker. And the bedroom. I didn't mean to upset you.'

'Take more than that to upset me.' His hand touched her hair. A patting motion. 'After all this time and you still don't know me, do you?'

She looked up at him, almost startled, and then quickly glanced away. 'It's not easy.' She spoke low. 'No, Derek, I don't know you. I don't understand you.' She gave a small sigh. 'Talking about knowing people, when am I going to meet your Mama?'

'When we've booked the priest and the church.'

'When pigs fly, eh?'

'God, we've been over it enough times, Sue.' The edge of exasperation. 'I can't even mention you to Mama, let alone introduce you.'

Torry could picture the scene and hear the voice.

'Marriage, Derek. Wonderful. Oh, if your father could be

here. Marriage.' Mama's voice still strident in spite of her age. 'A good Catholic girl, Derek? A Catholic?'

He could not lie to Mama, so he would not be able to tell her.

Torry looked down at Susan. 'For the hundred and fiftieth time, Sue; you know what Catholic families are like. You know what cockney families are like, and Italian families. Well, fuse the lot and what are you landed with? The Family with a big F. The Catholic Mafia's what you're landed with.'

'I'm willing to do it the other way.' She moved, a hesitant and self-conscious wiggle. 'You can take me any time. You know that.'

'I know. And I can't.'

'And why not, Derek? Why not? You can't marry me because Mama and your precious brothers would yell. They'd curse you if you didn't do it their way. So that doesn't stop you from screwing me ... '

'Susan!'

'You don't believe any of it, so why not?'

'I respect you.'

'Respect.' Anger in a spit. 'You mean that you get nervous without the talismans, the safeguards. Derek, you're like a little boy crossing his fingers when he walks under a ladder. I bet you played those silly games when you were a kid. Like it would be bad luck if you didn't reach a certain board in the stairs before the lavatory flushed.'

Torry nodded. 'So? Didn't you? Don't all of us? If you love me, Sue, you'll say yes and do it my way.'

'Your way. Christ, Derek, you make me sick. You're scared stiff. You ought to admit it. What do you do anyway? What do you do when you get sexed up? Mortify the flesh or get hold of some whore? Do you?' She was on her feet. In a second the backchat of two people had turned into war within a small room.

97

'A whore you pay money to? Then do you go to your little priest friend? Whatsisname? Father Conrad ... ?'

'Conrad.' Torry nodded, infuriatingly in command of his temper.

'You go to him, Derek, don't you? You don't believe in anything, oh no, but you have to hedge your bets. Just in case ... '

'Sue, try and understand.' He had said it all so many times before. 'Would it be so different if I were a Jew? There are some things that are demanded of you because you have been born into a certain environment. Hereditary actions ... '

'Don't you want to break with the past? Your environment ... ?'

'Not if it's going to hurt people.'

'What if it hurts me? Hereditary actions. To appease the gods? Christ, you might just as well sacrifice to the sun. How about a nice vestal virgin, Derek? How about putting me on the slab? Because if you don't do it soon I'm just not going to be around. Not as a virgin anyway. How can you respect yourself or expect me to respect you? A failed Catholic hanging on by his nails just in case. You make me bloody sick.'

'Sue. Please ... '

'You may be a lapsed Catholic, Derek, but I've got some feelings and I'm still a successful agnostic.'

Her foot caught the coffee cup as she turned. Liquid spilled over the carpet. A flurry of anger. She grabbed at the raincoat hanging by the door and slammed out of the flat.

Torry swore, then slowly rose and shuffled into the kitchen for a cloth to wipe up the mess. His mind spun in slow turmoil. Should he see it her way? Throw out the backdrop of a lifetime? He began to think in platitudes. Christian platitudes assimilated through the years. Christ did not find it easy walking to the Cross. There was real physical pain in the scourge and nails tearing His flesh. There was real blood on Golgotha and the parched loneliness of mortality. Was that what he wanted? To believe in all that again? To be what they called a good Catholic?

'Shit.' Torry cursed aloud. What was he trying to be anyway? The conscience of twentieth-century man? The Everyman of the 'seventies, struggling to find a way in a world without God?

The doorbell gave a short burr. Susan stood there, eyes ringed with watered mascara.

'I forgot my exercise books.' Like a small child.

Torry reached out for her.

The rain had gone by the morning, leaving a day fresh with the signs of spring. Even among the grimy façades, concrete, plate glass and the filth of exhaust fumes, the sunshine took on a fresh aspect. It was not the cold tired light of winter, but a new touch of warmth, the prophet of bursting colours and long dry days.

Torry thought he could sense the feeling of rebirth one is supposed to experience about the time of the vernal equinox. From his taxi he tried scrutinizing the faces of scurrying office workers. The sunlight would be playing on their minds as well. A good day for the travel agents. A good day for lovers. A tweak in his loins, the stirrings. Even with his somewhat pretentious respect for Susan's body, he knew that the break had to come. They would either split or consummate their emotions. Soon it had to come.

The taxi turned into Broadway, much smaller and so different from New York. Quite irrationally, Torry suddenly wondered about the colour of Susan's pants. Stupid, adolescent thought. He had caught a flash of black between her thighs last night. It was like a schoolboy sneaking looks in a lingerie shop window. He tried to flush the thought from his mind, but it remained, stronger and more disturbing. Hot and hard. He would have to call her. Talk to her. This was ridiculous. Teenage sexual fantasies had never troubled him before.

Wexton. Today was the first day of his search for Wexton. That did it; he was back in the maze of darkness with Ticker, Jumper, Morse, Hart, silly dead Lipperman and the Chief Superintendent. By the time the taxi pulled up at the Broadway entrance, Torry had his mind under control.

In his office three buff C.R.O. files and Sergeant Dumphy waited for him. Torry groaned to himself. Of all people he had to draw Dumphy, an old station sergeant who had been moved out of the uniform branch and into Crime One during a particularly short-handed period and had thence stuck like high-impact adhesive. An angular man in the late forties, Dumphy already looked as though he had seen the best side of fifty-five. For him, detection was a mystic hit, miss or hunch business. An avid reader, his library choices, often embarrassingly on display around the office, had remained at the *Death in the Refectory* fictional standard. Dumphy's one saving grace was that he knew form and procedure backwards. But he *would* talk. He began almost before Torry closed the door.

'Good morning, sir. Lovely morning. We have three files from C.R.O. and there's a personal Telex for you. From New York.' He would have continued, but Torry cut him down in mid-flow.

'What's in the Telex? Baseball results?'

'They have no Wextons that would be of interest. Strange, that, sir. We only have three.'

'Could've been three hundred. They've done a cross check with the aliases?'

'I asked them personally, sir. Nobody at present known using that alias. I've also had a quick look through those files, Mr Torry, and I'm just goin' through their present whereabouts ... '

'Good. Mr Tickerman called?'

'Not yet, sir. No.'

'Well, get on checking the whereabouts of this trio. I'll go through their files.'

'Not a likely bunch, sir. Not for this one.'

Patience, Derek. His irritable streak was rising, a running sore. 'Well, for heaven's sake let me get on with these. I'll call you.'

It was no good hinting to Dumphy, you had to tell him. No messing. The sergeant left unruffled. Susan floated back into Torry's consciousness, half naked this time. Running across sand in crimson underwear. Why sand? And why crimson? He put out his hand to pick up the telephone. She was coming round tomorrow night—he couldn't wait until then. Nine fifteen. Fool, she'd already be in school. His hand drew back. Susan erotically sprawled in front of the fire, the mini-skirt she'd worn last night pulled high, naked from the waist down, his body dropping in slow motion on to her, feeling her, entering her ... deep breath. The office window. He could just see across to C.R.O., the endless belts of moving files. Belts. Endless, moving. Susan and himself moving. Belting. The files ... files ... files. Another deep breath with Susan's face enveloping his brain.

Slowly, Torry picked up the three files. They were all slim. A bad sign. He opened the first stiff cover.

WEXTON, HENRY JONAS. Born: Kingston, Jamaica, August 21st, 1932. Entered G.B. via Heathrow January 3rd, 1960. (Only read the important bits.) Henry Wexton, a coloured immigrant working for London Transport, had fallen from grace in 1962. Six months' imprisonment for assault and G.B.H. Must have been a hilarious morning at the magistrate's court. The assault and grievous bodily harm had been perpetrated on Wexton's landlord, whom Henry Jonas accused of demanding money with menaces. Lower down the facts became more clear. The money was three months' unpaid rent. The menaces consisted of one sentence. 'If you don't pay up, man, I'll put the frighteners on you.' Henry Jonas had replied in kind, knocking out two of the landlord's teeth and breaking his wrist. Nothing since. Prison report: good. Full remission. A coloured master-mind? Black. Susan in black, from neck to toes, wrapped in a film through which he could see the heady curves. Torry, you're a policeman. The job. Have to see her. Prayer? St Francis was troubled like this, what did he do? Roll in the snow. Chucked himself into a bramble bush. 'What you need, lad, is a good cold shower.' An echo from long-gone schooldays. Jesus, a bramble bush. All those pricks. An adolescent mind, softening. Going soft and undisciplined over a woman. *From the spirit of uncleanness, Jesus deliver us.* But this wasn't uncleanness. It was wholesome. Alive. Love. *From the snares of the Devil, Jesus deliver us.* He'd always wanted her, there was nothing wrong in that. Part of the divinity of love. The mutual adoration. The outward expression of their feelings. Sacramental. But all this sudden power-dive into fantasy: was this what they called concupiscence? Lust? Work. Destroy it by sublimation. The next file.

WEXTON, GERALDINE ELIZABETH. Born: Godalming, Surrey, June 4th, 1943. Twenty-five years old. Good middle-class family. Three months in prison last year for stealing and forging two cheques. Mummy worried about what the neighbours would say, and oh, the disgrace. She shouldn't have let little Gerry go out into the wide world and get mixed up with the wrong people. It was her boyfriend's cheque book after all. Bet Daddy tried to buy him off. Full remission. Nothing since. No joy.

And who's the third?

WEXTON, ROWLAND FRANK. Born: Lower Eastwood, nr Newbury, Berkshire, March 3rd, 1949. A child. Three months, last October. Living in Hackney with a couple of other teenage layabouts. Big night out on the booze. Jeweller's window with all that pretty stuff behind it. Crash and nicked with twenty quids' worth of cheap rings. He'd be back. The telephone rang. Ticker.

'Hope you slept well and comfortably, Derek.'

'Very well, very comfortably and very much on my own, sir.' Ticker never let up. He was like a tape recording. You put one idea into his head, and if he thought it was funny, he played it back to you again and again. He was chuckling at the other end of the line. It had become a popular game. Bait Derek Torry. Or was his hide getting thinner?

'I was going to ring you, Tick. Any luck?'

'None you'd notice. Young Hart spent an hour with Jumper early on.'

'No joy?'

'Jumper says he thought that was the address but he may have been wrong.'

Hart wouldn't get far with a man like Jumper. Ticker wasn't saying it out loud but he knew nobody was going to get a straight story there.

'What about you?'

'Give me a chance, I've only been in half an hour. C.R.O.'ve turned up three Wextons. A spade who did his landlord, some little "Hallo Harriet" who pinched her boyfriend's cheques, and a boozy juvenile. They're not capable of raiding their own larders, any of them. I'm a sitting duck, Tick. The old man can fill me full of scatter shot any time he wants because young, vital, committed Torry ain't going to find a creepy master-mind planning things from a gothic Scottish castle among this lot. Look, Tick, have I got to check them?'

'Check and interview. Personally. Old man's orders.'

'Personally?'

'Yourself.'

'And it's yourself I love,' Torry muttered bitterly as he put down the phone. Blood they wanted. Wexton they wanted. And these were the only candidates. Neat little sheaves of paper in stiff folders. A few facts about three unlikely people. He pressed the intercom button for Dumphy. It sounded like the bell back in his flat. For a second Susan stood there in the doorway, tears filling her large brown eyes: two pools of pathetic searching.

'Got any of their addresses yet, or are they all holing up at the London Hilton loading their tommy guns and preparing to shoot their way out?'

'Sir?' questioned Dumphy, lost. He really should have stayed in the Army whence, Torry suspected, he had originally come. Dumphy always spoke too loudly on the intercom, a habit which resulted in a distorted Punch and Judy effect. Torry gathered he had not yet got young Rowland Frank Wexton's address but the other two were at his fingertips.

'You'd best come through,' said Torry.

The spade, Henry Jonas Wexton, had an address in Bermondsey and was listed as a night watchman at St Biddolph's General Hospital.

'Bermondsey?' mused Torry. 'He's not a Belsize Pakistani then?'

'He's Jamaican, sir,' said Dumphy, straight. Torry closed his eyes and rested his forehead on an open palm. 'O.K. Dumph. You win. I'd better go over and look him up first.'

'There's also Miss Geraldine Wexton, sir.'

'So?'

'She appears to reside in Paris.'

A golden glob of happiness spreading inside Torry's brain. A smile turning into a chuckle. 'Does she now? And what does she do to keep her body stocking and seamless soul together?'

'Works for B.E.A. at Le Bourget, has a flat in ... ' Pause to consult his notes. ' ... The Rue des Chevaux.' Dumphy pronounced it 'Chevawx'. 'That's somewhere near the Place de l'Opéra according to my map.'

'And that should be right, providing you're looking at a map of Paris and not Berlin. It would probably be the Pferdstrasse there.' Slow. Don't sound too delighted. 'Mr Tickerman's been on. The Chief Superintendent's orders are that I check and interview all three clients personally. Get the Paris thing in motion. Get it in motion now. Earliest possible flight. You know what authorities I need. Travellers' cheques. Hotel – try for the Opéra area.'

'Yes indeed, sir.' Dumphy of Interpol, excited and bursting with self-importance.

'And don't panic the Judiciaire,' Torry checked him. 'It's merely a routine inquiry, they tend to go mad and stir things. She still holds a British passport?'

'As far as I know. After all, she works for B.E.A.'

'Okay, get me fixed up. Shouldn't take long. One night away at the most unless I start stumbling over cartloads of clues like in private-eye movies.'

Paris. Funny how Paris, above other capitals, evoked all the coloured travel posters and gouged the romantic streak to the surface of one's mind. Sharp bright images, like a travelogue made by some brisk young director with a passion for tricksy camera angles – the Eiffel Tower tipping metronomically to and fro; a gendarme, white-gloved, whistling at the confusion of traffic; old elegant lamp standards, in close up, near the Louvre; Notre Dame majestic, dark and rising in the evening sunlight, then the slow pan down on to the Seine; the Garde Républicaine, mounted, clopping, flashing helmets and handsome faces along the Quai Saint Michel, the stalls of the *bouquinistes* behind them, hung with bulldog-clipped paintings. The Opéra, floodlit so that it seemed to be constructed from pure gold. Grief, you might be mooning over a line from 'These Foolish Things'. What was it? 'The Ile de France with all the gulls around it.' Gulls? *Gull: noun. Dupe or fool.* All you know about Paris, Torry, is the external tourist dishes. The slums, quaint and picturesque from a distance, you didn't want to know; nor the crime rate, nor those small cafés where they served up the usual muck. The frozen steak houses and chipperies. In Paris it had to be different, the wine, the bread, the mustard and the service. It might not be a whit better than London but, in the mind, it had to seem better. Shrug. Paris wouldn't be any fun without Susan anyway. So, today Paris. Tomorrow? Bermondsey probably.

Within the hour Torry was back in a taxi, dashing for the flat to pick up an overnight bag and his passport.

Dumphy had handed over a complete itinerary. 'The hotel's just behind the Opéra, sir. Not brilliant they tell me, but clean and that's what you really want in a place like that. Oh, and an Inspector Dumier has taken over until you arrive. He'll meet you at the airport.' Torry cursed silently, they were probably making a policeman's convention out of it. 'Check on her family for me,' was his parting shot.

Dumphy had booked him on the noon flight to Le Bourget and his mind skimmed the approach he would have to make on meeting Geraldine Wexton. What kind of a girl would she be? A sneaky ex-deb? Or simply a stupid young bitch who was sleeping around and decided to take a chance on her current bedmate's cheque book?

In the flat, standing with telephone in hand after sending a telegram to Susan ('Called away. Back tomorrow and will ring you. Love D.T.'), he looked up at the 'Haywain'. Was she there? The young girl in pink sitting with her lover on top of the hay? The naked Eve turning her face from the avenging angel in the left-hand panel? Maybe even the woman with the soothsayer, or one of those fat avaricious nuns stuffing their sacks full of hay filched from the wagon? The various characters of the complex painting merged and wove into one another, clear then fuzzy.

*

The Trident performed a perfect slow turn to the left, lining up on runway two-five, Le Bourget. Torry looked idly out of the window, watching the toy houses grow as the aircraft dropped fast through turbulent air. Then the open flat airfield. The first commercial airport ever to run services between London and Paris. A useless piece of information picked up somewhere. Streaking concrete. The judder, roar of reverse thrust, then quick deceleration.

Dumier was waiting, a nondescript man with a perpetually sad expression, like a bloodhound. A good face for a policeman. He led Torry to the bar.

'She doesn't come off duty until two thirty. It's better to talk over a drink.' His English was exceptional. Torry had a small whisky, Dumier ordered a vermouth cassis. 'Cheers,' he said, raising the glass, very British. 'What's it all about? Smuggling again?'

'Again? She's been on that game?'

'Not that you would notice, but when it's people connected with airlines one usually thinks of smuggling.'

'No, not smuggling. Routine check-out, as they say in the paperbacks. We're looking for someone called Wexton who might ... '

'Help you with your inquiries.' A mirthless smile, denoting that he too was familiar with the popular conception of police jargon.

'Right. We've got three on the books. She's one.'

'She is clean here. Lots of friends. Has a nice apartment ... '

'In the Rue des Chevaux.'

'As you say. Diligent. Quite a few boyfriends. One or two on intimate terms.' He did not stress 'intimate'. 'The concierge is talkative.'

'The boyfriends? Are they,' a shrug of the shoulders, 'clients?'

'A couple of pilots. A good-looking Air France radio officer.

Three chief stewards. That's why I thought maybe smuggling. They're all clean.'

'She go home much?'

'To England?'

A nod.

'A long week-end every three months or so. Her father visited her last month. You want to do the interview here or go back into my office?'

'The less official the better. Just in case.'

Dumier sipped his drink. 'The local people have put an office at our disposal and I have a female officer, an *assistante*, here.'

'Good.' Torry began to relax. With any luck he would get the business over by late afternoon. That would mean an evening flight back to London. What the hell. Make a night of it. You could take the dedicated bit too far. Play it off the cuff.

They waited in the main concourse opposite the B.E.A. counter. Geraldine Wexton looked pleasant and neat, blonde hair, short and pulled back a trifle severely behind the ears. Five foot six or seven, Torry thought. Good figure from what he could see. Her relief arrived just before two thirty. She was cheery, happy, smiling her farewells.

'Miss Geraldine Elizabeth Wexton?' Torry stepped in front of her just before she reached the door, trying to make it look like a friendly encounter. Dumier stood behind him. The woman police officer, late thirties, good foundation garments and a tight-fitting black suit, hovered in the background.

'Yes.' Her voice husky. Fear of the unknown. Mild shock. Her eyebrows were shaped like tiny scimitars.

'I'm sorry to trouble you, Miss Wexton. I'm a police officer. Detective Inspector Torry, New Scotland Yard ... '

'Oh God, something's happened. Daddy? Has something happened to Daddy?'

Why Daddy? What about Mummy? His first guess had been

108

right. Daddy had understood about the cheques. It was all wrong though, she looked too nice to go and do a thing like that. Torry, you should know better. You've met plenty of nice ones before.

'No, nothing like that. This is a routine matter. I'd like to ask you a few questions if you have no objection.'

'No. No, of course not, but ... Well, why me? I mean ... ' Torry saw the realization hit her behind the eyes. 'It's not about ... ? Not the trouble ... '

'Not really. This is Inspector Dumier of the Police Judiciaire. Shall we go somewhere quiet?'

The girl nodded. Her shoulders slumped. She'd been through it all before and, even with a clear conscience, expected the worst.

The small office was characterless, probably used for the occasional interview, or a place where one could tuck away a difficult member of the staff. Strange, Torry thought, one associated airports with sleek glass and clean lines. Here, the table was old and scratched, and a wooden filing cabinet, brass handles and a badly cracked side, stood in the corner. Dumier disappeared while the *assistante* stood dourly by the door. Torry motioned Geraldine Wexton into a chair and sat down on the other side of the table. Notebook out. Ball point at the ready. The policeman's lot.

'Miss Wexton, I'm going to ask you a number of questions. Think very carefully before you answer them, because a lot of time and trouble can be saved if you tell the truth.'

'I've got nothing to hide.' She paused. 'This time.' Distressed, twisting the big ring on her index finger, left hand.

'Are you personally acquainted or have you ever come into contact with a woman called Florence Annie Cust?'

She looked very attractive with a wrinkled brow. 'Cust? I don't think so ... '

'That's not good enough, I'm afraid. Yes or no.'

'It's not easy. Who is she anyway? No, I don't know anyone called Cust.'

'Wilfred Adam Grosvenor?'

'I know Bill Grosvenor. He's a second officer with the Company.'

Torry's hand slipped automatically into his pocket, removing the envelope with the photographs they were all carrying. 'That's Cust and the ugly one is Grosvenor.'

'It's not Bill. No, I've never seen either of them.' Frank and innocent. Or a grade-one liar? No. This was a dead end. A complete-state-of-death dead end. He went on with the questions. Jumper. Lipperman. Her visits to London. Half an hour passed.

'Can't you tell me what it's all about, Mr ... er ... ?'

'Torry.'

'I'm terrible with names. I never listen.'

'I don't think you've got much to worry about. We're looking for somebody called Wexton and, well, that's your name and it's on the files.'

'Yes.' She wasn't looking at him. 'Will it happen often? I mean the girls in prison used to say nobody would ever let me forget. The police ... '

'I shouldn't think you'll ever have any more bother. I'm quite satisfied. To be honest I was pretty sure before I even met you. But we have to make certain.'

She smiled. A splendid, friendly smile with the eyes as well as the face.

Torry glanced at his notebook again. 'If I do want to talk to you again your address is 37 Rue des Chevaux?'

'Yes. I shall be in for the rest of today and I'm on duty here at half-past two tomorrow afternoon.' Was she giving him some kind of encouragement? The look, and then the eyes quickly away.

'My telephone number is 073–8077.' Hesitation again. 'In case.'

'Thank you.' Just a little too calculated. Perish, as they say, the thought. Geraldine Wexton could be bad news. A girl you've just interrogated? You could get away with it. Following up inquiries. Or could you? He watched the slim figure walking away down the corridor. And Susan came glowing to the forefront of his thoughts. You wouldn't satisfy the devil lust with her, but with the Wexton woman … ?

'April in Paris. Chestnuts in blossom. Holiday tables under the trees.' Music and lyrics by Harburg and Duke. Torry had a couple of recordings of it. A standard by … who knows? Everyone had done it. The other was Sammy Davis with Sam Butera and the Witnesses; done live in Vegas. Well, this time Harburg and Duke had goofed.

Dumier ran a 1965 Peugeot and the windscreen wipers needed help from an expert. It didn't seem to worry Dumier who kept up a steady seventy along the Route Nationale 9 into Paris. It was April, okay, and the chestnuts were soggily in blossom, only a few holiday tables stood under the trees and they looked waterlogged. Even the shine seemed to have gone off the gilded Opéra as Dumier guided the car past and into the Rue Halévy. The hotel was fair, the service diffident. Torry had until ten twenty the following morning. Dumier was anxious to get back to his desk, wife or mistress. They said their farewells and made mutual thanking noises.

Once in his room Torry put in a call to Dumphy. They wouldn't like it on the expense sheet but he wasn't going all the way down to the Sûreté Nationale Headquarters.

'How's Paris, sir? Any luck?' Dumphy's voice was even more distorted on a long-distance line, as though he felt it had to carry across the Channel.

'It's wet and I don't think she would know how to start. Waste of time really. You checked her family?'

'I have, sir. Mother's an alcoholic, in and out of clinics. Father's retired Army. General Wexton. Clean as a whistle, good background and a lot of connections.'

'Sounds hopeful.'

'Connections in the City, sir. Honest as the day.'

'In the City? You're joking. Keep him on ice for me, will you? See if Mr Tickerman'll provide a tail.'

'Very good, Mr Torry, but I don't think ... '

'I should be back in the office around noon. Between noon and one. All right?'

'Very good, sir.'

So Daddy's a General. Precision. Planning. The City. It just could be. Half-knowing that it was a salve to his conscience, an excuse to use her as a woman, Torry picked up the telephone and asked for 073–8077.

She didn't seem at all surprised. 'I thought it would be either you or a call from England. Daddy's telephoning this evening.'

'I'm sorry to be a bother, but I wonder if I might see you again?'

'Professionally or socially?'

'A bit of both.'

'Make it more social and we can have dinner tonight.' Torry cautiously held the pause. From the window he could see nothing but rain against the background of an ornate façade fronting the building over the road.

'Where?' he plunged.

She laughed. 'Does Scotland Yard pay the bill?'

'More or less.'

'All right. Fouquet's at eight. I'll be wearing black so you'll recognize me.'

He'd underestimated Miss Wexton. She *was* the kind of girl

112

who'd pinch your cheque book. Your virtue and your cheque book. Holy Joseph, Fouquet's. It'd cost a fortune.

Torry was not much of a good-food-and-wine man, but Geraldine Wexton virtually took over. By the time the coffee and brandy arrived they were on Gerry and Derek terms, and Torry had begun to enjoy himself. Perhaps too much, he thought. Work,lad, work, even here in Fouquet's, all prosperous and a shrine to food, with waiters as bowing acolytes.

'You've done very well for yourself since your trouble,' he began.

'Derek.' The admonishing finger. 'My trouble. You sound like an elderly relation.' The smile froze on her face. 'I'm sorry. I shouldn't be flippant about my trouble.' Bitterness. 'Daddy helped a great deal.'

'Must've been nasty for him as well.'

'Worse for him than for me, really. Still, he's been super since.'

'How bad was it?'

'More unpleasant than bad. That was until they ... I didn't think they'd send me to prison.' She kept her eyes fixed on her coffee as she stirred. 'That was the shock. Time went quickly though. After the first couple of weeks they sent me to an open place. You don't really get used to it though. I still feel dirty.' She stubbed out her cigarette. 'You usually think of military people's children being awfully well disciplined and everything, but Daddy was never like that. Of course Mummy, well, Mummy's not a very well person ... '

'Mummy's a lush.' It slipped out. A reaction to the county style she had adopted. A revelation of Torry's streak of cruelty: how to make friends. He was ashamed but there wasn't a hint of anguish in her face. She gave a small jerky nod. 'Mummy's a lush.' Repetition. Agreement ...

'I'm sorry.'

'Why be sorry? Truth, about anything, doesn't hurt any more. At least, three months in jail did that for me. A sort of maturity.' Out it all came. An only child arriving late on the scene. First memories of living in Surrey, her father driving daily to Aldershot, a professional soldier who'd come up quickly during the war. The private school and that peculiar loneliness of only childhood. Teenage rebellion. The golden bowler for Daddy and then furious departure for London with an allowance too short for the long nights. The carnivorous young men. Money. Money. Debts and threats. Come home, Gerry, and all will be forgiven, all debts paid. Refusal. Longer nights, shorter tempers. Clive with lots of lovely money. Temptation. More fear. The grey unsmiling men arriving one morning. 'Anything you say may be taken down and used in evidence …'

'For people like me it's as good as that treatment they give in mental hospitals. You know, the electric thing.'

'E.C.T.'

'Yes. Oh, pay the bill, Derek, and come back to my place for some more coffee. I'm getting my own back on the police force tonight.'

An offer? A genuine bargain or a tender trap? Susan standing tall and sensual in his head wearing bra and pants. Lord, he needed a woman. Why not? Conscience. Out of the window. Conscience. On the plate with the big pile of ten-franc notes.

The flat wasn't spectacular. Cosy without the chintzyness he'd half expected. She popped a pile of records on the player and went into the kitchen to make coffee. It took less than five minutes, she wasn't the sort of girl who messed about with percolators. Sinatra was preparing the way.

> Come by for a drink, we're having a game,
> Wherever I go I'm glad that I came,
> The talk is quite gay, the company's fine,

There's laughter and life and glamour and wine,
And beautiful girls,
And some of them mine.

'And Daddy still misses you a lot,' said Torry as she placed his coffee on the low table in front of them.

'Misses and doesn't trust. He phones a lot and I'm sure he thinks the worst. He rang just before I came to meet you.'

'And what's he do with himself?'

'Potters in the country. Imagines he's no end of a financial wizard in town. He keeps busy.' She looked almost beautiful. Sad, as she added, 'He has to keep busy.'

General Wexton. Don't get carried away, but it would fit if he had enough money and influence.

'Hey.' Gerry pulled him out of the workaday dream. 'Now you tell me about yourself. You're not like any of the people who interviewed me before. In fact, you're nice.'

'There are people at Scotland Yard who'd disagree on the last count. They'd probably agree that I'm not like a policeman at all.' He laughed naturally for the first time for weeks.

'You've got a bit of an American accent too.'

'I was an American. For a time.'

'It sounds interesting. Tell.' She had moved a fraction closer.

'Okay. My Pa came over to England in, oh hell, when was it? Nineteen twenty-three.'

'From America?'

'Italy. A village near Riccione, that's just down the coast from Rimini. He was around twenty-eight years old and one morning, he used to tell us, he just tossed a coin. You know, heads America, tails London. His father's brother had a delicatessen in Greek Street. Torrini's. Torrini's the family name. He helped his uncle for a while. Had a look round, decided to go into business for himself, that's why there's still a delicatessen in the Earl's

Court Road called Torrini. It's run by my brother, Bobby.'

'Your mother's English?'

'Yes. Ma's a little cockney sparrow. They must have worked all the hours God sent. Built up the business, had three kids, planned our lives for us.'

'They planned for you to be a policeman?'

'No. They thought I'd be the brainy one so I got sent to a smart school in Kensington where I didn't really fit. That's where America comes in. The school had an evacuation arrangement to the States when war broke out.'

Suddenly they were looking at each other. 'I've never been kissed by an Italian-English-American policeman,' she said.

He wasn't prepared for the cool start. Lips firm but closed. Then it built. Fire. First the spark, then the licking tongues. Flame scorching his nerves. Their bodies were stretched over the couch and she began pushing the division of her thighs at him. He could feel her against him, the movement of her breasts, like a surge of waves, on his chest. She slipped her lips round to his ear, tracing damp up his cheek.

'Christ, Derek, you smell and feel like a real man.' He wasn't even worried by the blasphemy, his hand too busy sliding up the nylon, pushing her skirt up with his wrist. Fingers touching the hard suspender nipples, then bare flesh and a tremble of lace. The last flimsy barrier. He held his hand hard against her, wet with readiness.

'The bedroom's just through there, darling.'

He couldn't look at her as they crossed the room. She didn't bother with the lights. Sinatra still floated in through the quarter-open door.

> Love was a star, a song unsung,
> Life was so new, so real, so bright
> Ages ago,
> Last night.

116

Through the window came the omnipresent sounds of the city and in the living-room Sinatra stopped singing and the turntable was still.

7

SMITH sat on an upright Georgian chair. It was beginning to get uncomfortable. Numbing his buttocks.

Wexton lounged against the leather padding of a Sheraton which, as he never let anyone forget, was reputed to have been used by Queen Victoria. Wexton, thought Smith, is a snob about furniture.

The other men were only partly visible through the filter of cigarette smoke and beam of the movie projector. The film was coming to an end, the stilted commentary grinding to a dull matt finish.

'And as we leave this beautiful town, with its million memories, one feels that we have reached into the past and placed our hands on a man and a period which will be for ever timeless.'

The camera pulled away from the old stone bridge (a Pickford's van slowly crossing), then dipped towards the water where a couple of swans paddled, oblivious of their cinematic immortality. The credits came up and the lights went on. People were blinking. Smith looked around. For the first time since the Birthday Party had been planned he felt nervous. He had chosen the men. If anything went wrong it was on the cards that Wexton would hold him responsible. You could not tell with Wexton these days. He had become as unpredictable as a grasshopper.

'Well, if you've never been there, it gives you some idea of the hole.' Wexton sounded like a Commanding Officer. 'We'll have the final run through on Tuesday. By then there'll be more film. I'm having a few hundred feet shot this week-end so that we can be up to date. Archer'll be going down with his camera ... '

Archer, pink-shirted and ad-mannish, nodded.

Smith was quite proud of Archer. The man *was* in advertising, between jobs at the moment as they all were; but with Archer, Smith had collected a gem, an original twenty-two-carat middle-class nine-to-five commuter. You could not get better cover than that.

Wexton was still talking. 'We've been through the drill five times this morning, but I want you to see a final bit of film today. Stuff taken during last year's festivities. Any questions before that?'

'Yes.' Foxy Langdon who was going to drive the Army truck. Christ, don't say Foxy was going to be difficult. Red-haired Foxy was a country boy with the cunning mentality of a poacher. He had done very well at the training establishment, but Smith knew him as a man quick to bear grievances.

'Go ahead.' Wexton smiled. Unruffled but not friendly.

'I want to know why we've reduced the teams to three men each instead of four.'

Smith had warned Wexton about this one, but you just did not approach him like this. Foxy would have to learn the organization's discipline.

'I thought I'd made it plain.' Wexton's voice slid on black ice. His ruthlessness was becoming legendary. Especially since Lipperman. 'We've got enough men on the ground as it is. We're only dropping four, but I've decided this gives us a more reasonable safety margin. They're all being compensated, and if you want out, Langdon, let me know now and I'll arrange to have you compensated as well.'

Foxy locked eyes with his leader. Five seconds, then a nod of capitulation.

'Right. Let's go through the major jobs again, so that everyone knows exactly who's doing what and when.'

A murmur from the lads. A hint of stifled irritation.

Wexton began to rattle it off. Precise. Military. 'Number of men on the ground will now be twenty-two. Smith controls the operation from Point A on your maps. Look at it.' This last snapped out sharply at two of the men who were lighting cigarettes.

'White drives the Jaguar, Nolan the Westminster, Howel takes the Zodiac and McIvor the Humber. All right?' The four men nodded.

'Langdon,' Wexton paused for effect, 'will be in the Army truck with Donaldson in charge of the V.H.F. jamming equipment.' He paused again and looked around the faces. 'And if anyone's worried about that phase of the operation I would remind you that Donaldson's a radio mechanic in private life. He's also done a specialized course at the training establishment.'

Donaldson, pasty and inclined towards a weight problem, tried, without success, to look important.

'Wright drives the removal truck; Symonds and Crisp, of all people, will be in fancy dress inside the police Humber station-wagon.' A chuckle from the wags. 'That leaves us with the really important boys. The heads of sections. Barker, quite rightly I think, heads the Barclays team; King leads the Martins group; Short the National Provincial; and Evans, to keep the Welsh happy, will be in charge of the Lloyds section.'

Smith was aware of a small trigger of anxiety within him. He looked at the four men in turn. They were undoubtedly the key members of the operation. On the day, they would each command two other men, heavies to do the strong-arm stuff.

From the nervous web in his mind, Smith unravelled one question. Were those four the right men for the job?

Barker had been trained only six months ago. One of Wexton's recruiting officers had picked him up in a pub last November. Age, twenty-nine. Married with three children. A wages clerk. No record, but a private history of pilfering. He had been most responsive at the training establishment. Now, sitting here in Wexton's house with the others, he looked at ease. Confident, tall and muscular.

King looked less happy, but Smith was not particularly concerned about that. King's constant expression was one of abject misery. He was short, and reacted to life with quick, birdlike movements. Age, thirty-two. Unmarried, but with a succession of gorgeous girlfriends who seemed to be obsessed with the desire to mother him. A supermarket manager, King looked the most unlikely lad for this kind of caper. Smith knew otherwise. King had already proved himself. Twice before Christmas he had been second-in-command of a group which had successfully knocked off lorry-loads of whisky.

Short, the third section leader, belied his name. Tall and angular, 'Lofty' Short was another of Smith's prize pupils. Married with two children, the man had found it impossible to make ends meet on a bricklayer's pay. Never should have been a brickie in the first place, thought Smith. No disrespect to brickies, but Short was a man of abnormally astute intellect.

Evans was, perhaps, the borderline case. Married, aged thirty, with four children, he was the epitome of a stage Welshman, right down to his nickname. 'Taffy' Evans was everyone's idea of a bar-parlour lawyer, a stirrer, a trouble-maker with a mercurial temperament. His listed occupation was that of stores clerk, but 'Taff' had tried many ways of earning a living. He had spent some time in the Merchant Navy, had worked on the roads and even, for a while, as a stage hand with a provincial repertory company.

A clerk, a supermarket manager, a bricklayer and a jack-of-all-trades. Husbands, fathers, lovers. An odd combination, yet one which was well within Wexton's terms of reference. Honest, hardworking citizens to the outside world, yet all trained to a high degree of accuracy. And not one with a previous conviction, not even for parking in a restricted area.

Smith looked at the quartet again. Wondering. Worrying.

The lights went down and the screen came colourfully to life once more. This time they were looking at a street decked with flags and bordered by a horde of sightseers. Down the centre of the street moved a slow procession.

The sense of sin gnawed at Torry like an oversized maggot. The ache for satisfaction had now become the physical discomfort of post-sexual pleasure. The skin rough, sore and burning tight within his trousers. The muscles ached with the after-effects of strain. All reminders of fornication.

He looked down on the flat solid cloudscape as the Trident throttled back to begin its descent to Heathrow. Down there would be a grey day to match his own depression.

Gerry filled his mind. Sexually, she had temporarily ousted Susan in one long night of giving and receiving.

At dawn Gerry, sweat-smelling and warm, had slipped from the bed and made more coffee. Then they lay back together, nestling.

'When do I see you again, Derek?'

'You want to see me again?'

'Haven't I shown you?'

What was Dumier's information? A couple of pilots, an Air France radio operator and three chief stewards.

'Isn't there anybody else?' Sly, Torry, sly.

'Not like this, Derek. Nobody like this.'

'Sure?'

She sighed and moved a bare thigh against him. 'I forgot. Nothing's sacred. I suppose you've got all the details by now. I might have known, bloody coppers.' Her lips were pursed tight as she turned her head away.

'Gerry. It's not that.'

'No? I should have realized. Come on, you tell me, how many, where and how many times did we do it?'

'Look ... '

'Look me no looks, Detective Inspector in bed with me. You can tell me what positions as well. A few questions, Miss Wexton. I expect you've got a file, haven't you? Ex-cons? Easy lays? Your turn for a week-end, Inspector, trip to Paris. Gerry Wexton. She's been making time with pilots, radio officers, stewards. Get in there, copper, it's your birthday.'

'Gerry!' He rolled over and caught her by the shoulders, aware of the dangers of the situation. What the hell was he doing there anyway? A police officer with a suspect, a girl he'd interrogated only yesterday. First Jumper, now this, and he thought he was a good policeman. He ought to be bounced from the top floor of that bloody awful new New Scotland Yard. 'I promise you I was sent over here to question you. Oh, what the hell. Yes, I should've gone back last night but I was sorry for you. I liked you ... '

'You fancied me.'

'All right.'

'And you knew there were others.'

'Yes, I knew there were others. But I'm on a job. Important, very important. You could report this and they wouldn't even wait for me to pack my Junior Detective's Fingerprint and Disguise Outfit.'

'You'd get chopped?'

'Right down my soft backbone.'

She turned her head. The eyes held real tears. 'Derek. I'm ... Yes, there're other men I like, I sleep with. What the hell else is there to do with your youth? But you ... Well, it's not the same.' She looked at him for a moment. Clinging. Then, disillusioned, 'Anyway, I expect you have women.'

'No. I've got a girlfriend but we don't. I do occasionally but not with her.'

Gerry was spitting again. 'Saving her for the driven-snow wedding night and I'm a bit of spare.'

'That's the way it was last night. Now I don't know. Of course I want to see you again.' Torry bent over her, but the small tantrum on top of the night's pleasure had turned the fire to cooling embers.

Later, after he talked a lot about himself, she cut in. 'I'd come back to London for you, Derek.' A hand on his cheek, fingers sliding softly down.

They talked on. Gerry this time. The complete unabridged story of her arrest and trial. 'Daddy was wonderful. Some people think he's a hard man, but he understood. Really understood. And I'm sure it was him who kept so much out of the papers.'

I bet, thought Torry. Gerry's father was becoming an obsession. I bet his name wasn't even mentioned. General Wexton. She wouldn't be so keen to come back to London, to him, if his sense of smell was accurate. It wouldn't be the clang of wedding bells in her heart, not cookery classes but kukri classes, if he revealed her father as a respectable front, an angel, for vice, prostitution, protection, narcotics, murder. She'd thank him for that. Thank you very much for the life-long sentence, thank you very much, thank you very very very much.

He thought he could feel her hand on his cheek again now

124

as the aircraft bucked against the heavy cloud into which they dropped steadily. Below, there was a fine drizzle, red slates on roof tops, the tiny cars, a surge from the jets to take them across the threshold, then the familiar slight judder.

Nobody had bothered to send a car. Torry came back into London on the scheduled bus service, dropped his case off at the flat and, temper rising, took a cab to the Yard. It was almost twelve thirty by the time he got into the office. Dumphy was preparing to go off for lunch.

'Any luck, sir?'

'What do you mean, luck?' Torry's conscience read the question incorrectly. 'Sorry, Sergeant Dumphy. No. No luck with Miss Wexton, but a possible line. You get that stuff on her father?'

'Being compiled now, Mr Torry, but ... '

'No buts, Dumph. Please no buts. Today, especially, no buts.' Dumphy looked hurt.

'Anything new?' asked Torry as the sergeant followed him into the inner office.

'Not what *you'd* call new, sir. Mr Tickerman seemed disturbed when he heard you'd gone to Paris. Lot of people were worried when I passed on your instructions about Miss Wexton's father, General *Thornton Wexton*.' Dumphy stressed the name.

'He got shares in the Metropolitan Police or something?'

'He's influential.'

'So was Charlie One but he ended up on a cold January morning with his head singing I ain't got no body.'

The quip escaped Dumphy. 'I think your request for surveillance has been vetoed.'

'Has it now?' Torry's face hardened as his hand reached out for the telephone. Dumphy spoke again before he lifted the instrument.

'Mr Tickerman left word that the Chief Superintendent was

expecting your reports on the three Wexton interrogations by the morning, sir.'

Torry struggled. All right, be their lackey. Chat up the other two, then concentrate on General Thornton sparkling Wexton.

'Where'd you say the spade lived?'

'Sixty-five Sebastopol Road, Bermondsey. Should I get his Division to bring him in to the nearest nick for questioning?' Dumphy sounded like a television policeman. They were always bringing in people for questioning.

'No, Dumphy.' Restraint. It was a dull enough chore, best got over with quickly. 'I'll go out there after I've had a bite. If he's a night watchman he should spend the day at home. Unless he's doing the double-ended candle trick. Just tell the Division that I'll be on their patch and why.'

'You'll want a car?'

Torry nodded. 'In about an hour.'

'You want me, sir?'

'No.' Too quick, but the last person he wanted was Dumphy. 'See if his local nick'll co-operate and have the beat man meet me there. And not right on the doorstep like some of the silly buggers do. Bottom of the road. Somewhere I can see him at … ' He consulted his watch. ' … at two thirty. And, Dumph, for Pete's sake tell 'em it's just routine.'

Dumphy was already speaking into the telephone as Torry left for the canteen feeling wearily that the afternoon would be taken up with some unimportant episodic questioning.

Bermondsey, beautiful gateway to the London docks; where Charlie Dickens sent Bill Sikes to his fictional death and they held the 'rag fair' of a Friday and the population shuffled rather than shifted.

Sebastopol Road looked like it had been in the actual battle, while the inhabitants—such as were on display as Torry's car drew up at the corner—could have constituted a contingent of refugees mixed in with some of the walking wounded. The air was thick with poverty. But this was not real poverty, that condition which is sometimes overcome by a stiff class-conscious pride. Rather it was affluence gone wrong. Torry looked across the wide road at the flaking façades and grime-streaked windows. Not one house had a full set of panes. The shattered jagged edges and neat round holes told their own stories of a child's ball, a stone carelessly thrown; or worse, an internal wound, the climax of a bitter battle of words, the cold war that is marriage turned hot. One knew from experience that the cracked doorways, peeling paint and broken windows hid the extraordinary anomalies of the live-now-pay-later society: refrigerators and HiFi stereo, big-screen televisions and automatic washing machines.

Susan's washing. Frothing underwear. Even here in dingy Sebastopol Road.

Torry squeezed the unwanted thought to the far, dim rear of his consciousness. Luxury aplenty there would be behind the green bruised doors of Sebastopol Road. And on the kitchen tables? At best a scraggy piece of oilcloth—at worst yesterday's *Sun* greasy from last night's chips. In this road every tap on the door might mean the men from the H.P. and goodbye telly; farewell washing machine, fridge or even the sofa where our Mam goes with the lodger when Dad's off to work.

Halfway up the road, on the far side, two coloured men, loose-limbed and indolent, lounged against a bending brick wall. They muttered together, then one threw back his head, exposing a mouthful of exquisite teeth. A few paces from Torry's car a mixed group of children—black, white, and one little Chinese boy, elbows out of their thin jumpers, torn hems, jam stains, snot—started to re-enact the Lipperman murder, prompted by

127

the uniforms of the driver and the beat man who now approached Torry.

'Mr Torry?' The hand up to his helmet. Not a salute of any deference. Nod. Curt and full of superiority. God, he could be a bad-mannered bastard.

'Two-two-five Abrahams. Number sixty-five you're interested in, isn't it, sir?'

'Yes, sixty-five. He's a spade. Henry Jonas Wexton. Nothing to it. Only routine so we'll play it cool. Know him?'

'Afraid not, sir.' The young constable was well spoken. Sent down here to knock the edges off, thought Torry. The constable motioned with his arm.

'It's at the far end. Across the road, sir.'

'All right.' They began to walk up the street.

'Got a rear entrance?' asked Torry.

'Yes.'

'Get on ahead of me then, and round the back. I'll call you when I'm inside.' The constable nodded and quickened his pace as Torry slowed to a steady trudge.

The door of sixty-five had once been blue, the colour of the old Dolly Blue packets Torry's father used to sell in the delicatessen. Now, the door was faded, dirty, cracked and weathered with only traces of the original shade remaining. Torry knocked twice before he heard the shuffling from within and a reluctant bolt being drawn back.

She could have been a handsome woman and, in spite of her present appearance, there was still a hint of that racial pride and sensual character which so often graces coloured women. A couple of days with enough money and a reinjection of hope might have brought about a spectacular transformation. With the right foundation garments the sagging stomach and heavy breasts would have been neatly pulled in to give a firm line, the shapeless hanging floral print dress replaced by something more elegant. The matted straggle of hair could quite quickly be groomed into a stylish, smooth, black satin decoration, while the face would automatically brighten.

The first thing to really hold Torry's attention were her eyes: wide, dark and dead. The eyes of a zombie. Eyes which mirrored failure, disillusionment and a sense of despair. From behind the woman's herbaceous skirts another pair of eyes peeped, those of a small child, round with wonder and shifty fear at the sight of Torry.

'I'm looking for Mr Henry Wexton. Henry Jonas Wexton.' Torry tried to make it sound less formal but it still came out as an authoritative cliché.

'He ain't in,' said the woman, her voice as dead as the eyes. 'He ain't never in.'

'He ... ' began the girl child.

'You shush.'

'He does live here though?' Torry pushed the question firmly.

'If you calls it livin'.'

'This is his address?' Torry thought he caught a trace of cunning in the almost caricature acidity of the woman's last sentence.

'Yeah, it's his address. What you wanna know for?'

'We have to ask him a few questions.'

'Who is it, Martha? That Big Sam?' The voice came heavy and deep from somewhere behind her, within the bowels of the house.

'And who is that? The lodger?' Torry's foot was inside the door.

'Yeah, the lodger. We do well 'cos we take coloureds, mister.'

'Who is it, Martha, for Christ's sake? I just ... ' He was a tall man, heavy features and close-cropped hair, the body going a little to fat. Checked shirt and the almost traditional jeans. He appeared behind her and, after a moment's surprise at seeing

Torry on the doorstep, his face broke into a generous, friendly grin. There was almost a feeling of relief.

'Don't tell me.' He flashed his teeth. 'It's the fuzz?'

Torry nodded. 'Henry Jonas Wexton?'

'Yeah,man, come on in. Come and see how your wicked black brothers live.'

Torry moved forward. 'You keep a nice class of lodger, Mrs Wexton.' He looked unsmiling at the woman.

'You protects your man. Up to a point you protects him,' she said with that same air of one revelling in being underprivileged.

'You want to be careful. Protecting people is wrong.'

'So's eatin' people, but *you* do it all the time.'

There was a smell of stale vegetables in the dingy hallway, uncarpeted, furnished only with a dilapidated pram.

'Do me a favour, Mrs Wexton. There's a colleague of mine out in the back. Bring him in, would you?'

'You want me to put the kettle on so we can all sit cosy and have a powwow?'

'Git, woman.'

Torry detected an uncertainty in Wexton's command, as though the man expected not to be obeyed.

The woman looked at her husband, coming alive for the first time. 'What you been doin' to get the police in here, you good-for-nothin' black trash?'

Wexton leaned against the wall, smiling insolently. 'I ain't been doin' nothin', honey. Nothin' 'cept mindin' my own business, and you ain't got no call to be speakin' to me like that.'

Mrs Wexton made a disgusted face and moved off down the hall. She returned quickly with the constable.

'What can I do for you fellas, huh?' Wexton still leaned against the wall.

Torry showed his warrant card. 'Detective Inspector Torry.

Criminal Investigation Department, New Scotland Yard.' He paused. 'We'd just like a little talk.' Another pause. It was one of the tricks of the trade. Don't tell them anything. Say you want to talk and wait for them to unload, like going into a café and standing inside the door to see who makes the first dive for the gents.

Even in the dimness of the hall one picked up the smile disappearing from Wexton's face. It wasn't easy to read coloured faces. Some trivial bit of guilt could show itself as utter panic in some. Others seemed to have no response at all. He remembered Brandy, the big coloured cop they used to have down at the Fourth Precinct, joking about it in a mock Uncle Tom accent. 'Ah sure hate goin' to that line-up when they're all whites 'cos, man, Ah just cain't tell dose whites apart.'

Was it guilt now flickering across the dark face?

'We can talk.' A definite tremor in Wexton's voice, but that could mean anything. 'In here.' He opened a door to their left. 'In the parlour, and you stay out of it, Martha, huh?'

'If you've been up to your tricks again, Henry, I'm leavin' you, and I ain't kiddin' this time. I'm leavin' for good.' There was genuine distress behind the feline spitting.

'No tricks, Martha, no tricks.' A little too glib. Wexton shut the door firmly in his wife's face and turned towards Torry, who had resigned himself to the fact that this was a case for the social worker.

The room was tidy enough, if a little threadbare, but there was an indefinable sense of clutter. Perhaps it was a mixture of furniture. A good three-piece suite, chintz-covered to hide any defects, did not go with the empty beer crate in the corner. Torry had visited much worse than this. Because of the emotions, and one's own part in the communal rising guilt towards immigrants, it was natural to feel one's way carefully among these people, yet the Wextons certainly did not live in squalor.

'You wanted to talk, man?' Defiance? Arrogance?

'Yes. You know what it's about?' Once more the pause to bring him on. Then, quite suddenly, though with no sense of drama, the coloured man dropped into a chair and hid his face in his hands. Somehow it was pathetic. A broken giant. 'How you find out? How you find out so quick? I done it before and nobody found out, there weren't nobody lookin' in through any window.'

'What window, Henry?' This could be a gold mine. He wouldn't be the first police officer to stumble unknowingly on a hidden major crime.

'There ain't no window. You know that if you been there. And if there was a window nobody'd want to look in. Not at that time of night. Man, it's taken me long enough to get used to it. What happened? Didn't I clean her up proper? Poor young girl. I felt sorry for her. Real sorry. Like the others.'

Others? God in heaven, what have we got here? 'How many others, Henry?'

'Man, you just don't count things like that. Always the next day I feel it. I know I shouldn't have done a thing like that and I say, "Henry Wexton, why've you done somethin' dirty like that?" I just don't know. Maybe I need help.' He was blubbering now. 'I try to work it out up here.' A fist pounding his forehead. 'Sometimes I think it's just me, then other times I think like I'm tryin' to do them some good. Give them some life.'

'How many?'

'I don't know. Four. Five maybe.'

Think hard, Torry. Do you really know what he's talking about? Perhaps there were bodies, rotting, unfound. There were certainly no outstanding cases involving four or five linked killings. Girls? Go right back and play it from the start. The young constable's face looked green. He had a lot to learn.

'Can you remember where it happened?'

'Course I remember. You must know where it happened. Where they all happened. Right there where I work.'

'At St Biddolph's?'

'Where else would you get them?' Aggression taking the place of fear. 'Anyhow it's really all her fault.' He jerked his head towards the door. 'When I does it with her she just lies there like an old sack of potatoes. You white people think all black women got rhythm, well I'm telling you, you try her out. You got my full permission. And you'll come back and say, no man, no thank you, not even for practice.'

Sex, sex, sex. Torry, were you being dragged into some horrible nightmare perversion? You were already getting hung up with thoughts about Susan, could this be just a revolting extension? All roads seemed to lead to pounding sex.

'You work as a night watchman at St Biddolph's Hospital. For the record, whereabouts do you work? I mean what part of the hospital?'

'You know that. I'm the mortuary night watchman.'

Sense. If it was what he thought ... revolting. But this poor disorientated beast was off the hook as far as Lipperman, Armitage and all the others were concerned.

'Okay, Henry, you work in the mortuary. It sometimes helps if you tell people about it. So shoot. Tell us what happened last night. Or the other times if you like. Let's get down to the nitty gritty.'

The man seemed to brace himself. Then out it came, with a normality that made the whole thing more horrible.

Wexton's job consisted of sitting in a warm office. If a body had to be brought over from the hospital they rang through and he would either prepare one of the bins or open up the postmortem theatre. Quite often they brought in the remains of young women. The first time, it had been a girl of about eighteen, killed in a car accident but hardly marked. They had laid her out in the theatre and left Henry to put off the lights and lock up. He had touched the corpse's shoulder and found it still warm. With a macabre inquisitive terror he stripped back the sheets. 'She looked beautiful, like marble. Like a statue and she hadn't got stiff yet. I think I wanted to bring her back to life and it was the only way I knew.'

There had been several. Certainly more than five. Two had died during emergency operations, and there was an older woman. Torry felt the nausea rise in his throat. The constable was taking deep breaths. Torry let Wexton ramble on until he was talked out, tears streaking the ebony cheeks.

'You know, Henry, we'll have to do something about this.' It was a superfluous, stupid remark.

'I'm glad you came, man, real glad 'cos I couldn't have gone on. What'll they do to me?'

'I'm not sure, Henry, but you'll have to change your job and I think you're going to need treatment of some kind.'

'You mean I'm sick in the head?' He nodded, knowing the answer.

'We'd better go down to the station and talk. There are some other questions I've got to ask first though.'

'You go ahead and ask. Ask all you want.'

Torry went through his prepared questions about Lipperman, Jumper, the mythical Jones, Grosvenor, Cust, the whole organization, or at least the tiny part they knew about. He didn't press the questions. Wexton knew nothing of these people or of their lives. He wasn't even a criminal in the accepted sense, even though it was only a short step from Wexton's kind of necrophily to the act of destruction in order to provide himself with a body on which to practise the morbid perversion. You didn't have to be a genius to figure that one out. Henry Jonas Wexton was far too heavily bolted within his own evil to be the man they were looking for.

Torry talked quietly to Wexton's wife in the small kitchen, superficially clean but smelling strongly of rotting vegetables, an odour that impregnated the whole house. He did not go into details of Henry's private life, simply telling her that he was sick and needed treatment. But what kind of treatment did you give a guy like that? Some kind of aversion? Electric shocks while looking at the bodies of dead women? It was one for the doctors. Or was that just the easy way out? Passing the buck. It happened all the time to the problem people. The doctors passed them on, and the lawyers and the police, civil servants, even the government. In the end the vicious circle might drop Wexton once more at Torry's feet. Then it would be his problem again, with some lonely, wretched girl lying strangled and raped on a rain-soaked common. He had seen one of those only a couple of years ago. A pitiful little doll, broken, with the legs spread wide, an attitude, he remembered from the evidence, she was only too willing to assume during life.

Wexton's wife did not probe or question the manner of her man's illness. She simply accepted the situation and staggered off to give him what comfort she could.

In the car going down to the local station, sitting next to the big silent coloured man, Torry found himself becoming more bewildered. He was a man who had seen possibly every nauseating sight there was. His job made him reach out and touch corruption, the bodies, minds, beings of people. Yet his faith taught him, ordered him, to feel compassion. He had, himself, broken the moral rules of Holy Church so many times and, to some extent, the rules of society. Where do you begin to judge? At what point do you seek help or devise punishment? Susan flickered across the screen of his mind. Then Gerry. How great was his sin really? To have lustful thoughts about one girl and seek a kind of physiotherapy in another: how much greater or smaller was this compared to Henry Jonas Wexton? Or the

135

Wexton they were seeking, what of him? If the name Wexton had not materialized during his trip to New York, this afternoon's painful, disgusting episode would never have taken place. What then? A worse and more sickening episode in a year's time, with Henry Wexton being chased over three counties? And Tickerman told him not to get involved. You're already involved, Torry, like all men are involved.

His train of thought took him back to first base, his immediate precarious position within the Force. Jumper only had to start squeaking or Gerry get awkward, and he was without work or prospects. A forgotten man. If he was wrong about General Wexton, that would lead to the same thing. Torry could see a wall of rejection rising in front of him.

He looked at Henry Wexton. The coloured man tried to force a shy smile. Torry wanted to reply, show the animal that he had friends. But no smile came. Compassion didn't come that easy.

8

Two days and what had happened? One new friend who could turn into a treacherous enemy. The accidental discovery that an obscure coloured male was perverted. What sort of police work was this? Better forgotten. Not days to remember, yet the edginess of conflict gave him a feeling of exasperation, not simply with events but with himself and his dead-end life of clutching at people who had dropped lower than other men.

There was the red-tape statement to be made at the local station, then the ride back to the Yard. Torry did not get into his office until after five. A pile of work to be done. His report on Gerry, and another on this afternoon's filth. He really ought to make his confession. Perhaps there was an evening Mass at the Sacred Heart. That would mean sitting up half the night afterwards to get the reports filed. Dumphy greeted him.

'I presume Henry Jonas Wexton's not our man, sir?'

Why the hell couldn't Dumphy shut up? Torry walked quickly through to the inner office, the sergeant following like a trained spaniel.

'You presumed right. He spends his spare time boffing dead bodies. Oh, join the Metropolitan Police, Dumphy, and see the world.' More papers on his desk. Dumphy ignored his small tantrum.

'Two of the County C.R.O.s have come up with Wextons. You have them there.' The sergeant pointed to the papers.

Lord, no more. Please no more. 'How many?'

'Just the two. But I don't think you need worry, they're both inside.'

One was from Lancashire, an old lag now in the third year of a five-year sentence. In and out since the age of sixteen. Women's handbags, break-ins, one botched G.B.H. The other languished in Parkhurst. Life, for taking a length of lead piping to his stepmother who came out of the incident dead.

Torry picked up the telephone. Ticker was not available. He rang half an hour later as Torry was a third of the way through banging out his reports.

'Hear you had a deadly afternoon,' Ticker began with a dry chuckle.

'Cut it, Tick, please. It wasn't funny.'

'Touchy. What's wrong, Derek, the hounds of the bastard-villes sniffing at your heels?'

'I just don't find that sort of thing amusing.'

'Nor do I, lad. I don't find my officers leaping off to Paris funny.' Tickerman's tone changed.

'You passed the order. I'm the eternal yes-man around here or hadn't you heard? Tricky Torry's completely subservient.'

'Don't come it, Derek. You should have referred back to me.'

'I was told ... '

'Were you told to issue instructions regarding Geraldine Wexton's father? I'm sorry, Derek, but I'm beginning to wonder if the old man isn't right after all.'

'You want my resignation?'

'Don't be childish. Wexton may not be in the C.R.O. files but I don't think you're as stupid as that. He ties in somewhere.'

'What's new then? And what do I do about this brace of Wextons the County Forces have turned over?'

The two Wextons already inside could be safely left alone. For the time being anyway. Apart from that there was nothing new. No leads from the car or the Sterling. Nothing from Fingerprints or Forensic. No whispers from the pigeons. Jumper had been charged with being an accessory. Grosvenor and Cust were still silent. It was beginning to look as though everybody really was clinging to Torry's inquiries, as though some miracle might produce the right answer.

The church was still heavy with flowers from Easter. Father Conrad moved with the professional ease of one who has performed the same ritual act many times and yet managed to stay involved. A genuflexion and the Host, now the Body and Blood of Christ, a circle of mystic white, was held high in the air.

Torry, kneeling, stared towards the altar and the uplifted Host, his mind elsewhere. He had drifted, almost aimlessly, to the church. Then, on discovering that an evening Mass was to be celebrated, he had stayed. Again, almost in spite of himself, he had made his confession and received absolution. The ritual act did nothing to ease his depression and sense of bewilderment.

When he was younger, the Mass, above everything else, had been a prop in Torry's life. An anchor. The one certain thing. Now it seemed to have become an act divorced from life as he knew and lived it. The metaphysical arguments had ceased to sway him.

When it was over and Father Conrad had lifted his hand in the final blessing, Torry waited outside, pacing to and fro on the cobbles. This was more than just a habit out of which he had never grown. As a boy, Torry had made a practice of waiting for the priest after Mass. Tonight there was a good reason for it. He needed to talk, if only for a few minutes' consolation, to Father Conrad.

One or two people glanced suspiciously at him as they left the church.

'Derek. We haven't been seeing much of you lately.' There was no trace of reproach in the priest's voice as he came down the steps, cassock flapping in the light evening breeze.

This was, thought Torry, perhaps the reason why he could still cling to the outward signs of the Church while his mind and heart stubbornly refused any inward participation. The example that Father Conrad had set all these years could not be shrugged away. The priest was wholly dedicated to an idea, a faith of intricate complexity. Only a short time ago he had heard Torry's confession: Torry's faults, from small glib lies to the sensuality within his brain and the act in Gerry's bed. The things which the priest was forced to hear must be totally repugnant to the man, yet here he was, smiling and clasping Torry's hand as though he was a brother priest and steeped in sanctity.

'You're looking tired.' Father Conrad put an arm on Torry's shoulder.

'Just hard work. They say it never hurt anyone, Father. Anyway, I'm backing Britain.'

'Do they now? Well they're wrong about work never hurting anyone. It's one of the sops we hand out to the so-called working classes to which we all really belong. That's why we get so many managing directors and people with large responsibilities going down with coronaries.' The priest stopped and looked hard at Torry. 'You coming over for a chat?'

'I haven't really got time, Father.'

'No?' The priest started to pace his way towards the presbytery. Torry fell into step beside him.

'You look tired. Bad day?' asked Father Conrad.

'Depressing.' As he said it, Torry realized how depressed he really was. It shouldn't be like this. The case should have excited him, yet it simply seemed to be a dead end. You didn't play hunches like in the private-eye movies, or get involved in moments when the vital clue appeared out of the blue so that you could call together the suspects, reconstruct the crime and unmask the villain.

With the Wexton business there were a hundred crimes involved: extortion, murder, vice, drugs, thieving. You had to deal with all the shadowy little men, the narks and dirty unkempt whiners as well as the smooth boys. The only tools required were an inquiring mind, an observant streak and the hope that you could stay sane during weeks of boredom. Mixing in this strange world of human hulks and sharps brought its own kind of depression.

The priest had stopped. Once more he was giving Torry a hard look. 'I know, Derek,' he said. 'Priests and coppers share a similar load. We both share other people's sins. It can be disillusioning.'

Torry nodded. 'It is when you come up against the kind of thing I had to deal with today.'

'Yes?' Father Conrad waited for the story.

'Have you ever come across necrophily, Father?'

They had reached the presbytery steps. The priest did not answer directly but turned the question. 'Necrophily? You've met it before, Derek, surely? You were involved in the Hampstead Heath business, weren't you?'

'Yes.' Torry agreed. He would rather forget that one. The girl's body lying on the soaking grass. Obscene and revolting. 'Yes, but I'm not talking about the ones who kill in order to provide themselves with the means of satisfaction. This one today was a mortuary attendant. He hadn't reached the homicidal stage.'

The priest stood on the first step and put a hand on Torry's shoulder. 'I've known men who've lost their wives suddenly or tragically ... ' His voice petered out. 'Good God. Poor restless soul. You've got him?'

Torry nodded.

'Then you've performed a service, Derek. If you got him that early, think what a service you've performed. To him, to the innocents, the others, his relations.'

Relations ... relations. A service to Wexton's relations. Some· thing had been hounding Torry since he left Henry Jonas Wexton. He had never even bothered to check if the man had relations of the same name in the country. The tweezers of his mind nipped the thought and dropped it into the Cellophane envelope of action. The fictional clue under his nose. He had been quick enough with Gerry's father. His mind was becoming horribly single-tracked. Lazy. There could be another, more sophisticated, coloured Wexton within striking distance.

Torry muttered something about having to get back to the Yard, leaving Father Conrad with much to say standing on the presbytery steps looking after the retreating, tall figure hurrying across the square and out into the street to hail a taxi.

The Yard was practically deserted when Torry got into his office. He sat back at the desk, lit a cigarette and began to dial Tickerman's home number. Then, thinking better of it, he put his finger firmly on the receiver rests and called the station in Bermondsey. The C.I.D. man on duty knew hardly anything about the case but promised to talk personally to Wexton. Would Torry call back in an hour or so?

It took an hour and a quarter to complete his reports on Geraldine Wexton and Henry Wexton. When they were finished, Torry read them over, signed them and called Bermondsey again. The C.I.D. man had gone off duty but there was a message. Henry Wexton's only surviving relatives were the wife and two children in England, and an obscure uncle still in Jamaica. So much for that. A complete state of death to a possibility.

Wearily, Torry put the report files on Dumphy's desk, then,

as a last act of conscientiousness, he dialled Ticker's number. The Chief Inspector was watching his favourite television programme and the conversation was terse. Once more Torry felt the tensions of senior officers putting on the personal squeeze. There was still nothing new, unless you counted the one fact they had all begun to appreciate. Nobody wanted to talk, think or hint about a man called Wexton. Morse and smooth Hart were making a concentrated effort on interrogating Cust, Grosvenor and Jumper. The Chief Superintendent was chewing his nails and the parings were likely to be spat at Torry's feet any time now.

'You said that so fast I thought it was going to get away. Do I smell threats even from you, Tick?' Torry hit back.

'I don't need to make threats, Derek lad. I've done all I can for you.'

'And how does he repay me? I've worked and slaved for the boy and he turns round and kicks me in the teeth.' Torry said it straight and mocking.

'Kicks me in the teeth and goes off to Paris without checking, then orders a tail on a V.I.P.'

'As a frightener you're as adept as a cow with a gun, Tick. Back to your Western or Peyton Place or whatever it is.'

'And that's no way to talk to your senior officer.'

'Doesn't matter if I'm getting the Police Constable's farewell without even a handshake from the Commissioner or my presentation magnifying glass.'

'He'll give you more than a handshake, lad. Oh, and stand by for a major conference within a few days if nothing breaks.'

They parted on slightly better terms, yet Torry could not feel any great weight lifting from his mind. As he was about to leave the office he noticed his In-tray for the first time. On top of a hillock of papers lay a buff file with a paper-clipped slip attached.

*

Notes and latest information on General Thornton Wexton
M.C., D.S.O., O.B.E. Urgent for Detective Inspector J. D.
Torry.

Torry made a face and picked up the file. It might make interesting browsing in bed, when he'd finished with Jeff Hawke, Gun
Law, Carol Day and Flook.

'Glad you could make it, Tony.' A grey smile swept Al Vescari's
face as he ushered the lean man into his apartment.

Tony Champion set down his brief-case and slipped out of the
dark-blue raincoat before following Vescari through to the living
area. 'No one else?' he queried, sucking his teeth.

'Right first time, baby. Men's talk tonight. Just the two of us.'

Champion twisted his mouth, his manner of conveying uncertainty. 'What gives, Al? I been a naughty boy?'

'Just the opposite. No water?' Vescari stood by the bar.

'Same as always. No water.' Champion took the proffered
drink and lowered himself into a chair.

'No point in getting hung up.' Vescari had placed himself in a
chair across the fireplace. 'Looks as though Bertel was right. I
can't be certain, but it seems Wexton's private life is a shade
weird. Like you heard.'

'So what? You 'n' me've known plenty of weirdos, Al. Live
and let live. See how he pulls this Birthday Party caper. You've
had no beef till now.'

'No, but none of us can afford to see the British end fall
through.' Vescari leaned forward. 'My reading of the signs is that
Wexton's losing his marbles, Tony. He's beginning to get wild,
go to pieces. Like I said, we can't see the British end fall through.'

'Then just drop it quietly. I know you've dreamed dreams and
seen visions, Al. A coast-to-coast operation over here with big
controlling interests in Europe. Sometimes you have to cut down

144

on your dreams. Hell, how were you to know about Wexton? He came to us highly recommended and certainly had fresh ideas. You've got to admit he's touched genius in some of the plans. Anyone who can operate like him and not even get picked up on sus has to be brilliant.'

Vescari looked grim. 'We're in too deep over there. That's the problem, Tony. The police're getting nosy.'

'I warned you about letting him have old "Shoelace".'

'Stupid thing for me to have done. You were right. But Wexton was still showing common sense then. He didn't want any of his boys mixing with Lipperman.'

Champion took a swig at his drink. 'He used them just the same.'

'Had no option. Now they've cottoned on to his name, Tony. Got a cop working on it day and night.'

'A big gun?'

'Naw.' Vescari consulted a small leather-bound pocket book. 'Some Inspector Torry. John Derek Torry. If he uncovers anything ... '

'Al, don't be silly. It's not like the old days.'

'I know that. But he could have a price.'

'Torry,' mused Tony Champion. 'Torry hasn't got a price, we tried him already. He was the one who brought "Shoelace" back.'

'Well, maybe we didn't try high enough. My information says he's under pressure. They're threatening to get rid of him if he doesn't find anything under the garbage.'

Champion raised his eyes. 'And you don't want to go down in Bertel's estimation, so you're asking me nicely to take an airplane ride over to London and quieten Brother Torry?'

'And keep an eye on Wexton. If he does go to pieces you might ... '

'Make sure he flunks in living?'

Vescari smiled. 'I couldn't put it better.'

'I'm not a button man, Al. I'm up in the board room with you, remember?'

'That's why I'm asking you. It's a matter of trust. If anything's going wrong over there I want it stopped before they can tie in with us. Okay, Tony, so I may have to cut back on my dreams, but if the British end blows, then odds are that we've had it out here as well. Things have been fine, quiet, with everybody minding their own business until now. And the profits from the British market are big. You realize what we've done in London? Taken over a third of the gaming houses, a third of the major cat-houses, a third of the narcotics outlets. Half of the dough's being ploughed back into legit concerns and any heist job has got to be big before we okay it. Go try and save the family business, eh, Tony.'

'It'll cost you.' Champion smiled. He was as good as on the next flight out.

Smith tried to keep his eyes fixed on Wexton. Wexton, his leader, sitting upright across the desk. What was the point of hiding anything from him? Smithy, he thought, you reckon you're his right-hand man, but who knows? He may have three right-hand men. Wexton was devious. That was the word. Devious. Wexton was a devious person. Wexton's eyes holding his, combined with the silence, forced Smith into speech.

'They have no way of getting on to you, Mr Wexton.'

'No.' He was like a big block of stone sitting there, solid, impassive. 'No, they haven't got any real way. But they're on to the name. It's bad, Smith. Jumper?'

'I don't think Jumper's talked. Jumper's not a grass.'

Wexton moved, drumming his fingers on the polished desk top.

'I thought it was best to tell you,' Smith added.

'You did right. I had some information anyway.'

Christ, Wexton had access to so much.

'I hadn't heard about the coloured man, but I was told of the girl ... ' The fingers stopped drumming and reached for the leather cigarette box, fumbling slightly. Is he rattled, wondered Smith as Wexton continued, 'the girl in Paris. I knew about that.'

'Does it change anything?'

'You mean the Birthday Party? No, nothing'll change the Birthday Party. As for me, I have several choices.'

'Yes.' Sometimes, thought Smith, you didn't understand what Wexton was on about. 'Yes, I see,' he lied. 'Then the final briefing's on Tuesday.'

'On Tuesday.' Wexton was far away, retreating into his own strange forest of dreams where nightmare branches took hold of him and the rain lashed down. Just him and the little kicking, shrieking figure. It had come over him again last night. He'd even resorted to a kind of prayer, clutching at any straw that might stop him. Not again. He didn't want to go through all that again. If it was anything. Nothing was clear. It could have been a dream. Sometimes he was so certain that it was a dream, then there were the other moments when he knew ... Smith was looking at him. The vague questioning expression that could mean a hundred different things. Did Smith have any idea? Men like Smith were shrewd. They back-tracked over the years. Some of them were better than the police. He might ... just might think ...

'Smith,' said Wexton, 'there is one thing you can do for me.'

'Certainly, Mr Wexton. Anything.' Anything but look at your bloody eyes. Look up, Smithy lad, look up. Up at that picture there. The fellow all done up in Napoleonic gear on a horse, all gold frame and Harrods over the desk.

*

Torry telephoned Susan from the flat.

'Hallo, darling, you're back.'

'What's wrong with my back?'

'Thanks for the telegram. How was Paris?' She sounded stupidly happy compared to his own state of work-worry.

'Paris was Paris. Some guy tried to sell me a big rusty tower they have out on an old parking lot but I turned him down.'

'Good for you.'

'I bought the Louvre instead.'

'It'll make a nice place for week-ends.'

'Yes, and the cellars are good. Be great for nuclear disasters.'

'We'll have to hope they coincide.'

'What?'

'The week-ends and the nuclear disasters.'

'They will. It always rains on Sundays. What're you doing?'

Susan giggled. 'Well actually, darling, I'm washing my smalls. Why don't you come over?'

The wrong answer. Torry's mood and key changed. Fantasies. Soap powder and lace. Foam and …

'Tomorrow night, my place, Sue.'

Pause. 'You all right?'

'I'm fine. Job's bugging me, that's all.'

'What time tomorrow?'

'Seven do you? If I'm not there, let yourself in and wait.'

Torry cut any further conversation with a hurried goodbye.

He went into the kitchen to make coffee, then thought better of it, rescrewing the lid on to the jar of instant and making for the Scotch bottle in the living-room. Tonight was definitely a whisky night. He poured himself a moderate non-medicinal dosage, carried it, and the General Wexton file, into the bedroom and climbed out of his clothes. Once in bed, with the whisky in one hand, a cigarette in the other and the file open on the counterpane in front of him, Torry became conscious of his fatigue. He

148

had never really caught up with himself since the New York trip. Then as he glanced down the file's introductory page, the tiredness momentarily left him.

'Not *that* General Wexton.' Torry half said it aloud, his mind bursting with fragmented rage, fury aimed at himself, sentences, words, pictures condemning his own folly. A good cop? A good Catholic? You've become a bloody good introspective, that's all. No wonder there was a flap. Torry went cold at the thought of his presumption in ordering surveillance without even checking with Tickerman. Whatever else happened, the General Wexton file contained enough to put Torry bound and gagged at the wrong end of the Metropolitan Police pistol range. If there was one thing the British hierarchy understood it was power. And here, typed on the flimsy pages, was a keg full of power.

There had been a Wexton with Marlborough. Another with Lord Roberts at Paardeberg. A third died on the Somme. Thornton Wexton was a product of Sandhurst, a half-colonel with Montgomery and the Eighth Army in the desert before being promoted to Second-in-Command of an Airborne Division before D-Day. Three times wounded. Military Cross. Distinguished Service Order and bar. Order of the British Empire. A most senior and responsible post at Aldershot after the war.

Since the golden bowler, seven years ago, he had branched out, even been offered the job of Comptroller to one of the royal households. A knighthood in the offing, General Wexton was on the boards of four mighty concerns and the file left one in no doubt that he still acted in an advisory capacity to the Ministry of Defence.

Torry finished his drink in one jerky swallow, stubbed out the cigarette and lay back to take stock. General Thornton Wexton was a solid blockbuster of power and politics—no matter what side was in. Torry had no evidence to link the General's name with the Lipperman killing, or any other criminal activity. His wild instructions to have the man followed were based solely on a hunch as insubstantial as ectoplasm, and Torry didn't normally go for hunches. What was wrong with him? A good cop? A good Catholic? Once maybe, but not any more. Susan? One woman on his conscience and he was a goner, lost in a limbo of self-destruction.

He was shaking, for here in the silent room, on the verge of sleep, Torry had begun to reappraise his role. Did it start with his Catholicism, his Catholic conscience? By its very nature that conscience swept one into a slough of introspection where every mite of guilt became a monster mountain. That state of mind was not conducive to being a good cop. The two sides of his life had, perhaps, been at war with one another for years; Susan simply upset the balance and brought his defects to the surface. The thoughts crossed, separated and crossed again. Sleep began to take control.

Torry slept, but the Lipperman/Wexton case continued. The Chief Superintendent, assisted by Broadbent, Snaith, half of Crime One and the Flying Squad, was making it a round-the-clock job. Already the hard pressure of 'routine inquiries' had accidentally brought into the open two fences and a man wanted for fraud. In the early hours, pairs of C.I.D. men were sauntering into clubs, ranging from the near-beer no-sex Soho clip joints to the velvet night haunts of New Bond Street and Kensington.

Questions. Heads shaken.

'Protection? Who needs it?'

'Wexton? Knew a Wexford once. Charlie Wexford. Not a Wexton though. No.'

Then there were those officers who had exceptional contacts. The big informers.

'Sorry, guv, but you know how it is. 'Course I been shopping around, but there's not a peep about anyone wanting a shooter like that.'

On this particular night, of all those concerned, Snaith was the only one to draw any lead. Both Lipperman and Grosvenor had been seen together regularly at a private mixed club, The Carpet Bag, in the Sloane Square area. The place had a Rolls and Bentley carriage trade and an uncertain reputation so far untested by the Yard. But now the link with Lipperman and Grosvenor was noted. Soon The Carpet Bag would have to be done over.

Torry woke at five from a strangling dream in which Susan agreed to the wedding and then appeared in church wearing a stripper's outfit. He was sweating and unmercifully erect. It did not often happen, but there was only one thing for him to do. Afterwards, he felt unclean and wrapped himself in a shroud of sleep. Eventually his shelter was ripped open by the demanding and incessant telephone bell.

Torry sat up with a start, memory returning with the nasty feeling that he had not arranged his usual alarm call. For a second he did not take in the fact that his watch said ten thirty. He wrenched at the telephone. Dumphy was at the other end, conspiratorial.

'Thank heaven I've caught you, sir. You've never been late in before. I've had to stall him for half an hour already.'

'Stall who?'

'You've got a visitor, sir. Got to be handled with care. He's already been to the Commissioner who passed him on to Mr Tickerman who ... '

'Passed him on to me?'

'Sir.' Parade-ground agreement.

'Who is this kid-gloved character?' Sneering, not yet fully awake.

'General Wexton, sir. You've got General Thornton Wexton waiting here for you.'

9

GENERAL THORNTON WEXTON looked surprisingly young and fit. Spine like a musket barrel, a cold irritation building within him. You could feel it as Dumphy ushered him into the room.

Torry rose to meet him. He had shaved, dressed and made the dash to Scotland Yard in a time which would have shattered Batman.

'Good morning, General Wexton. I'm sorry to have kept you waiting.' The General ignored Torry's outstretched hand. 'Please sit down. My name's Torry. Detective Inspector.'

'So I gather.' The speech was precise, coloured with suppressed fury. 'I've been handed down the chain of command here like some delinquent corporal, Inspector. The Commissioner's a personal friend of mine and he assured me that your Superintendent would give me an explanation. He says you're the man I should see, and I've been waiting on you for one hour.' He paused with that petulance which is second nature to senior Army officers. 'Be that as it may, I'm told you can give me the facts.'

Torry summoned up his reserves of tolerance. Be tactful. Subservient. He just wants the facts, man. 'What facts are those, sir?'

'The facts about my daughter being interrogated for a considerable time in Paris the day before yesterday.'

'And your daughter's name?' Too late he realized the question smacked of insolence.

'Miss Geraldine Elizabeth Wexton.' Each word a prolonged stab of ice.

Torry held the pause a fraction too long then picked up the internal telephone and pressed the outer office button—it was more impressive than the intercom. It was stalling for time but he'd already made enough mistakes to send him back to bashing pavements, with or without his experience. Dumphy answered the phone.

'Sergeant Dumphy, did Mr Tickerman leave any instructions about General Wexton?'

'No, sir. Sergeant Gosling brought him down from Mr Tickerman's office. Mr Tickerman had already called me to say he wanted you to see him.'

'Thank you. Get me Mr Tickerman would you.' How do you play influential generals? Ticker came on the line, breezy.

'Good morning, sir. Torry here. I have a General Wexton with me. I wondered what your instructions were.'

'You only just seeing him?'

'Yes, sir.' Torry bearing down a little hard on the 'sir'. 'We've been trying to trace the address of the third interested party, Rowland Frank—you know the surname.' He lied, praying that Dumphy had not passed any information Tickerman's way.

'Have you now?' It was a shark's voice.

'What about the General, sir?' Torry did his best to sound glib.

Tickerman answered in a hiss. 'He is the wrath of God, Derek, which you have brought down upon us. So you, as a member of the One Holy Catholic and Apostolic Church, will have to exorcize him for us. I don't care how you do it but get him out of here, out of my hair and yours and his friend the Commissioner's. Lie, perjure yourself, cheat, fiddle and swindle, but get him out.'

'Very good, sir. How much may I disclose to him?'

'Disclose what you like. Don't assault him or give him cause for further anguish or action. Simply put his mind at rest. Otherwise, Derek, you are the deadest mallard on the pond. Do you follow?'

'Yes, sir. Mallard you said?' A cheeky attitude was Torry's last resort. He put the telephone down and looked hard at the General, an imitation of every detective he had seen on stage, screen or television.

'Your daughter, sir.'

'My daughter, Inspector,' said the General, matching Torry's mood.

Torry desperately wanted to meet the man with an unrestrained insolence. His seventh sense, the one policemen were always told to disregard, still tapped out 'Mayday' signals. The General could just possibly be the Wexton they wanted. Then Gerry sprawled across his consciousness. Big Gerry, magnificent Gerry. *Gerry Wexton, air hostess. Gerry Wexton, man-eater. Gerry Wexton, thief.* He had begun to doubt himself so much that he again started wondering about the girl. Had he gone to Paris in such a strained state of mind that he'd automatically cancelled Gerry Wexton from the list of possibles? Simply because she had a good figure and offered him bed and a sexual opiate? Remember, Torry, remember this could be your fish. Play him and remember it could be his daughter who was the fish. If it is, you're for the high jump anyway, Torry. Say something, you cretinous cop.

'Geraldine Elizabeth Wexton. She's over twenty-one I think, sir.'

'She's over twenty-one, Inspector.'

'And you're making some kind of complaint on her behalf?'

'I'm making a personal inquiry.'

'Not a complaint?'

'A complaint may follow. It depends very much on the answers I get from yourself, and the co-operation of other officers here.' The General chose his words carefully, controlling his temper to a hair's-breadth.

Torry gave an amicable half-shrug, as if to indicate that he had nothing to hide. 'What is it you want to know, General Wexton?'

The man, sitting bolt upright in the chair before Torry's desk, cleared his throat. 'Am I right in stating that my daughter was subjected to a lengthy and rigorous cross-examination, without warning, at Le Bourget airport on the afternoon of Thursday, eighteenth of April?'

'You are *not* right, sir.'

'Careful, Inspector, I understand you're in trouble already. I have many friends. A report from me to the Commissioner can break you ... '

'Like a stick?' Torry raised his eyebrows.

The General's chest heaved twice in a restraining movement. 'You deny my daughter was questioned?'

'No.' Bland, still playing for time.

'You've just denied it.'

'No. I denied that she was cross-questioned. I also deny that the questioning was rigorous and lengthy. Adjust your question and I'll go along with you.'

The General leaned forward, one hand on the desk. 'Then give me your version.'

Witness-box stuff, 'On Thursday April eighteenth, nineteen hundred and sixty-eight, I was instructed to carry out routine questioning of all persons by the name of Wexton who appeared on the Criminal Records at Scotland Yard. I was instructed to do this by Detective Superintendent Tickerman who had received his orders from the Detective Chief Superintendent of Crime One, New Scotland Yard. These routine interviews were to be made in connection with a major inquiry at this time being conducted by officers of the Criminal Investigation Department, C One, New Scotland Yard. I was furnished with a list of names after which I referred back to Superintendent Tickerman and asked if it was absolutely necessary for me to interview each of the persons named. He told me that the Detective Chief Superintendent had stipulated that I should carry out this inquiry personally. One of the names was a Miss Geraldine Elizabeth Wexton, employed as a ground hostess by British European Airways at Le Bourget airport, Paris.' Torry swallowed, mentally grinning at his next sentence.

'I proceeded to Le Bourget by air and was met there by Inspector Dumier of the Judiciaire and an *assistante*. Together we approached Miss Wexton and asked if she minded answering some questions. She agreed and later made a statement ... '

'What sort of a statement?'

'A statement which completely cleared her of any possible connection with our investigations. That clear enough for you, General?'

'A mite too clear. You may well have to repeat this rigmarole at an official inquiry.'

'On whose behalf are you acting, sir?'

'My daughter's, of course.'

'She has asked you to take the matter up?' Had the lovely carnivorous Gerry been stirring it?

'She has supplied me with certain information.'

'Such as?'

'That she was pestered by a C.I.D. officer.'

Pestered? Sinatra on the turntable, kisses returned, the walk to the bedroom. Pestered?

Torry put it into words. 'Pestered, sir?'

'You'd call it an interview. I call it pestering.'

Now was the moment to chance his arm. 'Your daughter's

simply told you that she was interviewed by me and you inter-
pret this as an act of pestering? An infringement of Civil Rights?
General, who do you think you are?'

There was a tic-like movement in the man's cheeks and, even
from the other side of the desk, Torry could see the pulse beat
in the General's temple.

'Don't push me too far, Inspector Tory.'

'Torry, sir. T-O-R-R-Y.' Aggressive now. Play him like the
big barracuda he could be. 'A Tory is what I suspect you are.'

The General rose, an indignant attitude. 'You'll be hearing
more about this ... '

'Sit down, General, please.' The words like four pistol shots.
'Now that you're here I've got some routine questions I have to
ask you.'

'You'll do no such thing.'

'I'm sorry, sir. I can't allow you to leave the building until I
have some answers from you.'

The General paused and looked at Torry with a contempt
usually reserved for molesters of children. 'I came here of my
own accord. I shall leave of my own accord.'

Dumphy, thought Torry, must be getting an earful. General
Wexton was using a vocal volume that would penetrate most
known types of soundproofing.

'General.' Torry did not have to raise his voice, he had long
caught the trick of the short sharp command. Wexton remained
standing, but still. Torry spoke quietly. 'Your daughter hasn't
asked for a complaint to be made against me. She hasn't even
suggested that I pestered her at the interview, has she?'

The General's lips moved. Then, almost capitulating, 'I've a
right to protect my own flesh and blood.'

'Which you did very nicely during the Second World War.
Don't you want to know how I'm aware of the fact that your
daughter isn't complaining about me?'

General Wexton took a step towards the desk. Torry continued in the same quiet tone. 'She isn't complaining about me because on the night of Thursday, the eighteenth of April, Gerry and I dined together in Paris. Socially, General. Socially and sociably. We're close friends ... '

'Close.' One word which summoned up all the disdain inherent in class consciousness.

'Close as clams,' Torry lied. To hell with everything. He refused to be intimidated by this strategic war horse.

'I shall forbid ... '

'You can forbid nothing.' Whiplash words. 'Gerry's over age. A grown woman. Full and blooming. One time, one time only, she acted stupidly, and paid for it. Unfortunately her name and yours tallies with someone we want to interview. It's not her. I don't suppose it's you. But it's my job to investigate any possibilities. My job, just like your job once, was killing Germans.'

The General, raging, muscles a-twitch, stabbed hatred across the room. In the quiet vortex of hurricane temper, he said, 'Inspector Torry, you've shifted this on to a personal level. I realize you have a job to do.' He stopped, took a step forward and returned to his chair. 'All right. I'll answer your questions. But after that, God help you.' A hard, harsh statement, not a threat.

Torry felt the hand of defeat on his shoulder. Even in the Welfare State one had few defences against power and the old-boy network of Wexton's class.

The following hour entrenched a deeper realization that Torry was tilting at reinforced concrete. Wexton, barely civil, answered all the standard questions with the candid honesty of a man who not only had nothing to hide but also could prove it with an avalanche of omnipotence.

By the time the interview was over General Wexton had regained his temper, but there was a genuine threat of reality in his parting words.

'I have co-operated, Torry, but my official complaint about your manner, your methods and your insolence will be on the Commissioner's desk first thing Monday morning.'

Torry sat back and lit a cigarette. In spite of the General's position and his seeming blamelessness, something still bothered him about the man. It could simply be the name, or his emotional hangover from Gerry – the feeling of insecurity and tension about his job. 'The Job'. That old dedicated sense began to well up inside him.

And there was war in heaven: Michael and his angels fought against the dragon; and the dragon fought and his angels, and prevailed not; neither was their place found any more in heaven. And the great dragon was cast out, that old serpent, called the Devil, and Satan, which deceiveth the whole world: he was cast out into the earth, and his angels were cast out with him.

Wasn't that what it was all about? A clear picture of the Bosch 'Haywain' focused firmly in Torry's mind, the top of the left-hand panel sharp in detail. The war in heaven with Satan and his vanquished angels conquered in some bizarre aerial dogfight, spiralling, spinning, swooping out of control like a plague of grotesque insects being swept from the sky by a virulent pest-controlling spray. This was the vivid battle. A biblical fairy-tale? A true, eternal allegory. The timeless battle between good and evil, law and order versus chaos.

Torry had three times pledged himself to the side of law and order – four, if he counted the big pledge of faith to Christ and His Body and the Church. And what had he been doing? Playing around with a bunch of names? Fiddling with reports. Submerging his body and mind in actions and thoughts which could only weaken his personal powers as a keeper of the peace. He grabbed at the telephone. His grip more firm than it had been for days.

Tick was just leaving his office.

'I've got rid of the pompous bastard, Tick, but he's putting in a personal complaint against me.'

'Oh God, Derek, you stupid git. What've you done now?'

'My duty, as I see it. And, as I see it, your duty's to stand by me.'

'What did you do?'

'Asked him some questions.'

'Wexton-type questions?'

'That's his name, isn't it? We're looking for someone called Wexton. A dirty, money-providing name behind a lot of names and a dunghill of activities. A wanted individual.'

'What else besides questions?'

'I told him to mind his own business about the interview with his daughter.'

Tickerman let out a long whistling sound. 'Then you might as well pack your bags, lad. He pulls a lot of strings.'

'I don't care if he pulls all the chains in Buck House, the House of Commons or the one in the Commissioner's private loo. That man was trying to influence the course of justice by interfering with my job.'

'Try to prove it,' said Tickerman wearily.

'I'll prove it. I'm about to write a report to the Commissioner. It'll land on his desk about the same time as the General's, and I'll even call the General's daughter as evidence.'

'Evidence?'

'For me, Tick. General Wexton's a suspected person as far as I'm concerned. We eliminate no person by the name Wexton until I bang the right boy, or girl, in the oven and turn it up to Regulo ten. Tick, I'm going to get this character, and when I've got him I'm going to tie him up so tight that it'll take Houdini and the whole of the Magic Circle plus the Cabinet to get him out.'

'You're still stupid enough to think General Wexton's the coppers' deb of the year?'

'Not necessarily the General ... but it's a Wexton. He may be in Bradford, Birmingham, Battersea or Bhubaneswar ... '

'Bhubaneswhat?'

'Bhubaneswar, it's in India. By Christ I'll get him though, and I mean by Christ.'

'Sheriff Torry rides again.'

'With his badge newly polished, so hard that you can see the plastic through the silver paint. Tick, I want you to back me up whatever I do.'

'Can't promise, lad, you know that. My neck's out further than a mug's wallet already.'

'Don't worry, I'm not going to blow up the Ministry of Defence or shoot Black Rod. I'll play it by the book, but I need your co-operation.'

There was a long pause. 'As far as I can, but you're under pressure, boy.'

'Of course I'm under pressure. Look, I'll refer everything to you, but keep me off the hook and on this case until it's closed.'

Again Tickerman did not answer straight away. 'I'll do what I can, Derek. What's your first move?'

'Grab a sandwich. Go through everything we've got so far. Everything the whole team's done, everything I've done. Oh, and I'll fit in the other Wexton interview as well — the lad, Rowland Frank. The report'll be with you by Monday. With you and the Chief Super.'

'And the Commissioner?'

'I've got a blank sheet ready for the typewriter now. Black Power's got nothing on my indictment of White Power.'

'Good luck, lad.' Tickerman replaced the receiver, uncommitted except in a general sense.

Torry followed suit, then pressed the intercom button. Loyal Dumphy was patiently waiting in the outer office.

'Sergeant Dumphy. Tea. Sandwiches. Now. Then every single

file we have on Wexton, Grosvenor, Cust, Lipperman, Lipperman's break and murder. The lot.'

'It's Saturday, Mr Torry. Some of the ... '

'I know it's Saturday but we do work round the dial in this Force. I want everything, including Rowland Frank Wexton's present address.'

'Very good, Mr Torry.'

Torry stubbed out his cigarette, twisting the butt viciously into the ashtray, and rolled a clean sheet of quarto into the typewriter. By the time Dumphy arrived, accompanied by a constable, tea, sandwiches and a formidable tower of files, he had written five pages of slashing condemnation.

'The constable can go. You wait, would you, Sergeant?' He read through his report to the Commissioner, initialling each page and signing the final result.

'Put that in an envelope, Dumph. Address it to the Commissioner and see that it gets to his office this afternoon.'

'He won't be in until Monday.'

'I know he won't be in until Monday, but Monday's the day I want him to get it. And I trust you've enough contacts to ensure this is one of the first things he sees when he places his bottom on the hot seat as dawn breaks on the new working week.'

'I'll mark it urgent, sir.'

'Mark it of cardinal urgency.'

'Cardinal?'

'Supreme urgency.'

Dumphy looked unhappy, took the document and departed. Torry bit on a sandwich and made a squeamish face. It was cold beef. Torry placed cold beef high on his register of dislikes.

Dumphy returned as he opened the first file. The sergeant crept, like a tracking Indian, to the desk and slid a slip of paper into Torry's view by his right elbow. Rowland Frank Wexton's address. Torry glanced at it. Some street off the King's Road. He recognized it instantly. Why the hell should he remember that street in particular? God, yes. When he'd first come to the Yard there was a case there. Something stupid, but the story went the rounds; an old girl who kissed every policeman she met in the street. The King's Road and Rowland Wexton. From the upper crust to the rancid gravy. What's the betting little Rowland's all done up with the Flower-Pot People or the Beadies or whatever name they go by now? Love. Love. Love and meditation. Meditation, like they've found something new even though the Church has been teaching it for centuries. Love, and keep the bells going, for God's sake, me flower's slipping out of me long tangled hair. He turned back to the case files.

Torry was still at it around four fifteen when the telephone went into action.

'Torry.' Sharp into the mouthpiece.

'Inspector Torry's the correct way for you to answer the telephone.' The Chief Superintendent, like a battering ram, at the other end.

'I'm sorry, sir. A bit wrapped up in work.'

'You're still dealing with the Wextons from C.R.O.?'

'Yes, sir, and keeping up to date with all other moves.'

'I've yet to have a report from you on Rowland Frank Wexton. Young lad, one of the three you've taken the best part of a week to interview.'

'We've had some trouble locating him, sir, but he's next on the list.'

'Well, you'll have to hurry, Inspector. It may seem melodramatic, even to you, but Rowland Wexton's just thrown himself out of a third-storey window after battering a girl to death. I can't get hold of Superintendent Tickerman but Mr Broadbent's already on his way with a team. As the boy's one of your mystic suspects you'd better get over there.'

'Right, sir. Where is he?' Already on his feet.

The old man gave the King's Road address. 'I don't even know if he's alive,' he added.

'Then I'll have to give him the kiss of life, sir, won't I? There's a lot at stake.' Torry banged down the phone and yelled for Dumphy to get a car.

Susan. Damn. She was due round at seven and this could be a late one. He'd told her to wait for him, but her mind would be easier if … A scribbled note with her number so that Dumphy could phone. At least you could trust Dumphy. With Dumphy it wouldn't be all over the department.

You could tell which house it was, not just because of the shattered window-frame high up, but by the knot of morbidly curious bystanders, a cluster of camera-ready newsmen and the ambulance.

Some of the team were already upstairs with the girl. Rowland Wexton had been carried into the nearest ground-floor flat where a shocked thin woman was doing the perpetual duty of the British housewife in moments of stress — brewing up. Torry showed his card. 'In there, sir.' The only uniformed constable in the living-room nodded to what must have been the bedroom door.

The doctor was just pulling a blood-spattered sheet back over the remains of young Wexton's head; the body was lying lumpy and empty on the bed. Torry mentally crossed himself and breathed *May he and all the souls of the departed rest in peace. In the name of Christ: Amen.*

His tranquil reverence was broken as he looked up and saw Sergeant Hart standing behind the doctor. The irrational feeling of dislike welled up. Hart turned and saw him as the doctor shook his head indicating they could do no more. Torry signed to Hart, and together they went out into the living-room now occupied by the constable, two ambulance men and a pair of shaken youths, long-haired, hippie-clothed and green-gilled.

'You come with Mr Broadbent?' Torry asked Hart with no hint of feeling.

'No. Heard the call on the radio. I was quite near. It was someone called Wexton so I thought I'd better take a look-see. I've asked them to pass a message to Mr Morse.'

They were standing by the brace of seated hippies.

'You know what happened?'

Before Hart had time to reply the tidier of the two boys spoke. The accent was good. 'They were both speed merchants. Rolly and the girl. Sylvia.'

'Yeah,' said the other one in a voice which sounded as though he would vomit at any moment. 'Yeah. Speed.'

'Speed,' repeated Torry.

It could have sounded like a question. Hart took it at face value. 'Methedrine, Mr Torry. They call Methedrine "speed".'

Torry looked at Hart with lingering pity, his lips consciously turned into a sneer. 'I've been around, Sergeant, and you know what I've discovered?'

'Sir?' The kind of mocking reply Torry recognized as one of his own ploys against difficult senior officers.

'I've found that in the investigation of criminal offences it's best to be accurate. Otherwise you end up in that little wooden box they have in Number One Court at the Bailey with some smart, educated lawyer spinning you round so fast you can smell your own entrails.'

'I don't follow, sir.' The cool gambit.

'Methedrine's a brand name. "Speed", as they call it, is meth-amphetamine hydrochloride.'

'That stuff gives you a bad ride,' mumbled the scruffier hippie.

Torry turned towards the hippie and looked at him thought-fully. 'It gives you the last long one as well, boy.' Then, back to Hart. 'Don't ever underestimate me, Sergeant. You can take notes if you want. Ever hear of James Hutchinson and Linda Fitzpatrick?'

'No, sir.' Teeth clenched.

To his intense pleasure Torry saw that Hart was seething with the anger of one being publicly intimidated. 'You ought to brush up on your druggy homework. Hutchinson was twenty-one years old; Fitzpatrick, eighteen. They were speed merchants. Ended up with their heads bashed in by bricks in a New York East Village cellar. The girl had figured sensationally in a gang-bang as well. You know what that is?'

'I know, and ... '

'If you want some more cases why not read up on the cattle-truck driver in Arizona riding high and crashing head on into a bus. Nine dead and thirty-four seriously injured.'

'Speed kills,' muttered the first hippie. 'Love's the message, man, not that stuff.'

Torry ignored him, heading for the kill, a brash matador who has made a few clumsy, but successful, passes. Now the bull stood, enraged but weak, waiting for the blade. 'You've probably never heard of the man who died after an overdose of speed. He'd been on the stuff for some time. The doctors wanted to preserve his brain, but at the autopsy it crumbled away like ... '

'Excuse me, Mr Torry.' Hart's face was the colour of a raw blister. 'I don't get time to study the American cases. I try to con-centrate on our own and I *do* know that Methedrine's a brand name but in my experience addicts tend to confuse their slang references. They call most of the amphetamines "speed", in the same way as they talk of others as "bennies", "splash", "cart-wheels". The slang isn't always synonymous with the same drug.'

'Stick to pot and you're safe,' added the second hippie.

'Yes, laddie, you look as safe as a condemned chimney.' Torry and Hart turned. The doctor had joined them and was looking sarcastically at the couple of specimens sitting pitifully by the two C.I.D. men. The first hippie looked angry. 'What's that mean?' he rasped at the doctor. 'Pot's okay. You're a doctor, aren't you? I've heard doctors say pot's okay.'

'I'm a doctor, boy, and I'm telling you that pot, or hash, or whatever you want to call it, is *not* okay.'

'It's safer than ciggies or booze.'

'So people never tire of telling me; and maybe it is, in some societies. Use your loaf, lad. Over here you start on pot and straight off you're mixing with people who've graduated to the hard stuff. You don't stand a chance, it's a hundred to one you'll deteriorate.'

'Balls, they ought to make it legal, like alcohol.'

The doctor had already started to walk away. He stopped by the door and turned. 'Don't come that one. Get your facts right. You don't have to be a meths drinker to be an alcoholic. Look at the figures some time: more people die in this country every year of alcoholism than they do of lung cancer. See you in the psycho ward or on the slab.'

'Afternoon, doctor.' Broadbent, efficient, sharp and steady, had come into the room. Torry became aware of the whole squalid atmosphere, the thin tea-making woman, ghost-white, whispering to the constable, chipped cups, oilcloth on the floor and a glimpse of the kitchen. Greasy, battered Bisto packet on the soiled stove and a huddle of filthy tins lining a newspaper-covered shelf.

'She worried about something?' Broadbent called across to the constable.

'Concerned about the bedding in there.' The uniformed man inclined his head towards the bedroom door. 'Doesn't know what her husband's going to say if it's stained. The blood, sir.'

'Don't worry, missus.' Broadbent, the people's friend. 'Sorry you've had all this upset. Nasty shock for you. We'll get him out of here in a minute and I'll see some fresh bedding's sent round.'

'I don't want that welfare lady round here.' She had a high-pitched, frightened voice. She'd live off this story for weeks.

Broadbent ignored Hart but nodded, indifferently, to Torry. 'The boy's a Wexton, one of yours, Inspector?'

'I'd planned to interview him today, yes. What're the details, sir?'

'I'd better go and look at the girl.' Distaste in the doctor's voice.

'Nasty,' warned Broadbent. 'Only screamed once apparently. God knows how. Suppose she must've passed out after he hit her the first time.'

'A mess?' asked Torry, the doctor's footsteps heavy on the stairs, shaking the thin wall near them.

'Nasty,' repeated Broadbent. 'He must've walloped her twenty or thirty times. Back of her neck's like bloody foam rubber. Broken.'

'Speed, man. That's the cause, speed.' The first hippie.

Broadbent gazed at him with a certain amount of tolerance. 'I didn't think they were doing it on Alka Seltzers. You two saw the boy come out?'

The second hippie looked nearer than ever to throwing up. 'Yeah. We were coming to call on Rolly and Sylvia. Just up the street, and the Goose Man here says, "Bodge, ain't that Rolly?" And I says, "Where?" And he says "Flyin', man." And there he was, naked and sort of in a red mist, like he was power-diving into the pavement.'

'Wow. Wheeee. Kerplop.' The other bedraggled character was impersonating the scene with his hands.

Broadbent gave a come-on nod to the uniformed man. 'Get

someone to help you. Take 'em both down to the local nick. The doctor'll be round and I'll talk to them later.'

'I can manage these two myself, sir.' He was a big copper. The old 'Hallo-then-what's-goin'-on-'ere' variety. He hustled the two boys out into the hall like a heavyweight champion with a brace of kittens. Broadbent grinned as the doctor returned looking miserable.

'Can we move the bodies?' asked the doctor.

'No point in keeping them lying around here. Unless you want anything, Derek?'

'Nothing odd, is there, sir?' Torry sensed that Broadbent could be an ally if worked upon.

'Open and shut, as they say in the Midnight Movie.'

'Take 'em away then, doc. Don't suppose anyone'll give you much for them.'

'Took a dislike to her, didn't he?' The doctor raised his eyes towards the ceiling. 'And to himself.'

'Instantaneous?' asked Broadbent.

'Near as damn it. Lacerations from the glass when he went out. Must've taken a header at the window. Fractured skull, several places I should think. Broken neck. The girl's neck's broken as well.'

'Best get on with the cleaning up, then.' Broadbent looked at his watch. 'Got a date with the wife tonight. Still, nothing much in it for me.'

Torry hovered. 'Could I have a word with you, sir?'

'As long as it doesn't turn into a forum on the legal aspects of drug addiction.'

They went into the hall where the ambulance men were negotiating a stretcher through the door. Outside the crowd had grown and a hushed, pseudo-shocked murmur floated in with the cold evening air. The lights were already coming on.

'Get those bloody people out of the way, they're obstructing

a thoroughfare,' Broadbent shouted towards the covey of uniformed men on the steps. 'Two complete states of death, eh,
Derek?' He grinned once more, a shade flip.

It's shaken him, thought Torry. By God, it's shaken him and
he doesn't want to let on. 'Shortened your odds on Wextons,
hasn't it?' Broadbent added.

'Depends, sir. Depends. That's what I wanted to talk about.
I'm checking back on all of them.'

'Microscopic examination of family trees.'

'Yes.'

'Real detective work. Sifting and searching. Makes a change
from the forms and reports.'

'I don't suppose you have anything on his next of kin yet?'

'Give us a chance, Derek. Nothing on his kin or kith. But
they'll be working on it.'

'I wonder if you could see that I get all available information as
it comes in? Next of kin. Anyone still living with the family
name. Everything. Anything. Reactions of relatives. You know
the sort of thing, sir.'

'Clutching at straws.'

'Maybe.'

'Minute details. They'll all be passed on, I'll see to it. Okay?'

'Fine, sir. Thank you.'

'Nothing. Twenty-four-hour service. One consolation, Derek.'
He inclined his head towards the room which led to the place
where Rowland Wexton's miserable corpse lay. 'That one wasn't
a master-mind. He couldn't even master his own mind.'

Tony Champion always stayed at the Savoy when he was in
London. The Hilton was too close to home, and inevitably the
Dorchester seemed stuffed with movie people. At the Savoy the
service was coloured by that extraordinary knack they had of

knowing what you required before you did. Though he would never admit it, staying at the Savoy made him feel like royalty, which was how he had to feel on this trip.

He had arrived at Heathrow around four. Now, bathed and freshly shaved, he sat back in his suite, sipping coffee and waiting.

Within half an hour of checking in, Tony Champion made three telephone calls. The first was routine; the second told him that Wexton was in London, not out at the country place; the third call was to Wexton himself. A royal command.

Champion looked at his watch. Six fifteen. Knowing Wexton, he knew that his visitor would not be late. Any moment now the telephone would ring and the hall porter at the other end would announce that a Mr Wexton was downstairs.

Obediently the telephone rang.

Champion had only met Wexton on three previous occasions, but he knew the man's character and background as well as he knew himself. Champion was not a pie-in-the-sky individual. His realism rested firmly on hard rock.

'Nice to see you again, Mr Wexton. Glad I caught you in London. You remember me?'

If Wexton was on the defensive he did not show it. 'Of course I remember you. We met twice in New York with Mr Vescari in '65, and you were there when we discussed further improvements to the British scheme in Miami in '66.'

'When we discussed your ideas of further improvements,' Champion corrected him.

'And you passed my plans.' Check and mate.

'Drink?' Champion crossed to a modestly furnished drinks table, waving Wexton into a chair. Once settled, again it was Wexton who took the initiative.

'What's the trouble, Mr Champion?'

'Trouble? I didn't know anyone mentioned trouble.'

'Nobody did, but I'm not a fool. You boys only come over here to congratulate or get tough.'

Champion stretched his legs out lazily. 'Come on. Maybe you don't know me too well, but I'm not like Al Vescari. I don't get tough as you call it.'

'No? What is it then?'

Champion took a sip of his bourbon. 'Look, Wexton, we've always been fair with you. Christ, we approached you when the whole thing was being set up. If anything goes wrong, then it's our fault.'

'And you think something's gone wrong?'

'There've been signs.'

'Lipperman?'

Champion nodded. 'Miss Cust and Mr Grosvenor, a guy called Jumper, so I hear.'

Wexton still betrayed no signs of surprise. 'It's been unfortunate, but trace the main cause, Mr Champion. Your people invited me to take control of what could be a flourishing enterprise. It involved practically every criminal activity known and, at the time, I couldn't very well say no.'

'You did have some problems, I recall.'

Wexton nodded grimly. 'One of the reasons you gave for choosing me was that I had no criminal record. I made it quite plain to you in Miami that this point germinated my own particular policy.'

'Okay, we'll take that as read. You wanted to train as much talent as you could. Talent unknown to the law. I'll tell you, Wexton, the idea was so good that Al's using the same method in New York, Chicago and San Francisco. But Cust, Grosvenor and Jumper were known to the law.'

'Precisely. It's been a tricky job phasing out these people. When Lipperman was caught he had only gone through a fraction of the training programme. I applied for help and who did you send?'

'Armitage. Yes. Don't blame me for that. It was the dumbest move Al's ever made. But some of the boys are edgy.'

'I don't see why they should be, they've been getting good profits.'

'Ach, I know. They appreciate that, but their argument is that you've continually put off the big take. You've done it again recently and substituted this Birthday Party thing.'

'It's a question of time and training. The bulk of the men who'll be on the Birthday Party have never done a thing before. They need the experience.'

Champion shrugged. 'Me, I like the idea, it's a dilly.'

'And you've been sent over to cover your assets if anything goes wrong.'

'You might say that, Mr Wexton. You might well say that. Thought you should know. Rather decent of me, isn't it?' He raised his glass and smirked rather than smiled.

The report on Rowland Wexton could wait. So could the pile of reading which lay on his desk back in the office. Like milkmen, coppers work on Sundays. Torry decided to go in and finish up after Mass in the morning.

He got back to the flat at seven fifteen. Not too late after all, but Susan was there and she had got his message from Dumphy. She sat in one of the armchairs, flicking through the *Catholic Herald*. She raised her head, and a cynical eyebrow, as Torry entered.

There was no attempt to offer embraces, yet her look brought out a rash of shame on his tender conscience. What was the old gag? 'What's she got that I haven't?' 'Nothing, but she's got it here.' Sue was here and with her that old feeling. Gerry's face slid into his mind and once more the Paris episode became a dirty memory.

'You look what my old Dad used to call "piss-happy".' She grinned.

For some reason Torry felt shocked. He should be used to Susan by now. 'Sorry,' he said glumly. 'It's been a great day. The Commissioner came down and did his Ken Dodd impressions for us. Then the Chief Super sang a couple of roistering ballads, 'Drake's Drum' and 'Boots'. You know the one ... ' He struck a fifth-rate baritone position and carolled a few bars. 'Then we had tea and jelly and I went down the King's Road and met Mr Broadbent and we had a look at some lovely dead bodies. It's a super day.'

He stood and looked at her, then held out his arms. She rose into them. Her hair on his cheek. Her own particular smell. He whispered her name and she pressed close. Once more he was being roused against his will, but there seemed nothing to stop it. The resolutions of only a few hours ago were ripped away. The ideal of purity turned to clay. Her lips, wet, slipped towards his. Her eyes were closed and he took her open mouth hard against his tongue. Tongues erect and sliding against each other. Torry relaxed, his abrasive personality slowly smoothed out to a satin finish as they struggled to get closer. Then Sue's body began to weigh in his arms as she forced downwards.

They were on the rug before the fireplace. She stretched out, her woollen kaftan riding up to display the dark elasticized top of her stay-up stockings, and an inch of flesh.

Again her mouth against his, the tongues constant in their movement, her breasts firm even through the combined clothing. Both breathed to a rhythm, the mouths twisting like two plants thrown together in a gale. Torry's hand dropped to her knee. Up. Up to the bare flesh. Higher into the crotch of her pants, wet with need. He twisted his mouth so that, opening his eyes, he could squint down their quivering bodies. White. Tight white nylon. Under his hand he could feel the fabric and the soft damp down of her. Then, suddenly her hand was on him, fingers scratching at his zip.

'Derek,' she whispered. 'We must. Now.'

'No.' His brain and body were screaming out the affirmative. His fingers began to probe.

Her hand now fastened on him, withdrawing him and pulling him towards her. Together. Closer. Panting. Squeezing.

Susan cried out, her body arching as she reached the peak, and, at the same moment, he felt the throb of satisfaction. It was not quite the true act, but they had only missed by a brief few seconds.

Torry rolled away from her and opened his eyes. He was looking up at the 'Haywain'. Adam and Eve in the Garden of Eden, ashamed, their hands covering themselves. His hand automatically dropped to his nakedness. Susan and himself. He turned his head. Susan was sitting up on her knees, her skirt high and her face turned away as she adjusted her clothes.

The first Sunday after Easter. Low Sunday the Church called it, and the introit for the Mass began: *As newborn babes, alleluia, desire the rational milk without guile, alleluia, alleluia, alleluia.*

Quasi modo geniti infantes, alleluia.

Quasimodo. The Hunchback of Notre Dame. Quasimodo. Salvatore Quasimodo, Italian Nobel Prizewinner 1959. Or was it 1960? And wasn't there something called the Quasimodo Complex? Something to do with murder statistics that American doctors had totted up. Six out of ten murderers in five American cities had some kind of deformity. Bully for the American doctors and after you with the wooden leg, Joe, I got an urge that's killing me.

Yesterday's drizzle had dropped over into the Sunday, making the London scene one of empty misery. The Yard did not have its customary number of officers at work on Sunday, but it was still a place of activity.

The pile of files still lay on Torry's desk. The In-tray had also become suspiciously full. On top was a memo from the Chief Superintendent.

> All officers concerned with investigations following the murder of Gustave Lipperman on Wednesday, April 17th, will attend a special conference and discussion at 10.00 hrs in the Briefing Room on Tuesday, April 22nd.

That would be an epic worth twice the price of admission.

Broadbent's report on the Rowland Wexton business was there, with the doctor's post-mortem notes. At the bottom, Broadbent had added a note in his own hand.

> Rowland Wexton seems to be the last of his doubtful line. Mother still alive in East Hendred, Berkshire. Local village constable broke the news. Had interesting reaction. Perhaps you would care to call him. P.C. Bates. East Hendred 6398, or the Berks Force can put you in touch.

Torry wrote his own short report on Rowland Wexton and read through an inch or so of the files before putting in his call to Bates. Safer nearer lunch-time. The village policeman had just come in.

'Oh yes, sir, they said last night you might be ringing. How can I help?'

'Mr Broadbent's left a note for me saying that you had an interesting reaction from the boy's mother.'

'Yes, well,that was a bit strange, sir. More unusual than strange, yet you can never tell, what with the shock and that.'

'What was it exactly?' Torry patient.

'Well, the old lady seemed more worried about the police being brought in than by her son's death. It was the disgrace more'n the actual death, if you see what I mean. She kept saying the family'd only had dealings with the police once before and that was bad enough.'

'That would be young Rowland's first brush with the forces of righteousness?'

'No, I don't think so, sir. Don't think she counted that. She was talking about trouble down here.'

'What was it then? You find out?'

'Oh yes, sir, no mystery there. Well, there is 'cos the case's never been closed, but practically everyone in the village was questioned. Certainly the Wextons would have been.'

'Tell me.'

'Well, they had a child murder here, couple of years back. The body, little girl, was found on Mr Dowding's land.'

'Dowding? Should I know him?'

'No, sir. Mr Rupert Dowding it was. Used to own a big house just outside here. Local celebrity, lord of the manor sort of thing. Hill Lodge the name of the house is. Before my time, though. Only been here a year. Mr Dowding left, what, about six months after the murder. Moved away and bought some estate in the Midlands, somewhere near Evesham in Worcestershire I believe.'

'And what's this got to do with the Wexton tribe?'

'Well, sir, old Fred Wexton would've been questioned. He was head gardener up at Hill Lodge for Mr Dowding.'

'Fred Wexton? That would be ... ?'

'Young Rowland's dad.'

'Yes. He's dead now though?' Torry felt he was getting past it.

'Oh yes, been dead and buried six, eight months now. 'Fact he'd given up the gardening job before Mr Dowding left. Cancer, I think it was.'

'Mmm,' noised Torry.

'Funny how the old lady couldn't get over the shame of having the police in on her son's death, sir.'

'Hilarious,' said Torry to himself.

'I suppose she identifies the child thing here with unpleasant questions, suspicions and the like. What with the case not being cleared up and that.'

Village bobbies becoming psychiatrically minded already. It was a few minutes before Torry extracted himself from the garrulous Bates. There did not seem to be much to go on in Rowland Wexton's background.

A sexy ground hostess and her father; a desperately weird spade; and a suicidal hophead whose late father had once been questioned, with many others, on a child-murder investigation. That was all one. Not a sniff of anything. Back to the drawing-board? No, they wouldn't even lend him a drawing-board, especially if his only bet was an uncertain hunch about General Thornton Wexton. Torry took the lift down and ate in the canteen. Before returning to the files, which he was still determined to read, he walked out into Broadway for a lungful of London air and drizzle. Aimlessly he glanced into shop windows until he found himself staring at a display of dainty lingerie.

The sign on the gate read CRIPPEN METALS. RESEARCH CENTRE. Below it, in red, was the legend, POSITIVELY NO ADMITTANCE. TRESPASSERS ENTER AT THEIR OWN RISK.

'You ever get any?' asked Champion, seated comfortably beside Wexton in the passenger seat of the Bentley.

'Any what?' Wexton lowered the electrically operated window to disclose his identity to the uniformed man at the gate. To left and right tall close hedges obscured any view. One could just discern high wire fences, curved at the top, behind the hedges. There was enough visible to dissuade professional and casual pryer alike.

178

'Trespassers,' answered Champion. 'I'd like to see you prosecuting them.'

'We had one,' said Wexton with no hint of humour. 'I'm not certain where they buried him. I prefer not to know things like that.' He slipped the car into drive and they moved slowly forward along an asphalt lane flanked by a jungle of evergreen shrubs.

'I'm surprised Al never made a trip to look over this training area of yours.' Champion had become impressed by the single-mindedness and devotion of the man he had been sent to watch.

'He saw the plans. I've given him every chance.'

The lane turned and spread into a driveway at the end of which stood a red-brick Georgian house, the big oblong window-frames smartly picked out in white. A full-sized dolls' house.

'You say you have fifteen in residence?'

'Fifteen to each course. Then six instructors. We've got one or two of the Birthday Party people here at the moment.' Wexton brought the Bentley to a smooth halt in front of the house.

'What about the local people? Villagers? Local cops?'

'Nobody's bothered us. Crippen Metals is a genuine company. I'm on the board, Mr Champion. No cause for suspicion.' Wexton slammed the car door and the two men started towards the house from which a tall, shambling man had emerged.

'Suttcliffe, our chief training officer,' said Wexton curtly. 'He's known, but keeps out of sight. Fifty years old, been inside eight times.'

'Specialist?' asked Champion.

'Big stuff. Banks. Smash and grab. Did five years of his time on the island.'

Suttcliffe's face had an open, sandpaper look. A face one did not carry well in the memory.

'Morning, Mr Wexton.'

'I've brought one of our associates down to have a quick look. What's on today?'

Suttcliffe fired a sharp questioning glance at Wexton. It was fractional, but still almost an entire oral examination.

'It's all right. Mr Champion's one of our backers. A professional. You can talk.'

Suttcliffe slid his eyes carefully up and down the American.

'We've got a pistol range out the back if you want to get in some practice with whatever you're carrying,' he said without menace.

Champion made a quizzical movement with his lips and turned to Wexton. 'He's good. I've got one of the best tailors in L.A. It shouldn't show.'

Wexton looked angry. 'For God's sake, man, what the hell do you want to come out with a shooter for? You're in England.'

'Doesn't show,' interpolated Suttcliffe. 'I've just got a nose for 'em. The way a man carries himself. But Mr Wexton's right, sir. Shouldn't go around with it on you.' He paused with deadly timing. 'Not unless you reckon to use it.'

Champion maintained his outwardly relaxed charm. 'Gets to be a habit,' he said, not giving way an inch. 'Now, what've you got for me to see?'

Suttcliffe waited for around fifteen seconds, looking down at his shoes, then up at Wexton who gave him the green light with his eyes.

'Couple of boys out on the track ... '

'Birthday Party drivers?' from Wexton.

'Uh-huh.' Affirmative. 'Chalky White and Freddie Nolan.'

'Good lads,' said Wexton in his brigadier voice. 'They're keen enough, Champion. One of the things we do manage to instil is a sense of self-preservation.'

'A necessary attitude in this wicked world.'

'Mmm. Especially when you have two great countries like your own and mine in such a brittle, gutless condition.'

'Wars and rumours of wars.' Champion spoke almost to himself as they approached the house. 'Funny how that big black Book has it all figured out. You know the passage, Wexton? "For nation shall rise against nation, and kingdom against kingdom: and there shall be famines and pestilences, and earthquakes, in divers places. All …" '

' "All these are the beginning of sorrows",' added Wexton. 'I was brought up with great respect for the Bible, Mr Champion. My family were Primitive Methodists.'

'Yep, it's a great book. That passage, Al quoted me that passage once. Al's a Catholic, of course, like all the wops and spics. Well, Al quoted that passage to me and he said, "Tony," he said, "it's all going to happen just like it says. It's going to happen soon and baby we've got to be organized for that, because when those politicians start messing up the deal that's when the whole world's going to be wide open for people like us." Me, I was an Episcopalian.'

They had reached the door and passed through into a large tiled hall, bare but for one table, a pay telephone, with a little curved semi-soundproof hood around it, and a picture of some autumn landscape with the sun shining weakly through gathering storm clouds.

'If we go straight through we might catch part of the lecture.' Suttcliffe was hurrying them on. 'It's the new course. Only been here since Friday. Just starting their basics.'

'How long's the course?' Champion to Suttcliffe.

'We keep 'em here nearly four months, then they go into ordinary jobs. We place them. Some stay on and do a specialist course. But normally we just call 'em in when they're needed. Give 'em a brief and any special stuff they may need. We got a regular little army. How many is it, Mr Wexton?'

'Just under forty on call. And half of them are university graduates.'

'Good.' Champion nodded. 'I like it. Very much I like it.'

They had reached a door, from behind which came the steady drone of a voice imparting information. Wexton nodded to Suttcliffe and they went in.

It was like any other classroom, probably once the drawing-room of the house, now transformed by rows of comfortable chairs, each with a sliding desk top attached. At the far end, a podium backed by blackboards. On the podium stood a small, middle-aged, sour-looking man with patent-leather hair. A book-keeper or, maybe, the representative of some small plastics firm? He stopped speaking as the three men entered. One or two of the fifteen young men who comprised his audience turned to have a look.

'Carry on.' Suttcliffe like a sergeant-major. The average age of the pupils was around twenty-five. They concentrated once more on the instructor who spoke in a painfully suburban accent.

'Harry Bowman,' muttered Wexton, nodding towards the instructor. 'One of the best petermen in the business. Comes here every morning from Wimbledon.'

Champion nodded.

For the next ten minutes they stood and listened to a sharp, witty lecture on safes, their construction, their locks and the means of getting to them and getting them open—by blowing, burning, ripping, punching, battering, carrying them away, or by a combination of two of the methods.

At last Champion indicated that he had heard enough.

'Let's see this driving track of yours.' Champion smiled once they were outside the door. 'Impressive, that lecture. Most impressive.'

'We like to give them the rudiments of all trades,' said Wexton, laughing.

At the far end of the lawn a small wood seemed to be pushing its growth towards the garden. From the wood came the sound of automobiles being driven at full stretch.

Wexton led the way into the wood. About fifty yards from the edge they broke into a long and wide clearing in which an oval metalled race track had been laid, about a quarter of a mile long and half that distance wide.

A Mark X Jaguar and a maroon Westminster were circuiting the track at speed.

'White and Nolan,' said Wexton. 'Both of them will be driving for the Birthday Party.'

'Not in those cars?' queried Champion.

'Those makes,' Suttcliffe answered. 'Nolan's trying to size up cornering at speed in the Westminster and White is just getting acclimatized to the general handling of the Jag.'

Out on the track Freddie Nolan took a right-hand bend at sixty, holding her steady then straightening and putting his foot down to lift her away on to the straight at seventy-five ... eighty. This was the life. Better than driving a delivery truck. Nolan had been doing just that a year ago. Now he worked part-time for an exclusive car-hire firm. That was when he did not have a job to do for Wexton. Pockets were usually full now. Wife and kids had smiling faces. And nobody asked too many questions. Nolan lined the Westminster up for the next bend. Through his teeth he whistled, 'Oh, for the wings of a dove'. Foot down, lad, here comes Chalky. Don't let him take you. He watched the Jaguar coming up behind.

Chalky White's eyes flicked between the offside edge of the track and the Westminster's rear lights. He grinned as the gap between them closed. Nerve, that was all you needed. In the final count Nolan's nerve would give before his. Nolan was nearly thirty. He was only twenty-one. Nolan had a wife and kids. He wasn't married. That's where you have the edge, said Chalky.

Youth and freedom. What would the lads of the village say now?

Champion nodded. 'They look great. But d'you know what I'd like to do now?' He grinned. 'Ah'd sho laike to try out ma pop gun on yoh range.' His smile was deadly.

Torry spent the afternoon with the files. Lines of words which spelled out the despicable side of man's nature. Individually, they were painstaking sorties into a world of darkness from which the inquirers emerged with little but tiny bits of dirt and mud. Put together, the files told part of a story. Ugly, black and slime-coated. The story would depress better men than Torry.

He got home around five, threw himself into a chair and contemplated the 'Haywain'. Adam and Eve, the Fall of the Angels in the background, the rich central load of hay with the queues of pillaging people. Lust, avarice, pride, covetousness, anger, sloth and envy jostled as though they could not wait to be carted off to the horrific nightmare of hell, on the painting's right panel, where monkey-like devils toiled, and the stench of death almost reached your nostrils from the towers and blood flames. A foresight of Belsen or Buchenwald? Has there never been anything else but this? Man, surely, had dignity somewhere, but that slice of mankind which he saw had lost its dignity centuries ago. Where was it now? The arts could not buy it and people did not seem to want it.

The telephone chirped. Torry jumped with the realization that he was waiting for something to happen. The feeling had been with him all day. He had read through the files not to detect something, or to make himself better informed. He had read them to pass the time. To wait for the moment when something would break, and violence would flare. Perhaps at the end of the ringing telephone.

184

Someone was speaking in French, then a voice in English asking if this was his number. A call from Paris.

'Derek?'

'Yes, who's that?'

'Gerry. How many other women have you got in Paris?'

'Gerry? Sorry. Shook me. A call from Paris.'

'You *are* an unsophisticated policeman, aren't you? I imagined you were something special, telephoning all over the world and leaping into aeroplanes at a moment's notice.'

Torry laughed. 'It's nice to hear you,' he stumbled.

'I tried to call this morning but you weren't in. I didn't think you'd be at work on a Sunday.'

'Don't you read the popular magazines? It's a draggy life, long hours, and low pay.'

'I wouldn't mind sharing it.' She meant it. Embarrassed silence, the twopence for 4.28 seconds slipping away. 'You still there, Derek?'

'Yes.'

'I hear Daddy gave you a rough time.'

'You heard wrong.' Steady, that was the old wop cop Torrini talking. 'What I mean is ... '

'You won. I know. I bawled him out as well. Poor old darling doesn't know which way to turn. I just wanted to say sorry about him coming along and making a fuss.'

'That's all right. Part of the job.'

'Why don't you ask me, Derek?'

'Ask you what?' Torry was lost.

'To come back to London. I could easily get a transfer.'

'You could ... ' began Torry, lapsing into silence.

'Okay. I tried.' Gerry gave a little sniff. 'Call me some time, Derek.'

'I'll call you.' He put down the receiver. Jesus God, what had he let himself in for? Why was he wasting his time? She was a cheap, easy lay. One day she'd hook someone like that. Torry put his hand to his forehead. He was sweating.

Susan arrived early, around six. Her kiss was warm, the proprietary brand.

'Treat tonight.' It was as though he had become frightened to stay in the flat alone with her. 'Food out.' He beamed.

'High living. Super. Where's it to be? Luxurious Lyons or prosperous Peter Evans?'

'Peter Evans on my pay?'

'Sorry, darling, we'll make it Lyons.'

They did. The Seven Stars Grill in the Coventry Street Corner House, with prawns, roast beefsteak, potatoes in their jackets garnished with a chives and cream dressing, and fruit salad.

'So this is how the poor people live,' remarked Torry.

Susan spent the evening looking uncertainly into Torry's eyes. Later she said that, as a policeman, he should take her into custody, or at least back to the flat to show her his handcuffs. At last, over coffee, she talked straight.

'Derek, do I really make it that difficult for you?'

'If you don't know by now … ' The edge of a snarl.

'Hey, put away your fangs.' She reached over and took his hand. 'I'd worked out what to say and everything.'

'What to … ? Well, say it.'

'Don't snap. What I'm trying to tell you is I think *we* are more important than ideals or traditions or rituals. I think we ought to get married. Anywhere. Anyhow. At Hyde Park Corner if you want it. Or in church.'

Now it had come, Torry found the act of capitulation something of an anticlimax. His stomach flicked over, but not at the thought of consummation with Susan. The sensation was becoming more frequent. A symptom of anxiety. The whole of the Wexton business was fast adding unseen pressures to him. Fraught, uncertain. Even unreasonable.

Back at the flat, with Sue close to him, Torry found his hand automatically sliding up the inside of her thigh. She closed her legs tight and pushed him away.

'Oh no. If we're playing this your way then we do everything from scratch.'

Torry, like many men before him, decided that he would never understand women. Their minds or bodies.

When Susan had gone he became enveloped in an awareness of being on the brink of action. The feeling was to stay with him throughout the following day.

'What you think I am, Derek? A nincompoop? When did you go to Mass last, eh? You tell me. Rushing about at all hours. So ashamed of us you had to change your name. When did you last go to Mass?'

'Mama. A couple of days ago.' Torry grinned.

The nearest Mama Torrini had ever got to Italy was drinking Chianti, yet the close and wonderful relationship she had had with her husband had, over the years, shifted her attitude. She now thought and spoke and saw things from an Italian point of view. Torry often thought she would have done well in show business.

For almost a year after he had changed his name, Torry had not been welcome in his mother's home with Roberto and his wife. Bobby had understood, and it was mainly through his pleadings that Mama Torrini finally opened her door again to her erring son. Now, he tried to get down for an occasional visit to the flat above the Earl's Court Road delicatessen. The evening invariably opened with a lashing from Mama Torrini's tongue.

'Derek, why aren't you like Bobby and Therese?' The little woman beamed as she looked across the table. Bobby, big and running to fat, beamed back. His small dark-haired wife gave an embarrassed shy smile. 'They're at Mass once a week regular as clockwork. You, Derek, I suppose you never have time for the priest or the church, what with your going around with criminals and low-life characters.'

'Oh Mama, give him a break.' Bobby chuckled. 'He goes to Mass when he can.'

'Sure. A couple of days ago. And I saw Father Conrad, Mama.'

'See, his hours aren't as regular as ours, Mama,' Therese broke in.

'No, and what kind of life is that for a man? In and out of other people's houses all the time. Never making a home of your own that you can invite your mother to. You ought to get hold of a good Catholic girl, Derek. That Catherine Cadogan who goes to St Saviour's. There's a nice girl. We should ask her round one night when Derek comes … '

'Mama, she's a hundred years old,' Therese clucked.

'I might as well tell you.' Derek hesitated for a second. 'I've got a girlfriend and we have talked about marriage.'

It was as though he had dropped a pile of diamonds on to the table. Too late, he realized that he should never have given them a hint.

Mama was thirsting to know if the girl was a good Catholic and what her family were like. She had automatically assumed that in other matters the girl was Torry's inferior.

In the ensuing chat Torry almost forgot the anxiety and danger which now lurked around him.

He should have told Tickerman about the telephone call. Not that it was anything new. Coppers are prone to calls from cranks. This one had come at the end of a hard day's paper work. Since first thing on Monday morning he had waited for a summons to the Commissioner's office. It never came. Then, as he was preparing to pack up and leave, his telephone rang for the first time.

He was convinced that this was the Commissioner. It took a couple of seconds for him to readjust to the strange broken voice on the line.

'Inspector Torry?'

'Speaking. Who is this?'

'Inspector John Derek Torry?'

'Yes. Who are you?'

'You have been searching for a Mr Wexton?'

'I have. How do you ... ?'

The security had been good. As far as he knew nobody outside the interrogated suspects and the officers working on the Lipperman case had knowledge of the drag for Wexton. But then a lot of people had been questioned in one way or another.

'May I make a suggestion, Mr Torry? A friendly warning? Cool things. Get off Wexton's back.'

'Why should I?'

'Because I'm telling you.'

'And who are you?' Dumphy was nowhere near. Torry could not even attempt to get the call traced.

'Never mind. Get them to stop the search for Wexton and we'll be lenient. If not ... '

'If not, what?'

'I don't fancy your chances.'

The line went dead. Threatening telephone calls were an occupational hazard. But this at least proved one thing. Someone was getting concerned. Undoubtedly Torry was on to something with the search for Wexton.

He looked at the dead receiver in his hand.

'Get lost,' he said to the telephone. Report it? No. He had enough problems without making out a report on a crazy phone call. At least he was now certain about Wexton.

The sinister implications of the call rose into his consciousness now as he sat with his mother, brother and sister-in-law.

'How's Paul?' He tried to draw the fire away from conversation regarding his possible union with Susan.

'Now there's a son for you.' Mama took the bait. 'Neat. Tidy. Goes with a nice Catholic girl. A real gentleman, now.'

'I'm sorry I've been such a disappointment to you, Mama.' The line was always good for cementing their relationship.

'Sorry? Disappointment? None of my sons are a disappointment. Only you should have done better for yourself, Derek, after all Papa and I did for you.'

'Come on, Mama, it's not that bad.' Bobby always played the game to humour the old lady.

'No,' said Torry. 'I know some good Catholic cops, Mama. You hear about one of our fellows last week? A really good Catholic. Saw a man on the ledge of a sixth-storey window going to throw himself off. "Hey, don't do anything stupid," he calls to the man. "I'm going to throw myself off," shouts the man. "Don't," shouts the cop. "Just think of the Blessed Virgin Mary." "Who's she?" the man yells. "Oh, throw yourself off," shouts the Catholic cop.'

It was almost midnight when Torry left the delicatessen. Bobby came through the shop to let him out. 'Don't let Mama bother you too much,' he said, hand on the door.

'She doesn't bother me. I only hope we've got the same amount of life in us when we're her age.'

'The girl?' Bobby lifted his eyebrows. 'You really going to get married?'

'I wish I knew. She wants to. Me, I don't know. I did when I first met her. Now I think maybe I've waited too long.'

'It would please Mama.'

'That's no reason for marriage, Bobby, and you know it.'

Roberto patted his shoulder. 'Look after yourself, Derek.'

190

'Always,' said Torry, stepping out into the Earl's Court Road.

Roberto closed the door behind him. Torry began to walk up the road towards the bright lights of Kensington High Street.

Earl's Court Road was strangely silent and deserted. He did not even hear the approaching car. The first he knew was a quick tingling warning among the short hairs on the back of his neck.

He whirled round. The car was coming up fast, lights out and heading for the pavement and Torry.

The driver must have seen him. The lights suddenly flashed on, blinding Torry. He crossed his arms over his face to shield his eyes.

The car was almost on top of him, then, in the split second before impact, Torry threw his body towards the nearest shop doorway. There was a scraping noise as the car's bumpers and side touched the wall below the shop window. Then the engine revved and the machine bounced unsteadily back on to the road, gathering speed as it took off, shooting the lights at the intersection with Kensington High Street.

It happened so quickly that Torry had no time even to identify the make of car, let alone get its number. He picked himself up, brushing the dirt off the side of his suit, and walked briskly towards the comparatively well-lit High Street.

An accident? A half-slewed driver? An attempt on his life? The frighteners? Torry knew what it was all about, but after the Chief Superintendent's attitude to his report on the affair at Kennedy Airport he was loth to call attention to this incident.

Back at the flat he took extra care in making sure of the locks and window-catches. Tomorrow was another day. Tomorrow was Tuesday, April 22nd. Tomorrow was a day of decision.

10

It was nine fifteen when Torry got in. Dumphy was flapping.

'The Assistant Commissioner wants to see you as soon as you arrive, sir.'

'Well, I've arrived so I'd better go and see him.'

The crunch moved closer. Torry was building a head of venom inside him. None of his normal escape valves seemed to be operating.

'You've only got three-quarters of an hour before the conference.'

Torry glanced at his watch, moving his arm like a knife expert going for the chiv in his sleeve. 'For crying out loud, Dumphy, stop acting like an old-age pensioner in a brothel.'

Dumphy did not even flinch. 'I've put all your Wexton reports into one file, Mr Torry. And everything we've got on the General. I think it's General Wexton the A.C. wants to see you about.'

'Wouldn't surprise me. And if he says what I think he's going to say then I shall tell him to take all the General's decorations and stuff them, item by item, up his ...'

'As I was saying, sir, is there anything else I can do for you?'

Torry thought for a moment, shook his head and made for the door. 'Oh yes.' He made it sound obscene. His hand on the door knob. 'Couple of things. I made some notes yesterday. Telephone conversation with a constable. Bates. Village bobby. East Hendred in Berkshire.'

'I saw them on the desk, sir.'

'Right. Young Rolly-polly Wexton's late father was interviewed about a child murder. A girl. Couple of years ago. The interview was routine, but dig up all you can on the case. Also check and make absolutely certain that Wexton senior's dead. The local man says he's buried at East Hendred, but nose around on the telephone.' He was halfway out of the door when the other point struck him. 'A Mr Rupert Dowding.'

'Dowding, sir? You spell that D-O ... '

'D-O-W-D-I-N-G as in Dowding. Used to own a place called Hill Lodge at East Hendred. The child's body was found there. In the grounds. Young Wexton's father was Dowding's head gardener at the time. Anyway he's moved ... Dowding's moved ... '

'Somewhere near Evesham, sir. It's in your notes. His name wasn't clear because of your writing, and ... '

'All right,' shouted Torry, 'get on to the Worcestershire Force ... '

'That's West Mercia Constabulary now, Mr Torry. Worcestershire, Shropshire and Herefordshire've combined.'

'Well, the appropriate one, Dumphy. Don't waste my bloody time.'

'No, sir.'

'Get on to them. Find out where Dowding lives. Telephone number. Status. You know.'

Torry did not look back or apologize to the civilian clerk into whom he bumped as he dashed towards the lift. What the hell did the Assistant Commissioner want? General Wexton? Jumper? The chop? Were they going to have his guts for duty armlets?

*

The Assistant Commissioner looked as though his breakfast eggs had been addled. Something had definitely disturbed his digestive tract. He stared at his watch a shade too long as Torry was shown in.

'Good morning, sir.' Calm non-aggression on the surface.

' 'Morning, Torry. Good of you to come.' Sarcastic. Fiddling with the papers on his desk. 'Sit down.'

Torry sat uneasily, the file flat on the knees, temper starting to burn visibly through his cheeks.

The A.C. continued to shuffle papers.

'I have some reports here, Inspector Torry. I see that on Thursday afternoon last, that would be the seventeenth, you instructed your sergeant — Sergeant Dumphy — to apply for a twenty-four-hour watch on General Thornton Wexton.'

'I did, sir.'

'On what authority did you do that?'

'On my own, sir. It was only an application. The Chief Superintendent gave me orders, via Superintendent Tickerman, that I was to check and personally interview all persons on file in C.R.O. by the name of Wexton. I was simply following a lead.'

'What sort of a lead, Inspector? You were only told to check and interview.'

'I considered it part of my checking.'

'How?'

Torry blew. 'I was using my initiative. For crying out loud, are we supposed to be detectives or defectives? I imagined this was a big one, not just confined to Lipperman. I've been pussy-footing around on a dead lead for the best part of a week.'

'So it has been pointed out to me, Mr Torry. I might as well tell you that your Chief Superintendent has asked for a replacement. A replacement for you. And General Wexton's reported by letter complaining that you were unspeakably rude to him during an interview ... '

194

'Unspeakably? I wasn't even trying. And if you want my resignation you're not going to get it, sir. You're going to have to kick me out.'

'Why pick on General Wexton?'

'I didn't pick on him. His daughter's on C.R.O. files. I interviewed her and concluded she was clean. But her father's name is Wexton. He's got the time and money to be involved. Whatever his background. Whether he was a soldier or a sodomite ... '

'You can stop that, Inspector.'

Torry paused, quivering. 'I withdraw it, sir. But I was under the impression we were dealing with a large-scale criminal operation. For that you need large-scale men and, if we're going to get anywhere, it's no good shielding men like General Wexton even if they're on speaking terms with the Almighty Himself.'

The Assistant Commissioner's eyes dropped to the papers in front of him. It was as though Torry had become invisible. Torry counted to forty before he spoke.

'I presume I'm suspended, sir.'

'Don't presume anything, Inspector. I'm not happy with these reports. I'm not happy with you. The Commissioner is not happy with your, somewhat emotional, report. Your temper's too fine for my comfort. But we need men on the ground. You'll carry on until I've had a chance to discuss the matter with your Chief Superintendent and others.'

'Do I get a say?'

'If the situation warrants it, you'll get every possible chance to defend your position.'

There was another silence. This time embarrassed. Then the A.C. looked up. He sounded surprised. 'That's all. You have a conference, haven't you?'

'May I ask if General Wexton is being watched?'

'That's out of your hands now, Torry. Just carry on.'

'What if I get any other leads?'
'Carry on.' Dismissal.

Half the Metropolitan Police C.I.D. seemed to be at the conference. The Briefing Room was packed and Torry did not have time to get back to his office before going in.

Tickerman looked his unperturbed self. There was a seat next to him, saved for Torry.

'What's new, Pussycat?' greeted Tickerman.

'You're about three years out of style, man, if that's meant to be a hip hallo.'

'It's my kids,' said Tickerman, looking poker-faced. 'They're growing up. Everyone gets dated.' He looked straight at Torry. 'So what is the new word?'

'For hallo, hi or how-dee-do-dee?'

Tickerman nodded solemnly. 'Yes. I like to put the kids down from time to time.'

'Last I heard, it was "goodbye", but you never can tell in pendulum city.'

'Here comes your friend.'

The Chief Superintendent was standing in the doorway, looking anxious, in violent conversation with Morse. Hart, Torry noted, was hanging around in the background, getting where the action was. The group suddenly split up as the Assistant Commissioner arrived and took over the talking where Morse left off. Finally, the Chief Superintendent and the Assistant Commissioner headed for the rostrum. It was the A.C. who was going to do the talking. Around the room eyebrows lifted in unison. The chatter died as the Assistant Commissioner looked around and began.

'Gentlemen. A large number of you have come from your parent divisions and the areas in which you have been working in order to attend this conference, so I want to make it as short as possible ... '

'Get on with it, then,' muttered Torry.

'You're all involved in a complex case which came to a head last Tuesday when Gustave Lipperman broke out of Her Majesty's prison, Wormwood Scrubs, and was murdered in Primula Street. However, I want to stress that this was only the final burst of something which has been worrying senior officers for some time.'

'We're going to be all morning,' thought Torry.

'This is no place to start lecturing on the structure of criminal gangs, or organizations, in the Metropolitan area. Most of you know all that anyway. In recent years we've had all sorts of attempts to take over certain areas in this city — I speak particularly of the Mafia policy in London. But the story of Lipperman's execution, because we all know that's what it was, goes back about two years. Officers in every division know, only too well, that in this time there has been evidence of a new and rising pressure involving protection, vice, drugs, skilled and well-planned robbery, even murder.'

The Briefing Room was still, everyone focusing on the A.C.

'We've at least thirty robberies which remain unsolved, and yet point to a central planner,' he continued. 'These include the three Hatton Garden thefts, two major jewellery thefts from security vans last year, and the Luton bank robbery. Your Chief Superintendent will speak to you in a moment, but those of us who have been correlating the information which you have been gathering so painstakingly are convinced that we are up against something relatively new in large criminal organizations.

'There is no doubt that here we have a central planner, or planning committee, with large sums of money easily available. If it's one man, as has been suggested to me this morning, then he could be a speculator with a precise and brilliant mind. The situation points to there being one man concerned with central planning. But there is also evidence that this whole scheme is being run with backing from America.'

Torry sat up as though jabbed by a pitchfork.

'In particular,' the Assistant Commissioner went on, 'there is the affair concerning our extradition of the man, Armitage, shortly before the Lipperman murder. Armitage was a known hired killer who was himself murdered, together with two F.B.I. agents, only a few hours after being returned to the United States. We also have the facts concerning Detective Inspector Torry. Someone attempted to bribe this officer in New York because he had been close to Armitage. We've heard the name Wexton bandied about as well. So it seems reasonable to assume that, however big the operations, they are being at least controlled from the United States.' He looked around the Briefing Room to let it sink in.

'A further point emerges from the way some of the known activities of the group have been conducted. If our thinking is accurate, known criminal experts are being used only in extreme cases. We don't think known men killed Lipperman, for instance, but we can be fairly sure that they are being utilized to train younger men who, as yet, have no criminal records. In other words a skilled criminal force is being trained and used ... '

He went on as Torry's mind picked up the central idea. It was a plan that would appeal especially to a military mind. Criminal Training H.Q. How about that? Instruction in driving, smash and grab, locks, weapons, in-fighting, documents, blowing a peter. Wexton at the head, using experts who'd be getting more money from him than from being continually on the trot. New methods. Men and women with no records trained for special jobs. Turned out as professional craftsmen. And, by God, the good ones were craftsmen. Insurance. Discipline, like Lipperman, if you stepped out of line. What a doddle. He came back to earth just as the Assistant Commissioner finished speaking.

The Chief Superintendent took over, ponderous as ever, constantly referring to notes, tediously going over the small pieces of information which had gone to make up the general pattern of the organization. The tips all seemed to have come from direct criminal sources. Old professionals who had not been used by the organization.

'As the Assistant Commissioner has revealed to you, the name Wexton has been talked about.' The old man looked straight down at Torry. 'It is still a name, gentlemen, that cannot be ruled out. Some officers have observed that their sources of information have become uncooperative, some even frightened, when the name Wexton has been mentioned.'

'You're not out of the running, then,' mouthed Tickerman.

'Don't look now but I think I've even pegged him,' replied Torry.

'Bet you don't get the credit for it.' Torry looked sidelong at Tickerman. The wily old Ticker was grinning.

Wexton watched the last two drive away. It had taken an hour for them all to leave in threes and fours. Now, like a moment before battle, he felt lonely and stuffed with apprehension. They were nearly all recruits doing their first operation. Were they ready? He'd followed their training carefully. Wexton visited the training area twice a week.

The final briefing had gone well. He crossed the hall into his study and sat down at the desk and again examined the street map. Everything else had been packed away – movie and slide projectors, the big maps. He was alone with only one map, the telephone and his watch. And the first call would not come until quite late.

God, it was starting already and he hadn't been waiting for

more than five minutes. Desperate. The night and the small creature. Sublimate. Sublimate. He'd read enough books on psychiatry to know it was the only way. Hands damp with sweat. Wexton reached over and dialled a London number. A woman answered, a low sexless voice.

'It's the General here,' said Wexton. The back of his throat felt dry, constricted.

'Oh yes, sir. What can we do for you?'

'The girl who came out last time ... '

'Sandra?'

'Yes. Sandra. Is she free?'

'Just one moment, General.'

His hand shook, fingers playing with the edge of the map. The woman came back on the line. 'Yes, she's free, sir. When would you like her to come over?'

'As soon as possible.'

'She knows all your requirements?'

'Yes. Tell her the same as last time.'

'Very good, sir. We'll get a hire car to bring her out to you. Any idea what time she'll be returning?'

'Tomorrow morning some time. If not, I'll call you.'

That should take care of it. God, get her here soon. It would all go before dusk then and he wouldn't have to ... the wind and bare branches. It was a wet night last time. Soaking wet with the moon in its first quarter and the wind sobbing in the branches — or was that another sobbing? Christ help me ... help me ... help me ...

In spite of the Assistant Commissioner's desire to make the conference short they were still at it until noon. Questions. Arguments. Two or three fresh pieces of information, sticky ones always being passed on to a higher level.

Torry ate lunch with Tickerman in the canteen and got back to the office just after one.

Dumphy arrived a few minutes later, beaming and rubbing his hands like an amateur Uriah Heep.

'Rowland Wexton's father's definitely dead, sir.' He looked pleased about it. 'Cancer in both lungs. I spoke to the doctor who signed the death certificate. The local man's sending copies of all relevant documents.'

'Good,' absent-mindedly, as his mind flicked back to the incident of the previous night. 'Good. What's outstanding?'

'Quite a lot of inter-departmental stuff and the mail that you didn't finish yesterday,' almost accusingly. That settled it, the afternoon would be whittled away on paper work.

'Okay.'

'Right, sir. Oh and I've got Mr Rupert Dowding's address and telephone number. You were right, it's near Evesham.'

'Bung it in the book.' Torry tossed his own private notebook across the desk.

Dumph chatted on while he wrote the address. 'That child murder in Berkshire. I've been checking on that too, sir. Haven't got the full story yet. Is it urgent?'

'I don't think so, not now.' Torry glanced at the address and telephone number that Dumphy had copper-plated into the notebook.

'January 24th, 1966, sir.'

'What?'

'The Berkshire child murder. Little girl. I'll have the file in the morning.'

'Oh yes. Good.' Torry had a mental picture of schoolchildren at play.

She looked like a child of sixteen, even younger. The Bentley hire car was driving away as Wexton opened the door.

'Thank you for asking for me,' was all she said, picking up her overnight case and walking in. Long blonde hair, babyish face. Young. Ripe. She looked more like a fifteen-year-old, Wexton decided. He knew she must be at least twenty.

'You know where the bedroom is?' He did not smile. Playing the part now.

Her hair bounced as she nodded and bit her bottom lip.

'Go and get ready then. I'll be up in five minutes.'

Another bounce of the hair as she began to climb the stairs. Wexton watched. You could see almost right up her skirt as she got to the turn of the stairs.

Five minutes later he followed. Opening the bedroom door firmly and closing it behind him with a bang. She stood by the window. The sophisticated coat and dress, in which she had arrived, now gone, replaced by what looked like a school gym slip, white blouse and striped tie, her hair pulled back and tied neatly in a bow. She turned to face him.

'Sandra.' Spoke sharply. 'You realize why you are here?'

'Yes, sir.' Half whispered, eyes down to the floor and teeth biting the lower lip. Hard.

'Come here then.' He sat on the oak chest at the bottom of the bed. The girl stood to his right.

'Is there any reason why I should not punish you?'

'No, sir.'

'No, sir. Right.'

Almost eagerly the girl bent forward across Wexton's knees.

'Sandra, you're a wicked, evil girl.' He lifted the gym slip. A sudden shudder in his body. 'And what's more, I see that you're not wearing the complete school uniform.' His hand rose.

By five thirty Torry felt beaten out. He had the beginnings of a headache and that bitter taste in the back of his mouth which could be the harbinger of 'flu or a cold. He also wanted to be alone. Or at least away from Susan. Away from Susan and all the others, his cordial workmates. He needed space in which he could work out the priorities of life. All things seemed to be a paradox. What was it with work? With Sue? With himself?

He had always believed that he was a man of dedication, married to law and order. A hater of evil. Now the taste of trying to overcome the unrighteous was turning sour. Even searching his heart, here in the office, he could not tell if he was living a lie: whether his desire for an ordered and orderly community was simply a side effect of lust. Was the magnetic attraction to Susan lust? Superiors were trying to get rid of him on the grounds that he was difficult. Soon he must talk it out. Pray it out? Now was the moment for placing the problems firmly into the hidden centre of the mind, 'at the still point of the turning world'. He smiled to himself, the literary Mr Torry quoting an Anglican poet, and began to tidy his desk.

Leaving the Yard he took a cab down to The Street, stopping the driver at Chancery Lane and walking the few steps to the Pizzala. There were only two couples in. Early evening is always the best time for the Pizzala.

Antonio, neat and grey, came quickly over to the door and began talking in rapid Italian. 'Mr Torrini' (Antonio would never acknowledge his change of name), 'where've you been? It's so long since we've seen you.'

Luigi beamed at him from the bar. He looked as though he'd just come back from sunning himself somewhere. He always did.

Most people have a secret place. Their own cell, private and known to nobody, just as a child may have a nest among the garden bushes. It is an internal secret which exists even in the middle of a crowd — a village, a house, room, clifftop, or even a theatre. This restaurant, the Pizzala, was Torry's secret place because, for him, it had a womb-like atmosphere. He was known;

there was mutual respect; some of the best Italian food in London. It was a cave in which one could hide from 'The Job'. Here Torry felt, at one and the same time, alone and at home.

He stayed until seven thirty and was back in the flat at eight to make his promised call to Susan, who was all tender and mothering. Torry's headache had gone, smoothed away by the food and contentment of the Pizzala, but he still used it as an excuse to fend her off. Tomorrow was going to be hell's busy but he'd call her. Yes, however busy he was, he'd call her. Possibly, just possibly, they could get together for the evening. Couldn't tell at this stage though. Yes, of course he'd do his best.

He had hardly replaced the telephone when it began to sound off again. It was Tickerman.

'Derek, two things.'

'Yes.' Torry detected a deflation of his own stomach muscles. The black cloud of either disaster or victory growing on the horizon.

'They've picked up a lad in Newcastle, drunk and throwing money around like a philanthropic fruit machine ... '

'Come again?'

'Forget it. The lad's been back from Aden for over a year, odd-job layabout since then. Missing most of last week. They picked him up in a pub brawl with the best part of two thousand quid on him ... '

'Had a good week. Must've looked like the Michelin man.'

'Very good. They've got a couple of witnesses who say he was shooting his mouth off about having been up the smoke using a Sterling sub-machine gun.'

'Progress is a wonderful thing.'

'Anyway, the old man's asked for him to be brought down here. He'll be arriving in the morning. No information to the press.'

'Okay, I'll call Bernie Levin now. What's the other news? They made me Commissioner?'

204

'West End Central's mounting three raids on probable Wexton properties. I'd like you with me. We're going into The Carpet Bag. Used to be a haunt of ... '

'Lipperman and Grosvenor. I read the files.'

'Dedication'll get you nowhere.'

'So I've discovered. What time are we going in?'

'The witching hour, old lad.'

'That's original.' At least something was happening.

Wexton could feel the girl's body next to him, her film of night-dress still pulled high around her breasts from their last act. He had not even dozed off. The girl was an incredible stimulant. Her bare thigh rubbed closer to his and, in her sleep, she started to move again. Then the telephone rang.

Wexton's arm leaped out. The clock on the bedside table gleamed. Ten thirty.

'Hallo?'

'General?'

'Speaking.'

'Romeo.'

'Yes, Romeo?'

'Leaving to take post now.'

'Thank you, Romeo.'

Quietly he replaced the receiver, but the bell had wakened the girl. She slid her hand between his thighs and he became fully aware.

'What's the time, darling?' asked Sandra.

'Half past ten.'

'What a lovely time to be wakened up.'

'You're earning your money, aren't you?'

'I don't mind earning it with someone like you. That's why I said thank you for asking for *me*. There are so many male masochists these days that I never get a proper share.' She squeezed closer and fastened her lips onto him. She felt like a leech.

'You want to be careful,' said Wexton. 'One day you'll meet a real kind and he'll do for you.'

'Not you though, darling.' She reached down from the bed and lifted a slim leather belt from the floor. 'Not you?' Sandra pressed the belt into his hand and shook off the bedclothes, spread-eagling herself across him.

The building which now operated as The Carpet Bag club originally belonged to a family as large as, and distinctly similar to, the Forsytes. The remaining members were now reduced to an eccentric old lady who tormented Bognor Regis with her gossip, and a pathetic scarecrow who can be seen on most evenings scavenging around Soho coffee bars.

From outside, the house looked normal. A four-storey dwelling with basement area and attic bedrooms. Some pop-culture Führer's London home. Except, of course, for the discreet sign on the portico, proclaiming THE CARPET BAG. MEMBERS ONLY.

Only a dozen or so of the members had gone up the steps during the fifteen minutes in which Torry had been watching. He sat in the back of the Q car, next to Tickerman. Morse, controlling the operation, sat in front with the driver. Hart, it seemed, was on another mission.

'I'd have said Tuesday was a bad night.' Torry spoke quietly.

'Tell it to the old man.' Morse did not turn in his seat. 'But what do you do? To us it's a last stand, an hysterical attempt to get evidence. To them it may be a signal that we're on to something.'

'And in the morning we're going to be apologizing to several harmless offended customers who've been searched and humiliated.' Tickerman had woken up.

Torry looked at the luminous dial of his watch. Eleven

fifty-five. A time when all peace-loving coppers should be in bed. The radio began to crackle.

'Alpha Sugar to Sugar One. All ready.'

Morse picked up the hand set. 'Sugar One to all Sugars. Move in.' He repeated the sentence, and then said something to the driver who started the engine. They pulled across the road, stopping in front of the club.

By the time the three of them were out of the car the whole road had filled with vehicles and uniformed officers. Morse stood square in the doorway, his right forefinger leaning on the bell.

The elderly porter who opened up stepped back in surprise. There was the usual difficulty of a large number of men trying to get through a narrow doorway. Torry could see the bar, dining-room and gaming-tables through an archway to the right. Scarlet velvet, marble, gold. A plush setting for flush people. There were a couple of shouts, but not the expected screams of conscience-stricken ladies realizing that Daddy or Hubby would read all about it in the morning.

Then the scene froze. Down the stairs facing them came a woman. She wore a flashing white hostess gown, blonde short hair and a face disfigured by living at an overdrive speed. She looked neither frightened nor offended. If anything there was a trace of amusement in her eyes.

'Superintendent Morse. How nice of you to drop in.'

' 'Evening, Ginnie,' said Morse, quite at home. 'Hope you don't mind.'

'Are you buying or window-shopping?'

'Depends what we see in the windows.'

'It would be stupid of me to ask you for your warrant?'

'Stupid but realistic.' Morse lifted the neatly folded paper from his inside pocket.

Torry moved towards the bar where they were starting to sort out the sexes. Five police-women stood calmly waiting, butch and itching to get their hands on the expensive ladies. Tickerman was playing the power game among the roulette wheels and chemmy tables. The clients' faces betrayed that they were merely put out, though occasionally Torry thought he interpreted fear in a twitching lip or moving eye.

The uniformed men were firm but polite. One or two customers tried to joke, but the boys knew better than to play that sort of game. Torry was crossing the bar again, where they were collecting the men together like a flock of sleek black sheep, when he saw a face. The man was tall, slim; his face lean, the colour of carefully polished light leather. A smooth man in a lightweight dark-grey suit. Torry slowed his pace, not looking at the man as he clawed through his memory. It was a face that should have a name or number stamped into his brain. Who? When? Why?

Torry stood back from the crowd and looked again. His memory did not throw up a single clue. It was something from a long time ago. He walked back, then up the queue of men again, this time pausing before the leathery face.

'Don't I know you?' Polite and not pushing.

'Not a chance.' The accent was American, the tone contemptuous.

'Name?'

'You asking officially?'

'Yes.'

'Then may I know who's asking? I don't normally talk to strangers.'

Torry lifted his warrant card to within an inch of the man's eyes. 'Detective Inspector John Derek Torry. C.I.D. New Scotland Yard.' He did not imagine it: the man stiffened. But when he spoke the words came out in the same relaxed style of disdain.

'Anthony Champion. United States citizen.'

The name, like the face, had a worrying familiarity, but there was no hook on which Torry could hang it.

'Can you prove that?'

'Do I have to?'

'Afraid so, Mr Champion.'

Champion's eyes never left Torry as he drew out his passport and handed it over.

Torry flipped through the pages. Visa was okay. He had only arrived two days ago and there were no special markings.

'Here on business?'

'I'm in the real estate business, officer.'

'Inspector,' Torry quietly corrected. There was aggression here somewhere. A personal thing. Or was that simply another bit of imagination? 'Yes, but I asked if you were here on business.'

'No. Just giving myself a rest.'

'For long?'

'Depends. Are we breaking the law being here or something?'

'No. We're checking, that's all.' Torry handed back the passport. 'Where are you staying, Mr Champion?'

'The Savoy, where else?'

'Thank you.' Torry felt the nagging irritation of trouble as he walked away. Morse was still standing at the foot of the stairs talking to the raddled lady in white.

'Come on, Ginny. The girls?' he said as Torry approached.

'I've already told you,' she said, her voice husky as ripe corn. 'I've got four girls living here. Staying here. I do allow them to come down and have a meal in the club, mix with the guests if they want to, but they are private individuals using my premises. They are not allowed to take members to their rooms. They pay me for their accommodation, and they all have respectable jobs.'

'And fully stamped insurance cards to prove it, no doubt,' said Torry.

'I presume so. That's up to them, isn't it? You won't get me for running a disorderly house, Superintendent.'

'I didn't think I would.' Morse sighed. 'We'll take a look just the same. You've given them plenty of time.'

Madame smiled and led the way up the stairs.

'Like old times, eh, Ginny? Walking upstairs with two men at your heels.'

She paused and turned to him with a smile which had lethal possibilities. 'Never two. One maybe. But never two. I was always precise and ladylike.'

They were wasting their time. The first three bedrooms contained young, fine, healthy and delectable girls, including one coloured dolly. All were sleepy. All produced the names of firms they worked for. Torry knew, as well as Morse, that they need not even check.

The fourth room was empty.

'Sandra must be out late or downstairs,' said the cool Ginny. 'You'd like to see my quarters?'

'Just a peep so we'll be able to think of you in your natural surroundings.' Morse had a poker-faced delivery.

There was an office with a door which led through to a bedroom with private bath. Torry lingered in the office, standing by the desk and letting his eyes drift over the papers and bills which seemed to be the normal backroom work of a club. Then he saw the telephone pad. On the top sheet there were two words scribbled in pencil. *Sandra. General.*

As Morse and the female came back into the study, Torry moved away from the desk. As they reached the door he spoke.

'Miss … er … ?'

'Mrs Crawley.' Morse smiled for the first time. 'I was at school with her late husband, would you believe it? Old "Creepy" Crawley.'

Dear God, thought Torry, thank heaven I've got Ticker. This one's a walking bundle of fun. 'Mrs Crawley,' he said. 'Who is the General?'

Morse's head whipped round, anger replacing the bonhomie. 'Torry!' Warning!

'It's all right, sir. I've got a reason for asking.'

'You'd better have, lad, or a report's going straight to the old man.'

La Crawley had recovered from the initial shock of the question. Her face showed that it had rocked her. 'I'm sorry,' she said with reasonable poise. 'I really don't know what you're talking about.'

'You're quite sure? I think you should consider this very carefully.'

'I do not know what you are talking about.' Firmly, her face flushed with either guilt or anger.

Torry crossed to the desk and picked up the telephone pad. 'There are two words written here. One is "Sandra", the other is "General". Is this your handwriting?'

She came over and looked at the pad. 'Yes, it is, but ... '

'Then what has your absent Sandra got in common with a general?'

'Not a great deal, I should think, judging by the generals I've seen.' She spoke to Morse. 'Really, what an objectionable young man.'

'I think you'd better answer the question, though.'

Good, Morse was backing him after the false start.

'I only use that pad occasionally. When I'm on the telephone I tend to write down odd words of the conversation, like some people doodle. I'm not sure when I wrote Sandra's name there. Some time last week, I think. I know I wrote the word "General" today, I was talking to my broker. Some shares were mentioned. General Electric.'

It was too glib.

'All right?' asked Morse, raising his eyebrows.

'Can I have the name of your broker, Mrs Crawley?'

'Certainly.' She rattled off the name, office address and tele-phone number of a man who, both Torry and Morse knew, was beyond any suspicion. Hell. But it was still too good. The American downstairs. Champion. Torry found himself lost in thought. Everything was wrong. Smelled wrong.

'Mind if I keep that?' he asked, raising the telephone pad.

'Do what you like with it.' Mrs Crawley left huffily.

Downstairs, Tickerman stood in the hall wrapped in personal gloom. 'They've got a couple in possession of cannabis. Nothing else. Any luck?'

'I don't know.' Torry told him quickly about the telephone pad and Champion.

'Put Champion on the Telex in the morning. I've got to go back to West End Central. Car can take you home if you like.'

'Thanks, Tick.'

'Tell you what. To put your mind at rest I'll call the Yard from Central and get them to put Champion on the Telex tonight. Okay?'

'Right. Thank you.' Tick was all right, but there had been a second upstairs when Morse had showed his true colours. Among the top brass there was going to be a lot of pressure.

The telephone was clamouring as Torry opened the door. During the last few hours he felt he had only used the flat as a message-receiving centre. He made a leap across the room, picked up the phone and recited the number.

'Derek?' It was Tickerman sounding agitated.

'Sir.' He would appreciate subservience.

Ticker was exact and fast. 'I wanted you to know this. I've been taken off the case. The Wexton case. They've had a bad one in the country. I'm going out of London now.'

'How bad?'

'Young girl. Seventeen or eighteen. Decided to call us in straight away. Came through while I was here. At Central. Oh, I've asked for that Telex to go to Washington.'

'Where'd they find the girl?'

Tickerman gave the place-name and area. For a second, Torry felt the familiar sensation of pre-knowledge. But it did not register, remaining a small irritation in the back of his mind.

'I'll be directly under Mr Broadbent, then?'

'Probably.' An embarrassed hesitation. 'Derek, you know the old man's asked for a replacement?'

'The A.C. told me.'

'It's just possible that Father might take you under his wing personally.'

'Guerrilla tactics.'

'Could be. So take care. I've borrowed young Hart by the way.'

'You've done ... ?'

'Hold on, Derek. He's coming to us anyway and he needs the experience.'

'The best of British ... ' Then it hit him. The jigsaw took shape. For a second the whole picture stood blazingly clear, the itch streaming out of his subconscious.

'You still there, Derek?'

'Tick, I've bloody got it.' Like a child gabbling with excitement.

'You got what?'

'Wexton. I've got it. Look, Tick, for once, just once, stick with me. Can you get me cleared to come with you?'

'Hart's coming with me.'

'I know. Him as well. But can't you insist on me as your staff officer?'

'Give me some reasons why I should.'

'Not on the telephone, but I think I can promise you Wexton in the bag. I must be right.'

'Tell me then, lad.'

'Not on the phone. Can you take me?'

'The old man won't like it.'

'He will when we're through. What's the drill?'

'I'm at Central. Hart's collecting the Bag from the Yard. Should be leaving here in fifteen minutes or so.'

'Will you do it, Tick? Pick me up on your way out?'

'Are you serious, Derek? No tricks?'

'Nothing up my bloody sleeve. Will you?'

'It's just gone two now. We'll be at your place by two thirty. I'll be a coward and leave a message for the old man. He'll have time to cool down before we see him again, but you'd better have something good.'

'The works, uncle. The whole works.' As he said it, Torry wondered if he was being over-confident.

Quarter past two in the morning. Four cars, parked placidly in different parts of London. The owner of each vehicle lying snug and asleep in bed, unconscious of everything, even the fact that their cars were fingered.

A young couple, homeward unsteadily from a night spent live, lithe and free in some discothèque or club, wove, clasped in each other's arms, into the entrance of a mews off Kensington High Street. They slewed to a halt and went into a long embrace, the girl pushing her boyfriend back against the blue Jaguar 3.8 which stood, as it usually did during the night, parked just inside the mews. The embrace became warmer, wild, twisting. Then it stopped as suddenly as it started. Oddly, the girl turned on her heel and walked away, her shoes neatly clipping the pavement, breaking the silence. Her friend, who had been working on the Jaguar's door lock, under cover of the embrace, slid into the driving seat and slipped a key into the ignition. (Ignition keys are no problem.) The Jag moved slowly, and with little noise, out of the Mews.

The young man in Down Street, a pebble's toss from Piccadilly, walked briskly and with confidence. He carried a brief-case and went straight to the claret Austin Westminster Automatic. Casually he put the brief-case on the ground while fumbling for the keys. Once in the driving seat he took his time adjusting the seat belt, then, with a grin, he leaned forward and felt under the glove compartment for the concealed switch. 'The best anti-theft device in the business,' his friend had boasted to him a few weeks before. 'Cuts out the transmission.'

The young man pushed the switch, inserted his duplicate key into the ignition and turned. A few minutes later the Westminster was moving steadily out towards Kensington.

The tubby, tousled-haired little man had been lurking for over an hour near East Heath Road, Hampstead, right on the edge of the Heath. He was nervous. Round here, if a copper saw you on your own at this time in the morning he'd pull you in soon as look at you. A final glance at his watch. Just coming up to the half-hour. Zero. He was far from casual, working too quickly. Nerves. First time for real. Jumper had trained him and they said Jumper was inside now. But Jumper wouldn't be pleased at the speed. Watch it. Black Zodiac. You had to work quick 'cos the owner slept in the house in front of which the car was parked. The bugger had one of those trombone bar locks going down from his wheel to the brake pedal. Guaranteed to keep your car safe from theft. Safe as a plastic strong-room. A kid could nip off the padlock. About as much use as a bicycle chain. See, comes away in your hand with a twist of the cutters. He removed the bar,

215

gently placed it on the passenger-side floor, out of sight, and like the other two, started the engine. Away a bit too quick but not enough noise to disturb the customers.

In sleeping Bloomsbury the Humber Hawk, polished and cherished, was an easy target. Its owner had not even locked it. At two thirty-five, after a nervous few moments waiting for the engine to warm, it pulled away, nosing comfortably through the streets towards the M 4 motorway.

Four cars. Four out of the forty-odd which would go missing in the Metropolitan area that night. None would be reported much before seven in the morning. A Jaguar, a Westminster Automatic, a Zodiac and a Humber Hawk. Four of the crowd which were a daily headache for the Metropolitan Police. These four would be a sick headache. And not just to the Metropolitan Police.

Two forty-five. The Jaguar, now with different licence plates, was exactly two miles up the M4. Chalky White at the wheel watched his speed and flashed his headlights quickly, three times.

Fifteen minutes later, at the same spot, the young man called Nolan, driving the Westminster, did exactly the same thing.

High on the embankment, a dirty figure stirred. He was unwashed and clothed in an old Army greatcoat, his hair matted, and the rucksack, against which he leaned, looked rotten with age. He added a second cross in pencil to a stained cigarette packet and noted the time from a suspiciously opulent wrist-watch. Three o'clock in the morning. He did not know that back there among the sporadic traffic was a police Humber Snipe bearing Detective Superintendent Tickerman, Detective Inspector Torry and Detective Sergeant Hart towards the body of a blonde girl in a gym-slip-like dress who lay mutilated in a country ditch.

216

They had listened to Torry almost non-stop since picking him up.

'It's possible,' said Tickerman. 'Quite an idea.' The car had reached the end of the M4 motorway and the driver manoeuvred it round the big roundabout. They took the Henley Road.

Hart said nothing.

'It's more than an idea, Tick.' Torry had turned fanatical. 'It fits.'

'You've got a substantial theory, Derek. That's all.'

'Have you got any idea about what else happened on the night of January 24th–25th, 1966? Apart from the child, I mean?'

'It's my sister-in-law's birthday, twenty-fourth of January.' Tickerman refused to get excited.

'The Luton bank happened. The one that the old man was talking about today. I checked with Crime Index while I was waiting for you. Wexton's a bloody maniac. Cracks that way under pressure.'

'The theory's sound, sir.' Hart, grudgingly.

'Thank you, Sergeant Hart. Thank you for your support. I'll wear it always. Of course the bloody theory's sound.'

'Circumstantial but sound.' Tickerman puffed at his pipe. 'It warrants investigation.'

Later, Hart changed the subject. 'Did you get any more on this one, sir?'

'Only that she was a girl, blonde, aged between seventeen and eighteen. She must've been in a bad mess because they decided it was a nutter and called us in straight away. Within an hour of finding her.'

Hart nodded and turned to Torry. 'I hear you were out at our old haunt, The Carpet Bag, tonight.'

'Whose old haunt?'

'Well, mine, really. I've been in there quite a bit. Undercover, as you might say.'

'I wondered why your boss didn't have you along. My God, he's a right little Yorick, isn't he?'

'I don't think you should compare Superintendent Morse to the former court jester of Denmark in my presence, Inspector Torry.' Then Tickerman laughed. 'You're right though. "A whoreson mad fellow".'

'Maybe. He's just that joker's type. I've always thought Yorick must have been a tricky bastard, pouring flagons of Rhenish over people's heads.'

'Mr Morse has been known to set the table on a roar from time to time,' said Hart primly.

'Christ, we've got a car-load of policemen with their A-levels in Eng. Lit.' Tickerman shuffled down into the corner.

'Did you have words with my little friend Sandra?' asked Hart.

'Sandra?' said Torry sharply. Tickerman stopped shuffling.

'Tell us about Sandra.' Tickerman showed the first signs of interest.

'What do you want to know? She's a prize little whore ... '

'What does she look like?'

'A million roubles. Blonde. She's twenty, looks around sixteen. Seventeen, eighteen at a ... '

'You with me, Tick?' Torry sounding as though he had won the pools.

'*Sandra. General,*' said Tickerman, fully awake. Then to the driver. 'Can you whip up those horses?'

'Like they taught me at Hendon, sir?'

'Better than they taught you at Hendon.'

'Impossible,' said Hart.

At three fifteen the Zodiac went through the same light-flashing procedure on the M4. Twenty minutes later the Humber Hawk followed suit. The tramp lying up on the embankment slid down out of sight and rummaged in the rucksack, pulling out a flat, oblong transceiver. He drew out the telescopic aerial, pressed the button and spoke in an accent which belied his filthy clothing.

'Alpha Fox to Romeo. Do you read?'

Back came the faint answer. 'Romeo. Alpha Fox, I read.'

'Alpha Fox. Romeo. Four out,' said the tramp.

'Four out. Thank you, Alpha Fox.'

'Four out. Thank you, Alpha Fox.' Smith spoke into the transceiver. He had pulled the car off the road, into a lay-by, ten minutes before. Now he pushed in the aerial on his transceiver, wound up the window, opened the door and walked slowly over to the telephone box.

The bell only rang once. Wexton had already waited for ten minutes. Ten minutes overdue did not matter much at this stage. There was plenty of time to spare. But he liked accurate timing.

'Hallo?' He spoke softly.

'General?'

'Speaking.'

'Romeo. Four out.'

A moment's pause as the tension relaxed a fraction. 'Good. Thank you.' Wexton replaced the receiver and listened to the silence in the old house.

They stopped in front of the Church Hall which was being used as a temporary murder H.Q. It was ten to five and still dark.

'Mr Tickerman?' asked the police constable on duty outside. Ticker nodded.

'Our Chief Super's up at the scene, sir. Said would you go straight up there when you arrived. Follow this road and fork left. About a hundred yards on there's a turn off to the left, more of a track than a road. You'll see them up there.'

'Thank you.'

'And there's a message for you, sir. From Scotland Yard.' The constable passed the memo through the window.

The driver flicked on the interior light. Tickerman read quickly and looked at Torry. 'Your mate, Champion. They've had a reply to my Telex. Washington's got him on file. Not wanted but suspected. Consorts with powerful syndicate and ex-syndicate members. Almost certainly involved in large illegal operations.' He leaned out of the car. 'You got a telephone link with the Yard yet?'

'No, sir, just one G.P.O. line.'

'That'll do. Don't leave without me.' He was out of the car.

'Who's Champion?' asked Hart.

'You heard. Some wheel I caught spinning at your club.'

Tickerman did not take long. 'Let's go,' to the driver as soon as he was back in the car. 'I've asked them to go down to the Savoy and discreetly ask Brother Champion to step along and have a little talk. Morse'll put him through his paces.' They came to the fork in the road. 'Derek.' Tickerman's voice went through a perceptible change. 'The old man's on the ball, even at this time in the morning. Someone's probably sold us out and been on to him at home.'

'About me?' Torry did not really have to ask.

'I've got to telephone him at my earliest convenience, and he wants a report in writing. My reasons for taking you out of the Metropolitan area as my staff officer without his authority.'

'I'd better be right about Wexton, then.' Torry tried to sound easy. Inside, he felt the pincers of tension beginning to intensify their pressure.

It was two minutes past five when Chalky White pulled the Jag off the main road and drove carefully up the narrow lane which rose to a point overlooking the town. At the top of the hill there was plenty of room to turn and position the car. He undid his seat belt, leaned back and lit a cigarette. The long wait began. Soon it would be dawn. A misty dawn by the look of it. The town, a faint tracing of subdued lights below, would not know what had hit it before the morning was out. Birthday Party. White began to laugh.

Half an hour later, a couple of miles away, on the other side of the town, Nolan drove the Westminster on to the grass verge from what was almost a cart track. Within the next hour he would be joined by Howel, the nervous one with the Zodiac, and McIvor in the Humber. Nolan also lit a cigarette and prayed that McIvor had remembered to pick up the surveying equipment. Wexton was right, the spot seemed deserted enough, but if anyone did think twice about what they were doing there they would need a cover. Nolan was a towny. He didn't like the wide open spaces on principle.

Visually, scenes of tragedy can normally be divided into two classes. There is either some spectacular horror of drunken metal, stone, wood, glass, or, as in this case, one can only sense a calm agony with little else to see.

The track was bordered by hedges. There was an unspectacular five-bar gate and a generator truck giving power to seven or eight floodlights which threw the area into an unreal relief, altering natural colours with their harsh blind of light. Most apparent was the lane of wooden stakes leading through the gate, stake linked to stake by thick string decorated, at intervals, with flapping pieces of white rag. It looked like a minefield through which a path had been cleared. But the cordoned area could easily be a treasure trove for clues. Already the lights picked up men muffled and gum-booted, bending cautiously over the ground.

Torry standing just inside the gateway, within the carefully defined pathway of stakes, string and rags, looked along the macabre line of hedge. Twenty yards away a rough structure of canvas flapped lazily. You could hear the slap of the material as the light wind caught it, billowing like sails on some small ship. There were men around the canvas screens. Two of them, seeing the newly arrived party, detached themselves from the knot of men and started to walk towards Tickerman, Torry and Hart. Torry swallowed. He knew what was coming. The ultimate in corruption. The complete state.

The two groups met halfway along the corridor of posts and string, like opposing parties exchanging political prisoners at some lonely check-point. There was a brief pause for introductions. No one was smiling.

The third telephone call. Wexton was again ready.
   'General?'
   'Yes.'
   'Romeo.'
   'Go ahead.'
   'Four in position.'
   'Good. Thank you, Romeo.'
   It was ten minutes to six. Just over five hours to zero.

Torry felt he should be moved by the thing lying in the ditch. At first sight it meant nothing to him. Two fragments of society had collided. One, presumably, was reasonably innocent, the other debased. His job was with that part of man which was debased. The result of man warped and twisted was there for all of them to see. Crime in all its aspects, criminals in all their perversity, scratched and tore at the carbuncle of his conscience. But, for the moment, he felt nothing.

He could sense Hart's immediate reaction, a sort of static emanating from a tightening of the emotions. Yet Hart had seemed all right in the room with Rowland Wexton's corpse. Torry had seen nastier things than this. People who threw themselves in front of subway trains, for instance. That was horrific. Double X certificate. What was this, in the glare from the lights? A thing, with arms and legs and a head, light hair, the face hidden in mud stained brown and red. Light hair. A thing, damp and useless. Something that had lived and laughed, cried, felt happy and sad, got excited at Christmas and its birthday.

Slowly the grip tightened on Torry. He began to feel it. He looked at Hart, their faces strangely altered by the light. For the first time, as their eyes met, they recognized each other. Now he could pray for the soul of the thing in the ditch.

For this and for all the souls of the faithful departed, may our Lord Jesus Christ have mercy. Slowly Torry made the sign of the Cross. The uniformed local Chief Super was looking at him. His eyes were saying, that man is emotional.

'Identification?' asked Ticker, a little sharply. Natural enough. Tick had a girl of sixteen.

'Not yet. Impossible yet.' The Chief Super sounded excessively worried. So would you, Torry, in his boots. Thinks he's got a homicidal maniac on his patch. He has as well, if it's Wexton, and, by God, it'd better be Wexton. Torry's Wexton.

'Well? Is it?' Ticker looked at Hart. There was no movement for a moment, then Hart slowly stepped forward and went down on one knee by the body, lifting the head gently. Torry turned away as what was left of the face came into view. Hart let go, as though even contact might poison him.

'Not pleasant,' said a big, hard-looking plainclothes man.

Hart shook his head. 'Can't tell.' He straightened up. 'It could be, but it's impossible to tell.'

'She got any other marks of identification you know of?' said Tickerman brusquely.

'I never got *that* close, sir. It wasn't in my brief.'

'This connected with something else?' The Chief Superintendent sounded even more alarmed.

'It could be, sir.' Tickerman stood, unable to take his eyes off the dead girl. 'I presume I'm going to be in charge now.'

'Yes please, Superintendent. Take over, if you would.'

Tickerman lifted his eyes and looked round the small circle of men. 'What's the story, then?'

The big plainclothes man replied. 'I'm Detective Inspector Player, sir. County C.I.D. This is a regular tunnel of love. At eleven twenty-five last night a young couple—John Henry Small, aged twenty, and Jennifer Davies, nineteen—stopped their car, Small's car, just up the track, there on the other side of the hedge. Small dipped his headlights. The girl thought she could see something strange through the hedge. It frightened both of them. They left the headlights on and, sensibly, went to investigate together. Luckily Small had a torch. They didn't have to look for long. They both turned out the village man at eleven thirty-eight.'

'And you all came up, had a peep, called in all necessary personnel, informed the Chief Constable and decided to send for us,' Tickerman finished for him.

'It seemed the obvious thing.' From the Chief Superintendent.

'Doctor examined her?'

'Perfunctorily.'

'Time of death?'

'Nothing definite. He thinks it couldn't have happened long before she was found.'

'Sexually assaulted?'

'Looks like it, doesn't it?' The Chief Superintendent nodded towards the body. The short skirt was ripped and the exposed underclothes torn.

'Can't tell from that.' Tickerman looked up at the sky. It was beginning to get light. 'No good with these damned arc lights. We've probably trampled a hundred things into the mud. You've got all facilities?'

'Everything.'

'All right. Soon as it's light I want the usual scene-of-crime stuff. Photographs taken ... '

'We've done photographs ... '

'I'd like them done again in daylight.' Rapped out. 'We'll go back to temporary H.Q. I've got a few things to find out there. As soon as the prelim's done I shall want the whole area gone over for anything. That facial damage wasn't done with his fist. He probably used a stone. Then get that,' inclining his head towards the corpse, 'to the pathologist. I'll want the lot by tonight. Forensic, fingerprints, everything. We'll be back later.'

'But sir ... ' started Torry.

'Later.' Tickerman cut, Gillette fashion. In the car, he said, 'Don't show your hand yet, Derek. Not yet.'

'Well, I know of him, sir, of course. Most people do around here.' The village constable looked uncertain, while the local Inspector's brow creased, hard wrinkles which came easily.

'You're not suggesting he's got anything to do with ... ?'

'Not only this.' Torry grimly. 'A few robberies, some high-class cat-houses, narcotics. And you can throw in the odd murder, if you like.'

'You must be joking. A man in his position.'

'You tell me what is his position? What you know about him.'

'What I know ... ? Well ... well, he's a charming man. Sits on several committees in the village. Takes part in things that concern the district as a whole. Generous to charities.'

'What's he do for a living?'

'A living? Torry, for God's sake, he's a wealthy man. Goes up to town, and abroad, quite a lot. I presume he's got a private income, or he may be a company director, or something. You don't ask people ... '

'Excuse me, sir.' The village man treading warily. 'Local folk say he's something big in the city. Has a lot of house parties. People down for the week-end sort of thing.'

'What about the resident cut-glass? They ever get asked to the parties?'

'Not to my knowledge, sir.' The constable smiled. They understood one another. 'That's not out of the ordinary, though. Village people're still a bit feudal and class-conscious. They'll accept a bloke with money buying a big house in the district ... '

'But the gents are more feudal?'

'You might say that, sir.'

'They don't accept people so readily?'

'Lot of wealthy people live around here, but they don't mix much with each other.'

'So,' Torry gave a cynical leer, 'nobody knows a great deal about a bigwig but they accept him because he's generous.' He pursed his lips, pompously. 'Generous to a fault.'

'Suppose you're right.' The Inspector from the County Force looked glum. They stood together inside the Church Hall, a place that had known happier functions. Outside, the Press had begun to gather. Already the first reports would probably be out on radio. The Church Hall clock said it was nearly ten past seven.

At the far end of the room, near the tiny stage backed by a crudely painted set depicting some unlikely living-room, the scene for the local amateur dramatic society's latest epic, a telephone rang. A uniformed sergeant, engaged in writing up the murder log, answered, then hurried over to Tickerman who had been engrossed in conversation with the top brass.

Torry tried to carry on the conversation and simultaneously

226

strain one ear towards Tickerman's telephone conversation. All he caught were odd words.

'Yes ... Yes ... Hell ... Has he? ... You've sent out a general? Good ... Now, that's more like it.' Tickerman put down the phone and headed quickly towards Torry, drawing him away from the village constable and the Inspector.

'They won't wear a search warrant, Derek. The bastard's a charitable institution in the neighbourhood.'

'A Nuffield centre forward.' Torry spoke low. 'And nobody knows a thing about him.'

'I got that impression.'

'The Yard on the phone?' Torry tentatively. He tried to ignore the fact that his career was at stake.

Tickerman nodded. 'Champion checked out of the Savoy in the early hours. They've put out a general but he's probably well away by now. There's good news, though.'

'Yes?'

'Morse's friend's former wife.'

'The Carpet Bag herself?'

'I asked them to put some pressure on. Amazing the results one gets in the early hours.'

'And?'

'She didn't exactly talk. But they got a violent reaction when your man's address was mentioned.'

'Wonder if he's up?'

'How would it be,' Tickerman took on the attitude of a man engaged in heavy gothic intrigue, 'how would it be if the three of us went up there?'

'Can't think of anything I'd rather do.' Torry all but sang the line.

'If he is playing Dracula he might run for it.'

'On the other hand ... '

'On the other hand, Inspector Torry, I play the nice under-standing one and you play the heavy. Okay?'

'I'll break the weighing machine.'

'Give me five minutes. We don't want half of Fleet Street following us.'

At seven twenty a five-ton removal van began its circumlocutary journey from Birmingham. One hundred yards behind it, keeping steady distance, was a half-ton Army lorry bearing the colours of the Royal Corps of Signals.

At seven twenty-five Wexton got another telephone call.

'General?'

'Speaking.'

'Romeo.'

'Go ahead, Romeo.'

'Deposit and Scrambler running.'

'Thank you, Romeo. Birthday Party on now. No more contact until it's over.'

'Roger, General.'

'Good luck.'

The Pan American 707 was still climbing above Ireland. In the first-class compartment there were only a dozen or so passengers. One sat dozing in his window seat. It had been a tiring night and he could not fall into a complete sleep, there was too much on his mind.

The man was tall and slim. He wore thick-rimmed glasses and needed a hair cut. His passport showed that he had been in Britain for three months visiting six universities: occupation, lecturer in economics. His name was Joseph Goldberg.

Tony Champion did not feel comfortable in a wig and glasses.

He was also concerned about meeting and reporting to Al Vescari in New York. It was also unpleasant to know that he was a fugitive.

Tickerman told the driver to stop inside the gates and follow up in ten minutes, unless any vital calls came through.

The house was large. A sprawling, ugly place built by some Victorian squire with unquestionable taste for that period. Torry felt their shoes were making too much noise on the gravel. Half a mile back down the road he had noted a signpost which said EVESHAM 6.

Tickerman rang the bell. Twice. Then, there was movement in the hall. The door opened. A sandy-haired man. Late thirties, tousled and wearing a dressing-gown over striped pyjamas. Unmistakably British striped pyjamas. Torry usually went for the eyes first. He did not like what he saw. These were blue and too bright. Too alert, despite the freshly wakened appearance. The eyes were dodgy without even moving.

'Good morning, sir,' said Tickerman like a breezy vacuum-cleaner salesman. 'We're looking for a Mr Dowding. A Mr Rupert Dowding.'

'I'm Rupert Dowding.' A professional voice. Cucumber cool.

'Good.' Tickerman's foot was sliding inside the door. 'Sorry to bother you so early, but we're police officers and we think you might be able to help us.'

The fractional silence was like that between seeing an explosion and hearing the terrible rumble.

11

'AFRAID I'm a bit conservative.' Dowding seemed completely at ease. Torry felt pangs of concern. If he was wrong? If his whole theory crumbled? 'Could I see your ... er ... your credentials?' Dowding was almost apologetic.

They reached for their warrant cards.

'Detective Superintendent Tickerman, Detective Inspector Torry, New Scotland Yard. And this is Detective Sergeant Hart, C Division, Metropolitan Police.'

Dowding nodded and held the door open, standing back. 'The Yard down here? Oh yes, this wretched business in the village.'

Tickerman moved forward. 'What business, sir?'

'Terrible thing. I've only just heard about it on the news. On the radio.'

Torry indicated to Hart that he would have to check on the seven o'clock news broadcast. Hart gave an almost imperceptible flick of the eyes showing that he understood.

'Yes, it's routine really. Is there somewhere we can talk?'

They were in a wide hall, nice solid staircase. Two doors to the left, one ahead and one to the right. Polished oak boards with skin rugs. Three large paintings. Oils. A four-masted schooner leaning heavily in a gale; a magnificent seascape with brooding clouds and the foam all but splashing the viewer; and an eighteenth-century gentleman, head and shoulders: a reptilian face. Small table to the right with a telephone extension. Mirror. Coat rack. All male coats. Couple of umbrellas and sticks.

'We'll go into my study.' Dowding led them to the door on the right. 'I don't see how I can help, but ... and I'm afraid I can't offer you anything, my housekeeper's away for a couple of days.'

'That's all right, sir. It shouldn't take long.' Tickerman carrying the casual approach to its limit.

The study was pleasant, looking out on to the lawn, velvet green. There would be a beautiful spring to that turf. In the distance two high pines. Inside, a large desk. Books. Another pair of oils. A second schooner and a village shrouded in snow. The last would look well on a box of Christmas chocolates. All the chairs were of padded leather except the one behind the desk, a huge upright, like a throne, with carved boars' heads on the arms and a boar lying within an oval on the back. Dowding went straight for the chair behind the desk. Boars, thought Torry. Richard of Gloucester's symbol. 'Now is the winter of our discontent.' Let's see if Mr Rupert Dowding's in the giving vein today.

Dowding sat back, waiting. Tickerman opened.

'I've already said we're sorry to bother you at this early hour, sir, but there are indications that the person we're looking for made off in this direction.'

'Good Lord.'

'You were in last night, Mr Dowding?'

'Yes. Yes. I was.'

'All night?'

'The whole evening.'

'We really want to know if you heard anything, or saw anything, between eleven and twelve.'

'Well, I went to bed quite early. I'd be asleep long before then.'

Tickerman did not slip in with a quick question. Time for Torry to start giving Dowding a Glasgow shave.

231

'Mr Dowding, have you anyone who can substantiate your claim to be in the house all night?'

None of them imagined the pause. When Dowding spoke it was with an element of uncertainty.

'No. Not really. No, I can't prove it.'

'You said not really. Is there some doubt?'

'No. I can't prove that I was in the house all night. But do I have to?'

'You might. Half a mile away, across the fields from the back of your house, between ten thirty and eleven twenty-five last night, someone caught a young girl. Caught her like an animal.'

Dowding shifted in his chair as Torry pressed it home. 'And like an animal he tore at her. We don't know how he killed her yet, Mr Dowding, but all of us here know why. During the operation he even managed to disfigure her.'

'Disfigure?'

'He battered her face in.' Torry said it as though the words hurt. 'We've just come from looking at the body. Anybody, Mr Dowding, who cannot prove what he was doing last night is suspect. Anybody in this area.'

'But surely … ?'

'Particularly gentlemen who live on their own.'

'I don't live on my own.' It came out fast. 'I have a house-keeper. She has to have some time off.'

'Big place for a lone bachelor.' Torry's voice was tinged with suspicion.

'I don't see … '

'All right, Mr Dowding,' Tickerman broke in, 'Mr Torry has a suspicious mind. Just to get things straight, what line of business are you in?'

'Line of business?'

'What do you do?'

'Do I have to answer that? This is getting like some kind of inquisition.'

'I'm sorry. It wasn't meant to be like that. Policemen. You know how it is.'

'I know exactly how it is, Mr ... er ... ?'

'Tickerman.'

'Yes, Mr Tickerman. You've got a most unpleasant case on your hands and you're stumbling about in the dark. The trouble with people in the dark is that they panic and start lashing out at the first thing they bump into.'

'Like a young girl out late in a country lane,' muttered Torry almost to himself.

'You're quite right, Mr Dowding,' said Tickerman quickly. 'Incidentally, what do you do?'

Dowding almost chuckled. 'Very little. My father was a shrewd man. I manage quite comfortably. Even with the taxation problems which beset us all, alas.'

'No occupation?'

'I am on the boards of two companies.'

Hart's notebook had been out from the moment Tickerman and Torry had started. 'Could I have the names of the companies?' The question was almost incidental. Hart's just too bloody good, thought Torry. Dowding did a reflex action with the names, tripping them nimbly off his tongue.

'So you have plenty of free time?' asked Tickerman.

'I should have, but it never seems to work like that. I ... ' Dowding was interrupted by the front door bell. 'Excuse me for a moment ... '

'It's all right,' said Hart, already making for the door. 'Probably one of our men.'

'A very nice place,' mused Tickerman as they waited for Hart. 'Makes my little semi look like a matchbox.'

'It's the devil to keep up.' Dowding leaned forward. 'Cigarette?'

'Stick to the pipe if you don't mind.' Tickerman affably took his pipe and began fiddling. A tap at the door and Hart was back. He looked a little green with patches of white around the gills. 'Message for you, sir.' He handed a slip of paper to Tickerman, whose face went grave as he read. 'That'll interest you, Derek, I think.'

Torry took the paper. Hart had scribbled:

Dead girl positively identified as a student nurse at the local cottage hospital. Went off duty at eleven last night. Always goes home the same way taking her past scene of crime.

Torry felt a wave of disintegration. If it wasn't Sandra, how did his case stand up? Hell, it stood up before they even knew about Sandra. So? Tickerman was speaking.

'Derek, you'd better join Sergeant Hart and check on those points. Use the car radio.'

Torry took the hint and left to join Hart in the hall.

'Nothing downstairs or in the outhouses.' Hart spoke softly. 'The driver's putting a radio call through. Getting Mr Broadbent to look into those companies.'

'Good.' Torry nodded towards the stairs. 'You willing to indulge in a spot of illegal sleuthing?'

'All part of the service.'

'Right. Let's see what the palatial bedrooms are like. I feel sleuth-inclined.'

The first door on the landing led to a guest room that had obviously been unoccupied for some time.

They opened the next door. Sitting at the dressing-table, half naked, was a young blonde. She made no protest and did not seem to mind the two men walking in on her.

'Well, well, well,' said Hart, carefully closing the door behind them. 'If it isn't our Sandra!'

'This is Sandra?' Torry expressing surprise and delight.

234

'This is Sandra. A very dolly lady, our Sandra. A pricey lady as well.'

'We've been looking for you, Sandra.' Torry with a big bad wolf voice.

'And what are you doing down here?' asked Hart. They were both leaning against the dressing-table, enjoying the situation, playing tough, Hollywood-type cops.

'I'm a house guest.' Sandra went on doing things to her eyebrows.

'For money you're a house guest?'

'Just a house guest.' She wiggled her nylon-covered bottom sexily on the stool.

'Whose house guest?'

'The owner's. And what business is it of yours? Can't I even come away from London for the night without some bloody great bogey sticking his nose into it?'

'Who is the owner of this house?'

'You know as well as I do, darling.'

'Yes, but we'd like to hear it from you, Sandra.'

'No comment.'

It was time for Torry to put the arm on. 'Okay. Get dressed, Sandra, you're coming with us.'

'You're joking, ducky. What for?'

'Accessory.'

'Accessory to what?'

'Murder.'

The tweezers remained poised between dressing-table and right eyebrow.

'I said get dressed.' Even Torry could hear the viciousness in his voice. 'Unless you want to walk out of here in your knickers.'

'Look, I haven't done anything. You're joking about the murder bit, aren't you?' Sandra looked from one to the other.

Hart eased himself into a standing position. 'Sandra Venice

also known as Sandra Volpone and Sandy Birch, I am charging you in that on the night of 22nd to 23rd April, 1969, you were an accessory to the murder of ... ' He continued through the full wording. ' ... may be used in evidence. That plain enough?' It was irregular but workable.

The girl was shaking. 'I never heard of her. I was here all night. I ... '

'Get dressed.' Torry raised his arm.

'It's no good doing that,' said Hart. 'She likes it.'

'You bastard.' She spat.

'Christ,' said the girl. 'I had nothing to do with nothing.'

'Who's the owner of this house, then?'

'The bloke. The one downstairs.'

'What's his name?'

'I'm not a grass.'

'All right. Come on, you've been charged.'

'I don't know his bloody name. They call him the General.'

The General. Torry had him. Cold, plucked and on a spit.

'You come here often?'

'Six times last night.' She giggled.

'Cut the funnies. When have you been here before?'

'Only once. Just before Christmas last year. He's good to me though, the General.'

'How long have you been here this time?'

'Yesterday afternoon. About half past four.'

'Anybody else here?'

'No. Just me and him. What about this bloody murder? Is it straight up?'

'Yes, it's straight up. Unless you give the right answers. You were with him, the General, from the time you arrived until this morning?'

'Yes. No. Nearly the whole time. He got dressed and went down to get us something to eat.'

'What time?'

'Must've been around half-past ten. Yes, he had a phone call at half ten. He went down after that.'

'Take long?'

'Yes. Funny thing that. I remember thinking it was funny him getting dressed. Took a hell of a time. Must've been an hour. I dozed, then he came back with the trays.' She pointed to a pair of silver trays, piled high with the debris of last night's meal, on the floor at the end of the dressing-table.

'But when he came back he'd changed again,' she continued. 'Pyjamas and dressing-gown.'

'Find them.' Torry snapping at Bart. 'Bathroom, anywhere. Find those clothes. Let me know, then get down to Ticker. I'll pull the surprises. Right?'

'Right, sir.' Hart was of the same mould as Torry. Now they were spoiling for the kill.

'Okay, Sandra.' Torry relaxed. 'Get your dress on and we'll give you a nice ride in a police car.'

'What about the charge?'

'You'll be all right. Probably have to give evidence.'

She began to climb into her skirt.

'What makes a girl like you … ?' Torry began.

'Don't come that chat with me, for Christ's sake. I get enough of it from my clerical clients, darling. Just get me away from this bloke here.'

She was doing her hair when Hart returned.

'Get 'em?' asked Torry.

'The idiot. Just left them in the bathroom down the passage. The lot. Suit's badly stained, mud on the shoes. It's all there. Name tags, everything.'

Torry took a deep breath. 'We've got him for that, but someone'll have to work on him to clinch the tie-in.' He was at the door. 'Don't wait up for me, will you? Call another car and get her out. I'm going to break him if it takes a week.'

Tickerman looked at ease puffing on his pipe. Dowding, still relaxed, was laughing.

'Sergeant Hart would like a word with you if you don't mind, sir,' said Torry.

'Fine.' Tickerman rose. 'I'd just about finished with Mr Dowding anyway. Unless you've got any questions.'

'I'd like a few words.'

Tickerman got the message.

'And do you want to see my birth certificate or something, Inspector?' Dowding looked at him with arrogance as the door closed.

'I'm more interested in death certificates.'

'What's that meant to imply?'

'You should know. Sir.'

Outside there was the sound of another car arriving.

'You wanted to ask me some more questions. I'd be grateful if you'd hurry up. I have some things to attend to.'

Torry nearly said, 'like burning a suit'.

'You say your father left you comfortably off?'

'I did.'

'But he didn't leave this house?'

'No.' Hesitation again. 'No, he didn't.'

'Before you came here, to the Vale of Evesham, you owned a property known as Hill Lodge at East Hendred in Berkshire.'

'Yes. You seem to know a good deal about me.'

'I know a lot more than you think.'

'Really?' Dowding pushed his chair back. Torry moved forward, sat on the edge of the desk and helped himself to a cigarette. An act of insolence.

238

'This isn't the first time you've been connected with a murder investigation, is it, Mr Dowding?'

Dowding did not flinch. 'I seem to be accident-prone. But that was a very different affair.'

'How different?'

'Tragic. A child.'

'The girl in that ditch over there wasn't much more than a child. I expect she put up a fight. Not like the other one.'

Dowding's hand moved towards the telephone. Torry caught him by the wrist. 'Not yet, sir, if you don't mind.'

'I would like to call my solicitor.'

'And why would you want to do a thing like that?'

'I don't particularly like the way this conversation's going. You seem to be accusing me of something. Something unpleasant.'

'I've said nothing to make you think that. Why would I be accusing you, Mr Dowding? What was the name of your head gardener at Hill Lodge?'

For a second Dowding's face crumpled. 'My head gardener? What a ... Fred, I think. Yes, Fred.'

'Surname?'

'Fred ... Fred. Damned if I can remember his ... '

'You should remember. His widow wrote to you when he died.' The long shot.

'His widow? You mean Fred Wexton's dead?' Dowding might just as well have clamped his hand over his mouth like a child who has let out some terrible secret.

'There you are, Mr Dowding. Funny how it comes back suddenly like that.' Let him think he's got away with it.

Dowding recovered quickly. 'Good gracious me. Of course. Wexton. Fred Wexton.'

Torry let it lie fallow for the best part of thirty seconds. 'We've got the lad who did Lipperman, you know.'

Dowding did not answer.

'And Jumper's told us quite a lot.'

'Jumper didn't ... '

'Jumper didn't what, Mr Wexton?'

'I don't know what you're talking about.'

'Why did you start using the name Wexton? Bit of pride was it? A code name in the underworld?'

'I'm sorry.'

'Not going to be talkative?'

'There's nothing to discuss.'

'Your American friends will let you down, you know. Champion's already bolted. In any case we've got you on the East Hendred thing and this. Really, Mr Wexton, you should have burned the clothes as soon as you came back. Sandra'll be a riot in the box.'

He did not see Dowding's hand move. The automatic must have been in a concealed partition under the desk. Torry was looking straight into the eye of death.

'You'll just keep very quiet, Inspector. I don't want any fuss.'

It was a moment that Torry had subconsciously dreaded ever since joining the Metropolitan Police. He knew the arguments both ways, but his background, in New York and with the Special Air Service, had always given him that extra psychological lift. He had always been armed. Now it was the classic situation. On television you talked your way out. But this was real and dangerous.

'You're not going to make it, Mr Dowding. There are more coppers out there than in a public convenience.' What sort of talk was that? You don't buy time or life with bad cheap talk.

'Move back from the desk, Mr Torry. I know I can't get away with it but I do need time. Right into the middle of the room, please.'

Torry obeyed. Dowding, or Wexton, or whoever he wanted to call himself, came out from behind the desk, his eyes never leaving Torry and the dull black piece of lethal metal staying firm and unwavering in his hand.

With an expertise Torry admired, Dowding backed towards the door. His left hand went to the dressing-gown pocket. A bunch of keys. Purely by feel, the man located the correct key and, still with his back to the door, inserted it into the lock. There was hardly a sound as it turned.

Torry tried talking again. 'Why did you pick the name Wexton? Was it just because of Fred Wexton or did you feel it might be a nice red herring — General Wexton? I spent a lot of time wondering about him?'

'I dare say, but this isn't the time for chat.' He was moving closer. Torry instinctively picked up the idea. He was to be disposed of. A sharp clip behind the ear. After which, Dowding would make a run for it through the window that looked out on to the side of the house. He could only pray that there was some-one watching the back. But Tickerman would have no idea of the danger.

'If you'd just turn round.'

Torry slowly began to turn. Then came the rattling of the door knob. A cry and pounding on the heavy door. It was enough. Dowding leapt, his arm raised with the automatic. Torry twisted to one side, felt a ghastly sickening blow on his right shoulder, then sprang in close, his left hand going for Dowding's gun arm. Contact. Fingers slipping against the material of the dressing-gown sleeve, then a hold, pushing the man's arm up.

Dowding was clawing at his face with his left hand. Torry flicked his body to the left, then hard to the right. They spun like a pair of exhibition dancers. Dowding's breath came in gulps against Torry's cheek. There was something of the maniac about the man's strength as he tried to force his gun hand down. Panting. The trembling power of two men locked together. A

241

crashing at the door. Then Torry suddenly found the advantage. Heaving with his left arm he brought Dowding's gun hand smashing down against the desk edge. Dowding grunted and the weapon thumped to the floor. Now, for the final moment. Torry let go and brought back his right arm. The fist caught Dowding in the mouth. He went back but kept his balance. Now the left, still to the face. That one was for the child in Berkshire. Another right, for the thing in the ditch, here. Dowding sprawled, whimpering against the wall. Torry's right knuckles smashed into his nose, the head going back and bumping against the wall. Blood. Lips screwed out of shape. Eyes glazed. Moaning. Torry pulled him up by the lapels of his dressing-gown, swung him round and connected again. For Lipperman, even if he deserved it. Dowding rocked back and fell. Torry on his knees, straddling the man's body, his hands out of control now, flashing down in wide backhand swipes to Dowding's face. For the whores and pimps, and every little man who had been terrorized by Dowding and his kind, for the poor stupid junkies, for the gullible, for everyone who came close to identification in the Bosch 'Haywain'. He did not hear the door crack in under a thick shoulder. It took a few seconds to realize that Hart was dragging him off and Tickerman was saying, 'Derek, that's enough. He's out now, lad. It's all right.'

All Torry wanted to do was to avenge that which was good in man by beating this symbol of that part of society which was wholly debased and had already begun to corrupt those who clung to the good, fair, just and right.

'We can't escape an inquiry, Derek. But we've got a lot in your favour.' Tickerman sat behind Dowding's desk. They had taken the unconscious man away in an ambulance. Torry's hands, now bathed and examined, felt sore, and the bruise on his shoulder ached as a nagging tooth reminds one constantly of its presence. He sat, slumped in a chair, unhappy with the anticlimax.

'We've got him, anyway.' Ticker spoke again.

'I'd like to get on to the American side as well.' Torry sounded sullen.

'We will. All in good time. We've got Wexton; Grosvenor and Cust are still in the bag, they might crack now. Then there's always Jumper and the lad they're bringing down from Newcastle.'

'Still something wrong,' said Torry. 'Dowding knew he hadn't a hope in hell but he wanted time. Time for something. Time for what?'

Hart came in with the local Inspector. 'Excuse me, sir, but I'm not very happy about the situation. I think Dowding was in the middle of a caper.'

'Oh?' From Tickerman.

'Sandra says he was laughing a lot last night. Kept saying that tomorrow—that is today—there was going to be one hell of a birthday party.'

'Birthday party?' Torry eased himself uncomfortably out of the chair. 'Birthday party?'

'He also had a telephone conversation at ten thirty last night with someone called Romeo.' Hart laughed. 'And she thinks there were several calls in the early hours. Wexton stayed awake apparently.'

Tickerman was already sifting through the few papers on Dowding's desk. 'To be truthful, that would be simple to do if you were here with Sandra.' Torry came and stood with him. Their faces both changed at the same moment.

'Christ,' blasphemed Tickerman.

Hart crossed to the desk. The Inspector, a shade slower, began to move. On the desk in front of them was a street map of Stratford-upon-Avon. The map was marked with enigmatic crosses.

'Stratford.' Tickerman.

'What's the date?' asked Torry to the air.

'Twenty-third. Twenty-third of April.' Hart had it. 'St George's Day and ... '

'Shakespeare's Birthday.'

'A-levels again,' said Tickerman. 'Don't they have some sort of carry-on at Stratford today?' to the Inspector.

'The Birthday Celebrations. Yes.' The Inspector was a little lost. 'Ceremony of the Flags. Big procession to the Birthplace and the Tomb. Slap-up banquet. They more or less close the centre of the town for an hour. Hundreds of people there today.'

'Birthday Party.' Torry almost gave off static. 'But is there anything there worth nicking? When does all this happen?'

'About now. In half an hour or so.' The Inspector glanced at his watch. 'Oh, a bit of time yet. It's twenty past ten. They'll be starting the procession soon. The Flag thing is at eleven, I think.'

'No chance of stopping it?'

'Not now. What, stop it? That'd be like stopping Christmas. The favoured Stratfordians would never survive.'

'Anyone important there?' Tickerman was on his feet.

'Lots of theatre people. You know, that fellow Monk or Nunn or whatever his name is, director of the theatre there. A lot of ambassadors.'

'How long to get there?'

'Half an hour. Forty minutes.'

Torry looked at Tickerman. It seemed an age before the Superintendent made up his mind. 'Best be safe,' he said finally. 'Mr Torry, Sergeant Hart with me. Inspector, will you get a warning off to Stratford that there might be some kind of criminal activity. Don't go mad, but warn 'em. And you'd better try and get permission for all mobiles to ring the area. Okay?'

'Very good, sir.' The Inspector did not really see what all the fuss was about. As far as he was concerned it meant several difficult telephone conversations. As he picked up the telephone, he heard the car from Scotland Yard accelerating up the drive. It was going like a jet. The time was ten thirty.

'We're going to look a right load of burkes if there's nothing,' shouted Tickerman as they took a bend, narrowly missing an 1100 that had strayed too far over on the corner.

'There's got to be something.' Torry sat in the front, next to the driver, half his mind on the road, half on the street map he had grabbed from Dowding's desk. 'They had a murder at Stratford once on Shakespeare's birthday and I'll never forgive them if nothing happens today.' They shot up a straight stretch of road, touching ninety.

The Duty Officer at Stratford received the message and sighed. 'Someone always gets panicky,' he said. 'Get a message to all mobiles and beat men not involved with the ceremonies. It'll be over soon, anyway. We've got enough on without people thinking up hare-brained criminal activities. What do they think's going to happen, anyway? Someone going to blow up the Bard's Tomb to prove he wasn't buried there?'

At ten fifteen the removal van backed into a side lane, off, and hidden from, the main road. Half a mile back the Army lorry had overtaken them and gone straight through. Now the driver secured the handbrake, opened the cab and dropped to the ground. When he reached the back of the van the men inside had already got the doors open and dropped the ramp. Slowly a white police Humber shooting-brake backed down the ramp. The two men, wearing police constables' uniforms, helped the driver to push up the ramp again and close the doors. They returned to the Humber, while the driver of the removal van climbed back into his cab.

The van driver adjusted two sets of seat belts and tightened the strap of a crash helmet under his chin. The van drew out into the main road and, very slowly, continued its journey. On the passenger seat lay a small transceiver, aerial extended.

One of the 'policemen' in the Humber had an identical piece of equipment on his knee.

White waited by the Jaguar, watching the hour hand creep to eleven. Two miles away, Nolan, Howel and McIvor went through the motions of doing a survey with compass and theodolite.

White, by the Jaguar, and Nolan, by the Westminster, had their ears tuned to the hissing transceivers which lay on their respective passenger seats.

The two men called Symonds and Crisp, uncomfortable in their police uniform fancy dress, were also listening in.

The removal van was now on the outskirts of Stratford-upon-Avon. So was the police car hurtling through the April morning with Tickerman, Torry and Hart.

In busy Guild Street, away from the area used for the annual Birthday Celebrations, the Army truck was parked near the kerb. It was not out of place. The Royal Corps of Engineers provided a band for the occasion. There was plenty of military transport around. The fact that this truck had broken down in a no-parking area did not much concern the police.

Foxy Langdon, in battledress, peered into the engine. In the back of the truck, Donaldson listened through headphones to the sporadic chat between police cars in the area. His left hand kept the set tuned, while his right hovered over the jamming switch.

12

Stratford-upon-Avon is proud, quite justly, of being the birthplace of William Shakespeare. In the Collegiate Church of the Holy Trinity, the Register of Baptisms distinctly says that on April 26th, 1564, the Vicar, then one John Bretchgirdle, christened *Guliemus filius Johannes Shakespeare*. The tradition is that this William Shakespeare was, in fact, born three days earlier, on April 23rd, Saint George's Day, the day now observed in Stratford as Shakespeare's birthday.

Each year, on April 23rd, hundreds of tourists and sightseers come to Stratford. The main streets of the town are closed to traffic and lined with a forest of white flagstaffs, each bearing a shield and painted emblem of the country whose flag will eventually be unfurled at the top of the staff.

Around ten thirty a long procession, headed by the town Beadle and Mayor, and consisting of diplomats from over a hundred countries, actors from the Royal Shakespeare Theatre Company, and other personalities, winds its way up the town's central street, Bridge Street, which is, by this time, packed with people lining the pavements.

Smith looked down on the scene from his hotel bedroom over Bridge Street. When he had booked the room, by telephone and confirmatory card, the receptionist had said cheekily, 'You won't mind if other people come in to watch the Birthday

Celebrations on the morning of the 23rd, will you, sir?'

'I most certainly will,' Smith replied. 'I want your room facing Bridge Street to shoot a movie of those celebrations and I'm not going to have people jogging my arm all the time.'

'Well, it isn't usual, sir. Visitors don't usually mind. There's a lot of call on front rooms for that day.'

'So raise the price,' Smith said. They did, and he was now squinting down the viewfinder of the Bolex H16 Reflex, set on a tripod pointing up the street. Wexton really knew what he was at. The Bolex with its long Paillard zoom lens was the perfect thing with which to control the operation. Smith was amazed at the number of people who had turned out. From everywhere. Saris and cheongsams, turbans. Americans and Russians. Black, white, yellow and red.

Nor did Smith expect this kind of colour, the glistening white of the flagstaffs along the pavements and straight up the centre of Bridge Street. The procession, each member carrying a wreath or posy of flowers, later to be placed on Shakespeare's grave. And the uniforms. The band at the top where the street forks into Wood and Henley Streets, and, directly to the left and right, High Street and Union Street.

Smith grinned. The band stood straight in front of the white, domed and imposing Barclays Bank tucked neatly into the cleft made by Wood and Henley Streets. On the roof of the bank there were more uniforms. The trumpeters. The upper windows were crowded with staff.

Slowly, Smith lowered the camera and zoomed in on the crowd standing directly outside the bank. Three faces stood out from the laughing, interested, mocking expressions. Barker was nicely on time with his team. Smith panned to the right across cordoned Henley Street. Martins Bank and three more faces. King in position with his boys. Right again. Next door to Martins stood the National Provincial. Again faces: 'Lofty' Short and his two boys. Pan right again across the narrow entrance to Union Street and into the thick crowd outside Lloyds Bank: Evans and his team were there.

Brilliant. Four banks crammed close together, carrying more money between them than usual on this one day, Shakespeare's Birthday: money which included Royal Corps of Engineers' pay. Outside each bank, mixed with the sardine-packed crowds, were three men, average tourists with their camera cases, shoulder-bags and rucksacks. Three trained especially for each bank.

Smith again viewed the upper-floor windows of the banks. Crowded. Four banks with only a skeleton staff behind their counters. All waiting for the trumpets. The signal for the flags to be unfurled, after which the band would play the National Anthem. The signal for the Birthday Party.

Smith zoomed out again and watched. The procession had begun to split up, going off in its twos, threes and fours. Each group to its appointed flagstaff. In the crowd people began edging each other, jostling for a good shooting position with their hand-held Super Eight cameras. Today some of them would get historic pictures.

The trumpeters raised their instruments, and just before the first bars of the fanfare cut through the murmur of the crowd, Smith's right hand moved to his transceiver. He pressed the transmit button and spoke.

'Romeo to all stations. Birthday Party. Go. Birthday Party. Go.'

They heard it in the flat lonely lane and began to pack up the surveyors' equipment. White heard it by the Jaguar and lit another cigarette. He just had time. Symonds and Crisp, in the bogus police Humber, started the engine and pulled into the main stream of traffic, Symonds driving and Crisp beside him with the stop watch. They had between four and five minutes.

Foxy Langdon heard Smith on the transceiver and banged the side of the truck. Inside, Donaldson threw the jamming switch. A distorted wave of static plunged the police 98 megacycle band into auditory darkness.

A hundred yards or so up the street from Langdon's Army truck, the removal van suddenly went out of control, slewing horribly across the road, then back again, mounting the pavement and crashing broadside on into the main doorway of Stratford police station, blocking the door and sealing off the exit road to the station's left. The driver was out of his cab and running before anyone could get near.

In Bridge Street everybody looked pleased. There is always a little joke about the flags which will not unfurl properly. All attention focused on the flags, gradually dropping, then rippling out from the mastheads. Nobody except Smith saw that the four banks had their main doors closed.

Smith did not like the look of the two coppers. They stood on the Barclays corner of Henley Street. Just hope to God they move when the National Anthem's finished.

Through the view-finder he scanned each of the banks for the fourth time, wishing he had some kind of magic eye that would allow him to see through the doors.

In Barclays, Barker and his two men had hit the jackpot. They had gone in as planned. Stockings over faces. Doors closed. Barker's number one with the hand grenade, by the door.

'Nobody's going to get hurt as long as they keep quiet and do as they're told. Otherwise, the grenade goes up and spreads itself among you.'

His number two went forward quickly with the sticky tape. Mouths, hands and ankles. One girl, four men. Faces lanced by shock and terror of unexpected violence. More staff than they had expected. Then it turned out that two of the men were the manager and his chief cashier. They held the vault keys between them. All the Army cash. Far more than they could hope to carry away. Working fast, the three men filled their camera cases, rucksacks, three brief-cases, the airline bags and their pockets with wads of folding money.

In Martins and the National Provincial things were quiet. As Wexton had pointed out, only a fool would argue with a hand grenade. Also the bank staff would naturally think they had an advantage. In all four banks someone had managed to press the direct police alarm bell. Nobody tried anything, but the teams had no chance of getting into the vaults. Still, there was a fair haul of cash behind the counters and in the upper offices.

Unhappily, in Lloyds Bank someone had a go. There was one customer at the counter when Evans and his men walked in. Now, he lay on the floor, a rivulet of blood spreading into an unpleasant mushroom shape on the floor. No trouble after that, and plenty of gelt. They had brought up two sacks for collection by security van and, just before the fanfare, one of Stratford's larger stores had paid in Tuesday's takings.

Smith panned the camera once more across the four banks. The band was nearing the end of the National Anthem. The dodgy moment. He reached for his transceiver. The teams in Martins, the National Provincial and Lloyds were all right. It should be easy enough. The banks stood in a row, Lloyds separated from the other two only by the entrance to Union Street. The three teams could make it down Union Street in fifteen seconds, and Union Street ran straight into Guild Street where Langdon waited with the Army truck. All teams had transceivers. The final note of the National Anthem. Now.

'Romeo. Two, three and four out.'

The doors of the three banks opened almost in unison. Nobody wise yet. There they go. King's team. Short's. Now Evans's.

'Romeo. Come on, cops, where've you got to?'

They're late. No, he could hear the klaxon. The crowd was

moving. Thank God those beat coppers had walked out towards
the Mayor who waited for the procession to re-form. Here we
go. The fake police Humber could be plainly heard now coming
down Henley Street.

'Romeo. Stand by one.'

They heard it in Barclays and stood by the door.

Now, this is where you've got to time it. The few people who
were not on the pavements in Henley Street had started to run as
the car came hee-hawing fast.

'Romeo. One out.'

Barker's team slipped from the bank doors. Christ, it's not just
one car. There's another. For a horrible moment Smith's mind
fogged over.

They had come into Stratford down the Evesham Road, flashing
into Rother Street. Torry still fiddled with the radio. 'It's not a
fault. Someone's jamming us.'

'Everybody.' Tickerman tense in the back with Hart.

'Which way, sir?'

They had come to the intersection and in the moment of com-
parative silence Torry heard the noise of a police klaxon from
behind the houses ahead.

'Straight across. Down there.' They shot forward. Torry
glanced up and saw the sign which said Meer Street. Almost an
alleyway. As they reached the top a white police shooting-brake
passed down the street in front of them, at speed.

'Follow him.' Tickerman, relatively cool.

'We're in Henley Street now, sir,' said the driver as he turned
right. 'Shakespeare's Birthplace there, on the left.'

'You're not a town guide, lad,' from Tickerman.

'The boys in front are pulling up,' Torry shouted. 'It's a bank.
What the ... ?'

The white Humber had slewed across to the right. They were almost abreast of them. Three men detached themselves from the crowd and leaped for the Humber.

'Head 'em off. They're not ours.' Tickerman got it first. The driver heaved at the wheel and put his foot down hard on the brake. They skidded in front of the long white car, a jarring grind as their side hit the front bumper.

Torry was out first. Chaos. The crowd backing away. One started to run and Torry saw Hart streak past him and tackle low. Then he was facing a short man, the stocking over his face pulling the features into a grotesque shape. The man was dragging a small piece of metal from his pocket. God, a hand grenade. Fingers closing on the pin. Torry's hand chopping down on the wrist. A clang as the little destructive oval ball hit the pavement and rolled away, the pin still intact. Torry lashed out again. This time at the face. The man screamed and put up his arms. Torry felt his fist going deep into the man's stomach. He doubled up into a perfect position to be chopped across the back of his neck. A woman screamed as the villain's face crunched on to the pavement.

Torry was torn away for a second by someone in uniform. Then it was a general scuffling; a helmeted uniformed man putting an arm lock on the driver of the Humber; Tickerman with his knee in the back of the other fake policeman; Hart standing with his foot on one man and holding another, struggling.

'Doing a bank on a day like this. How stupid can you get?' shouted Torry. Then, from behind him, panic broke loose with a shattered looking clerk yelling from Martins Bank doorway. Torry slowly turned and took in the fact that there were three banks in a row. He mouthed the most obscene word that came to mind.

'Romeo. Chalky. Out of it quick. Failure in One. They've blown one.'

Smith's breathless voice came over the transceivers. White threw away his cigarette, started the engine and drove as never before.

'Army clearing nicely.' Langdon kept his head, calm behind the wheel of the truck. The three teams from Martins, the National Provincial and Lloyds had arrived simultaneously. Now, while they got their gear organized in the back, he headed fast up the Warwick Road. About a mile to go before they would turn off into the lane that would eventually bring them to the three waiting cars.

The Westminster, Humber and Zodiac were all in position as the truck arrived at the lonely stretch of road. They moved quickly though without any undue rush that might allow things to be forgotten. The brief-cases, into which the three teams had now packed their money, were loaded into the Westminster, while the men themselves crammed into the Zodiac and Humber. The Zodiac took off in the direction from which they had come. The Humber headed away towards the little village of Hampton Lucy, where Will Shakespeare was once supposed to have been arrested for poaching.

Changed now from their battledress, Langdon and Donaldson climbed into the Westminster beside Nolan.

'Here goes then,' said Foxy. 'Give us a nice ride, won't you, mate.' Nolan gently put the car into gear and released the brake. They moved smoothly in the wake of the Humber.

By this time, the teams in the Humber and the Zodiac would be well on their way towards the various dropping zones. In twos and threes they would eventually arrive in Leamington and so, by train, to London. Not a single face among them for the police to recognize.

*

Smith left the transceiver on while he folded the tripod and packed away his camera. He felt nervous, edgy. But this was no time for panic. Below, there was confusion in the streets, but he would hardly be noticed elbowing through the crowds to the Royal Shakespeare Theatre car park where the little grey grocery van waited.

One last look from the window. The activity was around the Warwick and Banbury Roads. He had a more complicated route to take.

Three-quarters of an hour later, Smith turned off the main Stratford to Evesham Road. By now Nolan would have dropped Langdon and Donaldson at bus stops. Each had an overnight case and were booked, independently, into Stratford hotels. They would spend that night at the theatre.

Nolan, with the money, had three easy stops to make. By the time he got back to London he would be driving a clean car and the money would be safe. Pity about the Barclays lot. You could only hope that they wouldn't talk.

All Smith had to do was drive his roundabout route to London. The shock of Wexton's capture would come later.

'You'll make the headlines tonight, Derek.'

'We'll all make the headlines, and we'll all be asked how four banks can be done in broad daylight.'

'And there'll be repercussions about a lot of things.' It was still quite light and they were heading back to London. Dowding was being taken up separately and would appear at Bow Street in the morning.

It was over, yet Torry knew it was not over. They had only prised open one tiny flaw in the organization. For all they could tell, Tony Champion might be lying somewhere in a ditch.

Mutton. And that remark of one of the boys who had tried to do Barclays.

'This is nothing. We've only been rehearsing.'

Rehearsing for what? Around the corner there was more to follow and he felt only the bewilderment of a man who couldn't come to terms with himself and his circumstances.

'You won't need this anyway.' Tickerman handed over a newspaper cutting. It was a form for obtaining information on joining the Royal Air Force Police. 'I kept it for you just in case.'

' "Combat crime! Safeguard the secrets of the Service! Protect visiting Heads of State!" ' Torry read. 'They must be joking.'

'They're not joking,' said Tickerman. 'They believe it, just like we believe what we're doing or you believe what they tell you in church.'

Torry made a guttural noise in the back of his throat.

'I believe that I shall have a lot to drink when we get back,' said Hart quietly.

A Complete State of Death

Derek Torry, Detective Inspector
attached to Scotland Yard's "Crime
One," has earned a reputation for
brilliance and toughness, a reputation
earned in the jungles of Malaya and
in the police forces of two countries.
He is a man of ruthless dedication but
devious method. And he is a man
tormented by guilt and the inhibitions
of a Catholic conscience.

In *A Complete State of Death* Torry
is assigned to a top-priority case
involving a new, highly sophisticated
criminal organization operating with
increasing success throughout the
country. Two criminals die violently as
they are about to turn informers, and
a single name muttered in terror by one
of them provides the only lead:
Wexton. Torry's is the laborious chore
of checking the name against Criminal
Records Office files. It is a job that
leads him away from the demands of
his impatiently chaste girl friend Susan,
through the complexities and perver-
sions of other people's lives, into a
vortex of murder, drugs, and depravity.

Written by the creator of Boysie
Oakes in a style as sharp and sure as
rifle fire, *A Complete State of Death*
introduces a distinctive new character
to the established figures of modern
fiction—the solitary and tortured Torry,
a man with a mind and a moral code
uniquely his own.